LOST POWERS

BOOK 2

THE WOMAN'S WORLD SERIES

LYNNE HILL

1st Edition

Created with Vellum

OTHER BOOKS BY LYNNE

<u>The Lords and Commoners Series</u>

Of Lords and Commoners Book 1

Of Princes and Dragons Book 2

Of Gods and Goddesses Book 3

A Gods and Goddesses Novelette

<u>A Woman's World Series</u>

A Woman's World Book 1

Lost Powers Book 2

A Collision of Worlds Book 3

This book is dedicated to anyone who has ever been marginalized.

CHAPTER 1

Two suns sent streams of golden light through the infirmary's many windows.

Baya sat shoulder to shoulder with Vicaroy on his bed, where he was recovering from a head injury. She studied the handful of people who had gathered in the large room, the healer, two guards, a couple of servants and the ruler of Merth, Unawi Nacora, who was ... apparently Vicaroy's mother. Somehow, she'd managed to become the ruler, or the Unawi, of Merth.

The woman to the right of Nacora was the head of the guard. Adorned in armor, she held a spear with a sharp metal point as if it were a harmless walking stick. Baya was certain that the woman could have the spear pointed at her chest in the blink of an eye, especially if she thought the ruler was in danger.

The Unawi stood at the foot of Vicaroy's bed, lovely and regal, her back straight and head held high. Her mouth was set in a confident smile that seemed to highlight her high cheekbones. Black hair framed her face in tight ringlets that barely brushed against her shoulders. Clearly the woman had aged well. Only slight traces of lines at the corners of her eyes betrayed her years.

"The Unawi is your mother?" Baya's voice was incredulous. "But how ..."

The ruler gave Baya a fleeting glare.

Vicaroy's almond-shaped eyes remained narrowed on his mother. They flared with anger and ... something else. It took Baya a moment to recognize what it was — suspicion.

"That is a great question, Baya. How *did* you get here, Mother?" Vicaroy said.

"It is a long story, my son," Nacora said. "One for another time, perhaps. For now, you need to rest and heal. I thank the Goddess that you found us in time. The healer says that you will make a full recovery. In six weeks or so you will be as good as new."

Baya didn't know how Vicaroy could possibly look more angry but his eyes darkened and they flashed with pure hatred. Baya moved to stand beside his bed. She was unsure of what he might do. She had never seen him like this.

"Spare me the sympathy, Mother. You abandoned us and how, in the name of Ameris, did you end up here ... and a ruler?"

Gasps rang out from the onlookers in the room. Baya glanced around with discomfort. This was not how a man spoke to a woman, let alone to the ruler. Vicaroy appeared not to care or perhaps he didn't notice the others' reactions. All his attention was focused on the Unawi.

Baya had no trouble believing they were related as Vicaroy's looks resembled Nacora's. Unlike many of the people Baya had seen in Merth, Nacora had onyx colored skin much like Vicaroy's. Granted, her skin was a few shades lighter. They also had the same dramatically oval-shaped eyes. Everything else in this place was unusual and new, so there was some comfort in the familiarity of the ruler's features.

Nacora continued to smile, undeterred by her son's outburst. "You will not be angry once you hear my story. I never meant to leave you and I never thought I would see you again. You can't even begin to imagine how happy I am to be reunited with you. It is a miracle that you are alive."

The ruler placed her palms together and lowered her head in a brief prayer of thanks to the Goddess before continuing, "You managed to survive the journey from Pathins to Merth, despite traveling in all the wrong seasons. This is beyond my wildest dreams. It is nothing short of a miracle that you are here." She moved to take Vicaroy's hands but he quickly placed them out of her reach by wrapping them around Baya's waist and pulling her to him.

This erased the smile from Nacora's face. She gave Baya another quick glare but refused to acknowledge her further. Great, Baya thought. He hated his mother and she hated Baya. Their first day in Merth and things couldn't be worse.

"What has it been, at least ten years since we have seen each other?" Nacora said. "That would make you about nineteen years old, does that sound right?"

Vicaroy gave a slight nod. "You're stalling. I want answers."

"Once you have recovered, I will tell you my story but for now you need to rest." Nacora turned to leave. She gestured for her entourage to follow. "That includes you." Her eyes briefly flickered over Baya.

"No." Vicaroy's jaw was set with determination.

More gasps came from Nacora's court.

"I will not let Baya out of my sight. She's the only person I trust. Unlike you, she would never leave me. You always run away. I deserve to know why you left Pathins."

Baya's mouth had fallen open as she gazed at Vicaroy in wonder. Her lips slowly curved into a slight smile. She had never seen him so strong, standing up to a woman like that. She leaned into him and placed her arm around his shoulder. It was difficult to fight the urge to crawl on top of him and press her lips to his.

Baya was uncertain how to act in this place but his strength flowed into her.

"So be it. Leave us." On Nacora's command, the room emptied as people quietly filed out.

"Madam, if I may," the head of the guard ventured. "I do not think it wise for you to be alone with the outsiders. At the very least I should remain with you." The woman's accent was thick but Baya could gather the gist of the woman's concern.

"They are from Pathins, which is a peaceful society. I'm in no danger from my own son. I will be fine, Kuna. You can wait just outside."

Kuna's frown deepened, yet she headed for the door.

CHAPTER 2

When Baya, Vicaroy and his mother were the only ones who remained in the room, Nacora moved to the window. "Clearly a lot has happened in the past ten years. Where should I start?" She gave Vicaroy a warm smile. "I can only assume that you inherited my love for the ocean and for building things."

"Vicaroy is an amazing inventor," Baya offered. "You should have seen the boat he made for us."

Nacora continued to gaze at her son, ignoring Baya. "You don't know how proud I am of you. You managed to make it here through the hot season. That is unheard of."

"And the monsoon season," Baya added.

"It's remarkable that you survived." Nacora spoke only to her son.

"Enough! How did *you* get here?" Vicaroy snapped.

"Well ... like you, I too made myself a boat. I loved being out at sea. It was how I spent my free time. Eventually I added a small sail and learned how the wind moved the boat. It was not a large vessel."

Nacora sighed and shook her head. Baya could almost see the woman's memories as they flooded back.

"One afternoon the gentle waves rocked me to sleep," Nacora continued. "The wind must have picked up, catching the rigging on the sail, sending it up the mast and filling it with air that carried me away. When I woke, Pathins was gone. My home … lost. There was no sign of the island, only endless water."

Nacora studied her hands as if to distract herself from the horror of that moment so long ago. "I have never felt more panicked. I sailed around for an entire day, trying to find my way home — the way back to my family. Yet once you are on the outside, the island is next to impossible to find. As I'm sure you're aware, it is hidden by the priestesses' spell — rendering it invisible to outsiders. The second night I cried myself to sleep. I was sure I would die at sea. The worst part was that I didn't get to say goodbye to you and Azod."

Nacora's eyes shone bright with the threat of tears. "You see, my son. I did not mean to leave you."

Vicaroy's expression remained hard. "Azod said you left us because you'd found a new lover."

Nacora exhaled sharply and her shoulders sagged as if the air had been knocked out of her. "Why would he tell you such a horrible thing?"

"When you didn't return home, it was the most logical explanation. It's not uncommon for a woman to replace her theo." Theo was the word for a man who was spoken for.

For the first time, Nacora's expression grew stern. "You honestly believe that I would abandon you … on purpose?" She was no longer a concerned mother but a fierce ruler. Her son had finally pushed her too far.

Vicaroy's brow furrowed in confusion. Could it be that he had believed a lie all this time? Perhaps his mother had not meant to desert them? A sense of hope that he didn't want to trust swelled inside. There was a chance his mother loved him.

Nacora gazed out the window and released a sorrowful sigh. "Your father was always worried that I would leave him. He felt … unworthy of me … always carrying on about how powerful and beautiful I was. He often asked why I had chosen him. He never believed that I truly loved him … but I did."

"What's a fa … ther?" Baya struggled with the strange word.

This time the ruler's sigh was full of irritation. "I forget how ignorant people are in Pathins."

Baya's chest puffed up at the insult, even though it was not a very impressive gesture. When Unawi Shema, the leader of Pathins, had stuck her large breasts out, people paid attention. Baya was tall and thin, even more so after their harrowing journey to Merth. Soft brown hair hung down her back and her smooth skin was the color of amber. More than once she'd rendered people speechless with her unusual tri-colored eyes. They were a lovely honey color with a sunburst of green that transitioned to bright yellow around her pupil.

"We are *not* ignorant!" Baya said. "All women are highly educated in Pathins."

"Yes ... but not the boys. Such a backward place. In fact, you are so backward that you don't even know where children come from."

"Of course we know where they come from. They are a gift given to women from the Great Goddess."

"That is one of the many lies we were told in order to further suppress men."

"What are you talking about?" Baya was utterly lost.

"There are so many barbaric things about Pathins. They deny that men have anything to do with the conception of a child, just to further dominate them. Heaven forbid that women would have to admit that they need men to reproduce. In Pathins they believe that men are disposable. Yet, without them, people would cease to exist."

Baya shook her head — not understanding.

"Do you honestly think that it is a woman alone who makes a child?"

"Of course, men don't give birth," Baya said.

"They don't give birth but without them women would never become pregnant."

"So you're saying that it's not the Great Goddess who places babies inside women." Baya bit her lip. "Then how...?"

Nacora crossed her arms with impatience. "Do I honestly have to explain it to you?"

Baya and Vicaroy blinked at one another.

Nacora threw out her arms in exasperation. "Babies are conceived through the act of coupling."

The blank stares remained.

"For the sake of the Great Goddess, through sex. When a woman and a man —"

"Oh ..." Baya's eyes widened as recognition took over. Scenes from her childhood consumed her. In the blink of an eye she was once again a small child sitting on Rus's lap. *Why do my eyes look like yours?* she had asked him. "Rus is my father," Baya whispered. The next memory was of her mother's lover from the North and how, shortly afterwards, she grew large with Tash. "But Rus is not Tash's father." Her colorful eyes remained wide when she gazed at Nacora.

"Then Tash is your half-sister."

"That explains a lot, like how we look nothing alike." Baya turned to Vicaroy. "And Azod is your father."

"Of course, Azod is Vicaroy's father. Who else? I was never like the loose women of Pathins. You will find that things are different here. When a woman and a man are coupled, they are *both* expected to be faithful to their mate. Therefore, half-siblings are rare, as women should remain loyal to their theos. It is despicable how women can tramp about as they please in Pathins. Yet, a theo would be imprisoned for such disgusting acts." Nacora ended with a particularly sinister glare at Baya.

Vicaroy held up his hand as if to direct his mother's attention, or rather her fury, away from Baya. "That doesn't matter. What matters is how you managed to make it to land and then find your way here ... alone?"

"On the second day at sea I woke to the sound of a voice telling me to head east. I was led here by the Goddess Herself. She had bigger plans for me than a sheltered life on Pathins. I dare say, my journey was easier than yours. I did not travel during the monsoons and I didn't cross the vast desert plains in the Time of Daylight.

Nacora stared out the window without seeing. "The winds blew me to a small island. There were no people and few animals but it was a bountiful land. I was able to fill my small boat with supplies, food mostly. Nevertheless, I was all but emaciated when I finally saw land. I used my powers to protect me from predators and the voice led me ever Eastward."

"That sounds familiar," Baya muttered. "Like the voice that directed us here."

Vicaroy studied his mother with skepticism. He didn't like the way she treated Baya and how badly she spoke of their home. Of course, they had left because they were unhappy there. Yet, Vicaroy felt … personally attacked. It was still home or at least where they were from. "How did you come to rule this place?"

Nacora pursed her lips.

The uncomfortable silence that filled the room couldn't be ignored. Baya shifted her weight from one foot to the other.

"I had hoped to have more time to think about the best way to tell you. I pray that you can forgive me. You see, I thought you and Azod were lost to me forever. I never envisioned that I would see you again."

"You have chosen a new theo," Baya guessed.

"Spoken like the true barbarian that you are. You see, here men must agree to the coupling as well."

"That's enough, Mother. Stop insulting Baya. Do you know who she is? She's the daughter of —

"In Merth, she is no one!" Nacora snapped before issuing a tight-lipped smile. "But you, my eldest son … You are a prince."

CHAPTER 3

Baya couldn't process her thoughts fast enough. The Unawi's words rang in her head. "What is a ... prince?"

"The son of a ruler. They are nobility and held in high regard by the people of Merth," Nacora said.

Baya nodded slowly, trying to imagine a world that allowed men such status. "And you said *oldest* son, so you have more than one?"

Nacora's weak smile was directed at Vicaroy. "I hope you can forgive me. I have a new theo. His name is Wen. He is the eldest son of the former Unawi. We fell in love and ... he chose me as well. The previous Unawi had no daughters. So, at our coupling celebration I became the next in line for the throne. Wen's mother died about three years ago and I have ruled Merth ever since."

Vicaroy licked his teeth, lost in his thoughts. "And you had more children with this new theo."

"Please, call him Wen. He's the Unatheo of Merth. I can't wait for you to meet him. And yes, we have two sons. We are hoping for a daughter, so she can take my place one day." There was a new light in Nacora's dark eyes as she spoke of her family.

"Leaders are chosen by their lineage and not by a divine calling?" Baya asked.

Nacora nodded.

"And they're allowed to have children ... apparently. This is all so different from Pathins."

Vicaroy placed his hand over the bandage on his head and laid back on the pillows. "I have brothers?"

"This is a lot to take in. You need to rest, my son." More sternly she added, "Baya, come with me. We must let him sleep."

Vicaroy reached for Baya, taking her hand. "No. Don't leave," he whispered. His eyes were drooped at the corners.

Baya gently kissed his forehead. "Get some rest. I won't go far. Besides, I need to check on Tara." Plus, she wanted some time to process all she had learned.

Nacora crossed her arms.

"Mother. Please take her to the animal. The creature means a lot to her."

"Very well."

Vicaroy's eyes were closed before the two women were fully out of the room.

Nacora kept her eyes forward and her faithful guard, Kuna, fell in behind them as they headed down the long hallway lit by torches that had been mounted to the walls. Their footsteps echoed off the stone walls. The hallway ahead of them was dark but as they approached Nacora lit more torches with the wave of her hand.

"Thank you for saving Vicaroy," Baya said.

No response.

"I'm sorry. Perhaps I didn't make the best first impression. I hope you will like me once you get to know me."

"I will *not* get to know you and you will not be with my son."

Baya's mouth fell open. "What ... Why not —"

"I will not allow my son to be with a backward woman from Pathins."

"I'm not backward!"

A sinister smile crossed Nacora's lips. "Soon you will discover that you don't need or even want each other."

"What does that mean?"

Nacora ignored her. "Yes, Vicaroy will couple with a well-raised woman from Merth." Nacora wore a content expression as if her eldest son were already betrothed.

Baya's knuckles drained of blood as her fists tightened into balls. She had just gotten Vicaroy back and she was not about to lose him … again. One thing her long friendship with Vicaroy had taught her was that they were meant to be together. This had only been reinforced these past months when they relied on one another to survive.

He is mine and I'm his, Baya thought. "Nothing has ever been able to keep us apart and nothing ever will." Not even death.

Nacora shook her head and muttered, "Silly girl."

A low growl escaped from Baya's throat. "You're from Pathins and you clearly don't think of yourself as 'backward.' What makes you think I am? I've always treated Vicaroy with respect. You can ask him."

But Nacora stared straight ahead, lost in her own thoughts.

Baya let out a frustrated sigh and decided to change the subject. "What do you do with the animals you keep in captivity?"

Nacora didn't answer. She gave a command to Kuna, then to Baya she added, "Go with her. She will take you to the beast. I must get back to work."

Baya watched the back of Nacora's shimmering gown as the Unawi continued down the hall without her. She shook her head in hopes of pushing away the sinking feeling in her stomach.

Baya and Kuna rounded a corner only to find another hall. They moved down several sets of stone stairs in silence, until Baya felt like she would explode if she didn't say something. "Why do you wear metal breastplates and carry spears? Is it truly that dangerous here?"

Kuna glanced at Baya with a heavy frown and confusion in her brown eyes. Baya figured that she hadn't fully understood her and that the frown was not directed entirely at Baya. Rather Kuna was most likely not happy about being away from the Unawi. It was obvious that the woman was fanatical about her job of keeping Nacora safe. An image of Tara sticking close to Baya came to mind. Kuna was loyal to Nacora, just as Tara was to Baya.

The head of the guard even kept her brown hair cropped short.

She most likely didn't want it getting in her way. Baya found this odd as women usually flaunted their long hair. But not Kuna. She was all about her work. To add to her tough appearance, a piece of Kuna's ear was missing and a jagged scar ran diagonally across it.

She finally came to an abrupt stop and opened a door for Baya. Gesturing for her to enter, Kuna grunted something that sounded like, "In there."

Baya cautiously entered the room. The first thing she noticed was the smell. Stale air filled her nose, like a small room that had been filled with too many people cooped up for far too long. Yet, the chamber was large with a low roof and stone floor. The walls on either side were lined with cages. Through the metal bars, several different types of animals turned their attention to Baya. Most resembled Tara. Baya was reminded of the place where Mook was kept, back in Pathins. Yet, this room housed far more animals.

She moved slowly toward the cages and was relieved to see that they were clean and that the creatures appeared to be well fed.

Tara's cage was near the back. She was the smallest of her kind as she was still young. Yet, even if she were not, Baya would have known it was her.

"Tara!" She sprinted for her cage.

As she drew close, the guard let out a yell from behind. Baya could only make out some of the words and guessed at others. It was something about "stupid girl, dangerous beast" and "stay back."

Baya didn't slow her pace.

The light in Tara's four black eyes danced when they focused on Baya. Tara placed her forehead against the bars and Baya threw her arms around the animal the best she could with the barrier between them.

Kuna let out another cautionary holler, which Baya ignored.

"Are you okay?" Baya whispered. "They haven't hurt you have they? Do you have plenty of food and water?"

I'm okay. Not hurt, just sad. Don't like this place. Tara's voice sounded in Baya's head.

"I'm so sorry, Tara."

Where you been?

"Sleeping mostly. I would've gotten here sooner if I could have." Baya stroked her lovely rainbow-colored feathers and a relieved laugh caught in her throat. "You're unharmed! But I have to figure out a way to get you out of here."

CHAPTER 4

Nacora held Vicaroy's chin firmly as she examined his head. He no longer needed a bandage and the long, curved scar was a healthy pink color.

"How do you feel?" she asked.

"I feel great. Good as new." Vicaroy freed his chin from her grip and moved to one of the many full-length windows in the infirmary room.

"Your hair is growing back nicely as well." Nacora joined her son and gazed out the window at her vast gardens below. "As soon as you are able, you must start your education. You have much to learn; not only the education you were deprived of in Pathins but you must also learn the ways of Merth."

Vicaroy frowned. He had never had to sit in a classroom. How had Baya endured all that grueling time seated on a school bench? "I belong in a garden."

"Don't be ridiculous, my son. You are no longer a garden boy. You must take your place at my side, as a proper member of the royal family."

Vicaroy lowered his head in dismay. He had no idea what that would entail.

"I've been given a chance I never could have dreamed of," Nacora said. "I can finally give you the gift of knowledge." She gave him a nudge with her shoulder. "It's important for a prince to be highly educated."

"Oh," Vicaroy said but it came out as more of a grunt.

* * *

OVER THE NEXT several weeks Nacora had a language instructor work with Vicaroy and Baya. She taught them the basics of Merth's language. Thankfully, Pathean and Merthean had many similarities, and once they learned the main differences it was not difficult to pick up. Some words were entirely the same, while most sounded only slightly different. It was like speaking with a heavy accent. It didn't take long before they could understand what most Mertheans said.

However, these lessons had been hard for Vicaroy to endure.

Vicaroy sighed and turned his attention out the window to the lush gardens below. He watched as Baya threw a stick as far as she could. Tara bounded after it. Her powerful back leg propelled her almost faster than the eye could follow. Tara had doubled in size since he'd last seen the animal. It had taken a lot of convincing but finally Nacora agreed that Baya could take Tara out of her cage once a day for a brief reprieve.

Vicaroy noticed a saper bush that was being overtaken by the surrounding vegetation. There was so much work to be done and he was stuck inside. "I would give anything to be out there with them."

"Soon, My Dear Son. We have to wait until the healer informs us that you are well enough to go outside."

The first order of business would be to rescue the poor saper bush, Vicaroy thought. The saper flower was Baya's favorite. If he were allowed to, he would pick a bouquet of the lovely purple flowers for her. Vicaroy exhaled in frustration. At least Tara was able to play in the garden every day. Vicaroy was not allowed to take one step outside his cage.

* * *

After an hour of frolicking in the royal gardens, Tara lay with her three paws in the air while Baya ran her fingers along the animal's feathery neck to her scaly underbelly. When Baya's arm tired, she used Tara as a pillow. The sparse clouds were wisps of bright orange in the deep purple sky. Both suns gently warmed her skin. It was the Time of Daylight, when the days were long and warm, although it was not as hot in Merth as it was on their island home of Pathins.

I don't want to go back. Tara's voice sounded sleepy in Baya's mind.

"I know. Yet, I'm grateful they allow me this time with you."

Tell that woman that I belong with you.

"I have. The problem is Nacora doesn't like me and she doesn't trust animals."

Why?

"Your kind is wild and untamable. But I found you as a baby and raised you myself. Vicaroy and I are all that you know. I'll keep trying to convince her that you are not a threat."

I need to be ... in the open ... with you.

"Soon. Hang in there. This is temporary." Although, Baya had no idea how to permanently get Tara out of her cage.

Baya felt as if someone was staring at her. She glanced up at the tall palace behind her. Its large glass surface hurt her eyes as it reflected the suns' light. She squinted and searched the tall, pointed spires for signs of someone watching her. Her heart jumped when she spotted Vicaroy. He stood next to Nacora.

Baya gave them an enthusiastic wave. "I bet Vicaroy wishes he could be out here."

Vicaroy smiled and returned the wave.

His mother frowned in greeting.

* * *

Baya was told that she had to sleep in her own room in another part of the palace. Her room was small, consisting of only a bed, a dresser and a chair. There was a communal bath down the hall. Nacora had explained that it was forbidden for an unattached man to sleep in the same room as a female. On top of this there was a strict curfew for all uncoupled people. They were to be in their rooms by dark every night.

Vicaroy and Baya had protested when Nacora demanded that they sleep apart. She'd gone on a diatribe about how this culture was much more virtuous than Pathins. They'd had to listen to her rant about how sex before being officially coupled was a sin ... whatever that meant.

This was ironic as Vicaroy and Baya had journeyed to Merth alone. Well, they'd been the only humans on their travels. Of course, Doba and Tara had been their animal companions. They'd spent a lot of time alone together but now that was no longer acceptable. Regardless, their stressful journey hadn't given them the chance to be intimate.

At least Baya was allowed to visit Vicaroy's room during the day.

"Do you think things will be better here?" Baya asked

"I don't know. They have a lot of rules." Vicaroy spent most of his time pacing like Tara in her cage or staring blankly out the window, as he was doing now.

"Yeah and they're weird about sex. I feel like I'm a mistress again, confined to the palace grounds at all times."

"You think *you* feel trapped..."

"I know. At least I can go outside."

A shadow had fallen over Vicaroy's face. This conversation wasn't helpful. "I could read to you or would you rather play a game?" She had to do something to cheer him up.

Vicaroy shrugged. "Neither, I guess."

"I don't understand why they won't let you go for a walk in the garden."

"Mom and the healer are worried that I'll 'overdo it.' For some reason, they think I'm not ready." His lovely almond-shaped eyes, which were normally a golden brown, had darkened.

Baya placed a hand on his shoulder. "I hate seeing you like this. I could sneak you out for a bit. We won't do any gardening, just a harmless stroll. Some fresh air would be good for you."

"No. Mother has forbidden me to leave this room."

"What happened to the strong man who stood up to his mother only a couple of weeks ago?"

Vicaroy lowered his head as if ashamed of his behavior that day. "I was angry but I had no reason to be. Mother didn't mean to abandon me."

Baya's brow furrowed. "Don't."

"Don't what?"

"Fall back into those old habits. You don't have to do everything your mother says."

"Of course I do. You had to do as your mother said and you're a woman. *I* certainly don't have a choice."

Baya gently pushed his chin up with her index finger to gaze into his eyes. "I hope that things are truly different here and we won't have others telling us what to do all the time. After all, that's why we left home." Baya's full lips curved into a playful smile. "I know what we can do." She stepped in close.

Vicaroy's expression lightened as he admired the playful twinkle in her eyes. "And what is that?" he asked, knowing the answer.

She pressed her lips to his.

Vicaroy wrapped his arms around her waist, pulling her against him. His lips responded with ease, eager to explore hers.

She kissed him harder before stopping to breathe in his scent at the hollow of his neck. He smelled of the earth, like a pile of fresh leaves, with a hint of sweetness. She gently placed her arms around his neck and found his lips again.

The door swung open and in came Nacora and Kuna.

Vicaroy pulled away from Baya, his cheeks flushed.

Baya kept her arms around his neck. "You really should knock."

"And Vicaroy should be resting, not doing … that." Nacora shook her finger at them. "You see why we can't allow you to sleep in the same room?" She crossed her arms and glowered at Baya. "Perhaps I should have a guard chaperone you?"

Baya held her gaze with raised eyebrows — a challenge. It wasn't until Baya noticed others filing into the room that she reluctantly slid her hands down Vicaroy's chest, releasing him.

"Now that you are feeling better, I felt it was time that you met Wen and your brothers." Nacora gestured to the man who stood at her side. "Wen, this is Vicaroy."

Wen was tall with curly blond hair, pale skin and piercing blue eyes. Vicaroy's lips parted in amazement. Wen was so … different and it was not only the color of his skin and hair. His head was held high and his gaze was steady. Wen never cast his eyes downward — an educated man who belonged in the world of powerful women. Vicaroy wondered if he could learn to be like that.

"It is wonderful to finally meet you, Vicaroy. Your mother has always spoken highly of you and since your arrival she has spoken of nothing *but* you. I'm relieved that her heartache at losing you is no longer a burden."

Vicaroy opened his mouth to speak but couldn't think of anything nearly as elegant to say so he forced a smile and nodded his greeting.

Nacora squatted down and placed her arms around the two young boys on either side of her. "And these are your brothers, Rand and Nefer."

They had curly light-brown hair and their father's crystalline eyes. Their skin was a lovely hazel color, not as dark as Nacora's and not as light as Wen's.

"Hello," Rand, the slightly taller boy, squeaked. He gave Vicaroy a quick wave.

Nefer moved to hide behind Wen.

"Now, don't be shy, Nefer," Nacora said. "Please excuse him. Nefer is only five years old. Rand is eight."

"And you must be the lovely Baya?" Wen stepped forward and took Baya's hand, gently placing his lips against her knuckles.

Baya felt heat rush into her cheeks. She hoped the others hadn't noticed her blush. No one had ever greeted her like that before. "It's a pleasure to meet you."

CHAPTER 5

Two more excruciating weeks passed before Vicaroy was allowed to leave his glass prison. When the healer announced that he was well enough to venture outside, no one could have stopped him from heading for the door.

Baya watched with delight as Vicaroy inhaled the sweet garden air and stopped to smell every flower on his way to the gardener's shed. He all but shook with excitement as he went to work trimming bushes and pulling weeds. He'd had a long time to map out his plan of attack on the garden while gazing down from his window.

When he finally fell into bed that evening, he was asleep before Baya could say goodnight. She had to pull his boots off and cover him up. She smiled as she watched him sleep. He would be sore tomorrow but happy. This was why they had been afraid to let him leave his room before he was fully healed. They knew he would work too hard. After a kiss on the cheek, she headed for her room.

Baya was growing accustomed to sleeping without Vicaroy by her side but if she'd had her way she would have curled up next to him and fallen fast asleep.

* * *

MUCH TO VICAROY'S DISMAY, his mother insisted that he start classes the very next day. "There's still so much work to be done," he insisted.

"I have gardeners, you know," Nacora said.

"But they're not very good," he said.

The corners of Baya's lips turned upward.

Nacora chuckled. "I'm sure they are not as good as you but my gardens are fine and your education is sorely lacking."

Nacora herself escorted Vicaroy and Baya to their first lesson.

"You will study in the palace with other members of the royal family." Nacora's arms moved with excitement as she spoke. "Many of the students are Wen's relatives. For some lessons, such as history, you will study with the regular class, while for other subjects you'll need a private tutor."

Vicaroy's frown deepened. "You mean for the subjects I'm way behind in?"

Nacora nodded. "So you won't have to be in classes with the younger students."

"I can teach him," Baya chimed.

"Vicaroy needs to be exposed ..." Nacora paused as if to choose her words more carefully, "exposed to others."

When they entered the classroom all heads turned to greet them. Every student got to her ... or his feet at the sight of the Unawi, their backs straight and heads held high.

Nacora didn't bother to apologize for interrupting the class. With confidence she strode to the front of the modest room. Baya noted that the desks were different from the ones she was used to. They were individual wooden chairs, unlike the long benches back in Pathins. Each one had its own small writing area attached to the chair, like a miniature table for each student. She couldn't help but admire the design.

"It is with great pride that I introduce you to my eldest son, Vicaroy. He and his friend will join you in class from now on. Please help them to feel welcome." Then to Vicaroy she added, "This is your instructor, Priestess Var."

Var's long blond hair fell across her face as she gave Vicaroy a nod. "It will be a pleasure having you in my class."

All the students surveyed Vicaroy and Baya with wide eyes.

Baya knew that boys were allowed to be educated in Merth but she still found it odd to see them in a classroom. Perhaps she had expected that they would be educated separately from girls but there they were — all together in one class.

Beads of sweat formed on Vicaroy's brow. He was used to being invisible in Pathins, yet here he was anything but. Baya figured that he could never have imagined being in a full classroom, let alone standing front and center with forty eyes pinned on him. She tried to reassure him with a smile.

The girls in the front row appeared to melt as they stared up at Vicaroy — the tall dark prince from some mysterious faraway land. Baya turned toward him and away from the girls in hopes that they would go away, somehow.

A girl with blond hair waved her hand and an empty desk slid across the floor only to land right beside her. "You can sit here," she said to Vicaroy. Her voice was as smooth as silk — seductive even.

Baya's stomach knotted.

Vicaroy remained frozen in place.

It was all Baya could do not to glare at the lovely young girl, whose long golden hair and large blue eyes reminded her of her half-sister, Tash. This didn't help the stomach-wrenching sensation brewing inside Baya.

A boy in the back of the class gestured to a chair next to him. "She can sit here." His broad smile revealed that he was thrilled to be seated next to an empty desk. He was hard to miss. His bright red hair was unlike anything Baya had seen before.

Nacora's expression was stoic but her eyes betrayed her amusement. She gave Baya a cursory glance that seemed to say, "I warned you this would happen." Nacora gestured for Vicaroy to take the seat next to the blond. "So thoughtful of you, Osa. Osa is Var's daughter."

Great, Baya thought as she ground her teeth. Osa would naturally be the teacher's favorite.

Vicaroy stiffly did as he was told.

"Wonderful! Now I will let you get back to your lesson," Nacora said.

Baya moved to the back of the room to sit next to the still beaming, red-haired boy. She glared at Nacora's back as the woman made a graceful exit. Things were already working out the way the Unawi wanted — Baya and Vicaroy, torn apart.

The students sat as soon as Nacora was gone.

A flash of light caught Baya's eye, causing her to do a double-take. For a moment everything stopped, her thoughts, the boiling jealously — all of it ceased as Baya stilled. The hair of the boy next to her caught the light and changed colors, from deep red to a light blond. It was even more stunning up close. It fell down to his shoulders in shimmering waves — nothing like Vicaroy's course black hair.

Her mouth had fallen open.

The boy stared at her with equal intensity. "Your ... eyes ..." But he seemed to lose the ability to speak.

Baya blinked and forced herself to look away.

"I mean your eyes are so ... colorful. I've never seen ..." Again the boy seemed to lose his words.

Baya ventured another sideways glance at the boy. His eyes were an intense green, his skin was milky-white and covered with reddish-brown freckles — entirely different from anyone in Pathins. "And I've never seen eyes like yours."

"But yours are brown, dark green *and* ... golden." He sounded completely awestruck.

"Yeah, it's rare." In fact, the only people she knew with eyes like hers were her father, Rus and her brother, Bek. "I'm Baya, by the way." Baya didn't know what was wrong with her voice but her words came out clumsy and awkward.

"Mek," the boy replied. "It's nice to meet you."

Mek, rhymes with Bek. A different emotion overwhelmed Baya, an intense longing for home — to see her father and brother. Baya placed her hand over her stomach, which felt like it was doing somersaults. She tried to distract herself by surveying her surroundings but that didn't help. Most of the girls were staring at Vicaroy and most of the boys were staring at her.

They looked so different from her and Vicaroy. Most of them had light skin and brown or blond hair. Many had blue eyes as well. They were relatives of Wen's, so that made sense, Baya thought.

Her attention fell on the blond seated next to Vicaroy ... Osa. She flicked her long hair and leaned toward him. Vicaroy shifted himself away as best he could.

The instructor, Var, had a difficult time drawing everyone's attention back to the front of the class. Baya didn't hear a word she said. She spent the entire class glaring at the back of the blonde next to Vicaroy.

She could feel Mek's stare at times but she didn't return the gesture.

"Hey, Baya, I can show you where we eat. You know, after class," Mek whispered.

Baya didn't want to draw any more attention to herself by talking or, worse, interrupting the class. Not to mention, the very last thing she wanted to do was eat. So, she ignored Mek.

By the end of class, her jaw ached from being clenched and Vicaroy had almost been forced out of his seat as he tried to inch away from the ever-encroaching Osa. His leg never ceased its nervous twitch.

As soon as Var dismissed the class Baya sped for the exit.

Vicaroy jumped to his feet, only to find himself surrounded by mostly girls but even a few boys appeared eager to get to know the new prince.

Baya was almost to the door when she stopped to see if Vicaroy was coming. She bumped into Mek, as he had apparently been right behind her.

"Hey, do you want to get something to eat?"

His sparkling jade eyes caught hers and held them. It was as if she simply couldn't look away. Mek's expression pleaded with her to say yes. She shook her head and glanced around him at Vicaroy. Several people spoke at once. The chatter escalated as they fought to get

Vicaroy's attention. He looked like a wild animal that had been caught in a net. Sweat ran down his forehead. He was backed against the adjacent wall.

"Sorry. I have to save him."

Mek's face fell.

Baya swiftly moved around him and a handful of other boys whose eyes followed her with anticipation — apparently waiting for their chance to talk to her. She pushed her way through the crowd. "Excuse me! Pardon me!" Baya yelled over the chorus of voices. "Give him some space."

The two girls standing directly in front of Vicaroy would not budge. Baya had to shove one of them aside. It was Osa, the lovely blond who had spent the entire class leaning into Vicaroy.

"Watch it!" she yelled at Baya.

"You're overwhelming him." Baya took Vicaroy's hand and pulled him from where he had been frozen with fear. She headed for the door at a fast pace, which forced people to move out of her way. Neither one of them exhaled until they were out in the hall. But their reprieve was short-lived. Voices grew louder as they headed toward them.

"Don't look back, just pick up the pace," Baya said. When they rounded the first corner, she added, "Run!"

Vicaroy was all too glad to do so. They took a wrong turn, which may have helped to lose anyone who was still following them. Eventually they ended up back in his room.

Panting, Vicaroy fell onto his bed.

Baya slammed his door shut.

"That was ... insane." Baya collapsed next to him.

"You saved my life for the twentieth time."

"But who's counting?" Baya propped her head up with one arm and gave him a playful smile. "My famous Prince."

He rolled his eyes and took her by the waist, pulling her onto him. Baya rested her head on his chest and breathed him in. His familiar earthy scent consumed her. Every muscle in her body relaxed. He smelled like home. It didn't matter where they were, as long as she was with him she would always be at home.

"I love you," he whispered.

The knot of jealousy in her stomach loosened. "We belong together." She ran her fingers through his thick hair and their lips met.

They were in a tangle of arms and legs when the door flew open. Vicaroy was topless and Baya was about to be.

"Honestly, you need to knock," Baya said.

CHAPTER 6

"You two are always together." Nacora modestly looked away while Baya straightened her top and Vicaroy reached for his tunic, quickly pulling it over his head.

"I can never find a moment alone with my son."

Vicaroy lowered his head at the irritation in his mother's voice.

Baya elbowed him.

"I wanted to find out how your first lesson went."

Vicaroy's head shot up and he got to his feet. "I can't do this. I'm too old and the other students are too ... different. I need to be outside ... doing things, not sitting in a classroom." His words poured out in a torrent.

Nacora sighed. "My dear boy, an education is the greatest gift I can give you." She moved to the window and gazed out thoughtfully. "Maybe we can come to some sort of a compromise. I want you both to learn the history of Merth, which is the head Priestess Var's class. So one hour a day in her class, plus two hours learning other subjects like reading and math with a private tutor. You can skip the afternoon classes and have the rest of the day to yourself."

She took her son's hand. "I will make room for you in one of the storage buildings outside — a place all to yourself, where you can build ... whatever you like."

Vicaroy's eyes lit up at the possibility of having his own work area. "Only three hours a day, then I'm free?"

Nacora nodded.

"I suppose I can give that class another try. The other students were ... overwhelming. I've never ..."

"Been the focus of such attention." Nacora finished his sentence. "Don't worry, the novelty will wear off as they get used to you."

* * *

THE NEXT MORNING Baya and Vicaroy decided to get to Var's class early so they could choose desks next to each other. Anyway ... it seemed like a good idea.

As students filed into the class, they placed themselves around the new-comers, instantly invading their space. A girl with light brown hair took the seat next to Vicaroy. She leaned over his desk. "Hi, Vicaroy. Remember me?" Her voice was playful.

He leaned away from the girl. "Ah?" was all he got out before he was pushed toward her as Osa shoved a desk between Baya and Vicaroy. They had made the mistake of leaving all of five inches between them and apparently that was all Osa needed.

Baya almost fell out of her desk as Osa thrust her desk in between them.

"Hi, Vicaroy," Osa said in the sweetest voice.

Baya adjusted herself in her seat only to find that Mek had raced another boy in order to claim the desk next to her. He scooted his desk as close as possible to Baya. If Baya moved one inch to her right she would brush shoulders with Osa. To the left she would touch Mek. She opted to sit perfectly still so she would do neither. In fact, she hardly took a breath.

"Hi, Baya!" Mek beamed.

"Hey, Mek. Something tells me that you all are not usually this excited to get to your history lesson," Baya's voice was flat. When Mek didn't reply, she gave him a glance. But he was looking at Vicaroy.

Baya and Osa both looked to Vicaroy at the same time.

His eyes were narrowed on Mek. "What did you do to your hair … to make it that color?"

Mek ran is fingers through his hair. "Nothing, I was born this way."

"I've never seen hair that color before."

"And I've never seen skin as dark as yours."

Vicaroy's almond eyes darkened and narrowed farther.

"I mean, not even your mother's skin is that black."

Vicaroy's fingers curled into a fist.

"Drop it, Mek," Baya said.

Osa turned her back to Baya and Mek, blocking Vicaroy's piercing glare at Mek. "I have great news, Vicaroy. Your mother has chosen me to be your private tutor." Osa giggled. "After all, I am the top in my class. Your mother told me all about the awful place you came from and how you were denied an education. I can't even imagine such a horrid place."

Vicaroy crossed his arms and stared toward the front of the class.

Baya did the same. Surely there was nothing worse than Osa, the beautiful blond with big blue eyes, giving Vicaroy private lessons. Yet, things were about to get even worse.

"Baya," Mek said. "I know it's not for a couple of weeks but I have to ask … you know, before someone else does …"

"What's not for a couple of weeks?"

"The big banquet that Unawi Nacora is planning. You know, to celebrate her son's arrival and to officially introduce him to the court and, well, all of Merth."

Baya's scowl deepened.

"Anyway, I was wondering if you would go with me." Mek's words came out fast.

This shocked Baya out of her miserable reverie. She blinked and turned wide eyes to Mek.

Mek's breath hitched. His pleading sea-green eyes pulled her in.

"I —" Baya started.

"That's perfect!" Osa beamed. "You can go with Mek to the banquet and Vicaroy can be my escort."

Mek's nod of agreement was overly enthusiastic.

Baya sighed and Vicaroy's jaw flexed with irritation.

Thankfully, their instructor, Var, called the class to attention. "It is good to see you again, Vicaroy. I have prepared a special lesson for you today." Her eyes roamed over Vicaroy for a bit too long. There was a playful glint in her eye.

Baya crossed her arms over her chest and focused on the desk in front of her. It seemed to be the only safe thing in the room as even their teacher wanted Vicaroy. Gross, Baya thought. She was old enough to be his mother.

"You see," Var addressed the class. "Our new guests come from an isolated island where they are taught many lies."

Baya's eyes snapped up to the instructor.

"The biggest lie being that they believe Ameris is *the* Great Goddess."

Chuckles erupted from some of the students.

"Of course Ameris is the Goddess," Baya blurted.

Gasps came from the class.

Osa laughed. "Ridiculous."

"Yes, Osa. It is a ridiculous belief. Thank you, Baya, for demonstrating my point." She gave Baya a wicked smile. "We, in Merth, know of the *real* Ameris, as she was born here over one thousand years ago. She was a woman, just like any other. She was powerful, yes, but no Goddess. She is nothing more than an important historical figure. Can anyone tell me why?"

Osa's back straightened. "Because she caused a terrible war, the only one in a thousand years. She's responsible for hundreds of deaths."

"Correct again, Osa." Var smiled with pride at her daughter.

Baya shook her head. This couldn't possibly be right.

"Ameris was nothing more than a power-hungry warlord. She killed anyone who did not agree with her. There was a large uprising in Merth, as the people had had enough of her tyranny."

"That's not true!" Baya blurted. "Ameris was a loving and kind leader. She saved her people by taking them to Pathins, providing safety from the wild beasts that roamed the earth."

"Again, Baya, thank you for demonstrating your ignorance. As we all know, the truth is Ameris was defeated in The Great Uprising. She and her pathetic followers were forced to flee the city. She ended up in Pathins where she started a new society, one that blindly followed her and even believed her delusion of being divine."

Baya's face had turned an angry shade of purple as her blue blood rushed to her face. Her chair scraped against the floor when she abruptly stood. "What proof do you have."

Var had to gaze up at Baya as the young woman was a foot taller than most of the girls in the room. Var's expression was one of indifferent confidence. "It is all clearly laid out in our sacred scrolls."

"We have sacred texts as well and they say otherwise." Baya stormed toward the door.

"The delusional Ameris wrote those scrolls herself, making up whatever suited her, while our texts are unadulterated," Var declared loudly to Baya's back.

Vicaroy stood and moved to follow Baya.

"Vicaroy, your mother demands that you stay in my class."

He lowered his eyes to the floor and returned to his seat. He glanced to the door longingly but Baya was gone. Vicaroy couldn't focus on the rest of the lesson and was about to doze off by the end. This was more out of a need to escape rather than tiredness. He couldn't shake the feeling that he needed to be with Baya — to comfort her.

As soon as Var dismissed the class, Osa was quick to put her arm in Vicaroy's and lead him toward the door. She shooed his admirers away and dismissed all the questions from students about what he thought now that he knew the truth about the "evil" Ameris.

"It's time for me to give you your math lesson." Osa was so full of cheer that Vicaroy wondered if she might explode.

"Great," he mumbled.

CHAPTER 7

Baya headed straight for her room after storming out of Var's class. She scooped Doba up in her arms. "Do you want to come with me? We'll get Tara and head for the gardens?"

Doba usually preferred the quiet of Baya's room but on occasion he would choose to explore the gardens with Baya.

You look like you could use my company. Doba's voice sounded in Baya's ears.

"I sure could." She rubbed his favorite spot under his chin.

In no time, she was playing with Tara while Doba roamed around under some shrubs.

As Tara bounded off after a stick, Baya heard someone call her name.

She glanced behind her to find Mek jogging toward her. Baya resisted a moan.

"They said you would be here."

"Shouldn't you be in class," Baya said.

"Nah. It's over. I came looking for you as soon as I could. Are you …" Mek rubbed the back of his neck. "I just wanted to make sure you were okay?"

"Sure. Fine. Couldn't be better."

"That was ... unconvincing."

"Yeah, well I just learned that everything I was taught to believe may be a lie."

Mek's eyes were full of compassion and maybe even understanding. That all changed in an instant when he caught a glimpse of something behind Baya. His eye's widened and the faint color in his cheeks faded. "Baya ..." He pointed behind her.

Is this boy bothering you? Tara asked.

Baya spun around to face Tara. "No. He's fine." She put her hands up, indicating for Tara to stay back.

Mek grabbed Baya's arm. "Run!"

Tara growled and lunged forward.

Baya pulled loose of Mek's grip and jumped in front of Tara. "No!"

Mek slowly backed away. "Baya. Get away from that thing."

Tara bared her long teeth at Mek.

"Tara. Behave. This is no way to show people that you're harmless."

Fine. Tara closed her mouth and sat down hard on her back leg. *But if he touches you again...*

"He wasn't going to hurt me. He was trying to save me."

Save you from what? Tara looked around for a threat.

"From you. He's terrified of you. This is what I've been telling you."

"Are you ... talking to that thing?" Mek asked.

"It's not a thing. H*er* name is Tara. She's my friend and, yes, we can read each other's thoughts."

But Mek was not listening. He slowly reached for a stick. "Baya. ... There's something on your shoulder."

"I know. That's Doba. He's also a friend."

Mek straightened and slowly lowered the stick.

Not another boy. Are you collecting them now? Doba said.

"Doba! Be nice," Baya chastised.

Mek continued to back away. "Sorry, I thought you were ... alone."

"Well, I'm not." Baya gestured to her companions with a reassuring smile.

"I'll ... be going."

"What was it you wanted? I mean you came all the way out here for a reason, I assume."

With wide eyes, Mek looked between Doba and Tara.

The two animals never took their numerous black beady eyes off of him and Tara's sharp pointed tail flicked in warning.

Mek shook his head. "I ... um, wanted to make sure you were okay ...you know, after Priestess Var was so rough on you."

"That's nice of you."

"Oh ... and I wanted to finish our conversation."

"About what?"

"The celebration and ... well, Osa's idea was pretty good. She's my first cousin, you know."

Baya's eyes narrowed at the mention of Osa. She had forgotten, most likely on purpose, about the dance.

"I'd better get Tara back. I didn't realize we had been out here so long."

"So will you go with me?" His words came out fast.

Baya couldn't avoid the question forever. "Mek, I'm with Vicaroy. I'll be going with him." It dawned on her that she and Vicaroy hadn't actually discussed this. This caused a flutter of panic to move through her. At least she *hoped* they would be going together.

Mek's shoulders dropped. "Sure. Of course."

Baya sighed. "You seem like a really nice guy ... I'm sorry."

Mek lowered his head and turned to leave. "No. It's fine," his tone implied that it was anything *but* fine.

Baya had the sudden urge to stop him, to tell him ... what? She shook her head and watched him leave.

What was that about? Doba asked.

"What?" Baya snapped.

You like that boy.

"No I don't. His determination is ... sweet. He stayed to ask me to the dance ... again, even after being scared to death by you two." Baya looked thoughtful. "And he's so different and handsome — I mean, he looks unlike anyone I've ever seen —"

I'll stop you there because you're not helping your case. It appears I was right. You are collecting them, Doba said.

Baya growled. "Shut up. Why did I bring you along anyway? Come on, Tara. I have to take you back."

Tara's head hung low as she lumbered after Baya.

When Baya was leaving the animal room she noticed that the two cages at the far end were empty. She must've been lost in her own thoughts on the way in, not noticing them. She paused and stared at the empty pens. They had been well cleaned. Only the bare stone floor remained.

"Tara?" Baya jogged back to her cage.

Tara jumped about excitedly at Baya's quick return. *Do we get to go out again?*

"What did they do with the animals in the far cages?"

No one knows. Some men came and took them away this morning.

They never come back. A dull voice rasped in Baya's head.

Baya jerked her body toward the animal in the cage next to Tara.

"Where do they take them?"

Who knows? The only thing that is for sure is that Tara is the only one of us to ever leave this place and return.

Baya's brow furrowed as she rubbed behind Tara's ears. "You stay safe. Let me know if they ... try to do anything to you."

I'm sure those other animals will come back, Tara said.

The crease in Baya's forehead deepened. "Yeah..."

CHAPTER 8

Baya took Doba back to her room. She had had enough of his prying into her mind.

She headed to Vicaroy's room at once. Peeking her head around his door, she found him with his elbows on the desk and his fingers in his hair as if he were trying to pull it out. His face brightened when he looked up to find Baya.

Osa sat across the desk from him and glared at Baya. "In case you forgot, *we* are in the middle of a math lesson. You should show some respect by not disturbing his important studies."

"And it looks like it's going well," Baya said. Her voice softened when she spoke to Vicaroy, "Are you okay?"

"I don't understand any of this. There's no way I'll learn math." He jabbed at the parchment in front of him.

"Let me take a look," Baya said.

"That's not necessary," Osa said. "I'm his tutor and I've already made it clear that you should leave."

Baya ignored her and moved to stand next to Vicaroy.

She glanced at the numbers on the page. "Oh, I remember this. Shema had an easy way of teaching this. Look ..." Baya took the ink quill. "Arrange the numbers like this and then you can add them easier, then carry this number over here."

"Let me see that again." Vicaroy sat up straight and watched with intent.

Baya wrote a new set of numbers and slowly went through the steps again. "Now you try it with this one." Baya scribbled on the paper.

Vicaroy studied it for a moment.

"That's not the right way to do it," Osa scoffed.

Vicaroy slowly went through the steps Baya had shown him. "Is this right?"

"Outstanding! See, you *can* do this. Here, find the correct answer for these problems." Baya set out writing as fast as she could.

"I will give him the problems." Osa grabbed the quill out of Baya's hand.

"But I understand Baya's way better," Vicaroy lowered his head.

Baya gave him a swift kick under the desk.

Vicaroy knew Baya was not happy about his timid behavior. So he forced himself to meet Osa's gaze. "Maybe Baya should teach me."

"Of course I should. No one knows Vicaroy better than I."

Osa glared between the two of them before throwing the quill onto the desk, sending ink splattering everywhere. "Fine. We'll see what your mother has to say about this."

She moved around the desk to pass close to Baya on her way out. "You don't want to get in my way," she whispered.

Baya rolled her eyes. "I've dealt with girls like you before."

"I guarantee ... you haven't."

When Osa slammed the door on her way out, Vicaroy and Baya burst into laughter.

"Thanks for saving me."

"Any time." Baya sat on his knee.

"I really did understand when you showed me. It's even ... kind of fun."

"It is fun. I always liked math. Here..." Baya got a fresh scroll and wrote out more problems. "Try these, using the method I showed you."

In no time, Vicaroy had two parchments full of math problems answered correctly and he grew quicker with each problem. Baya could hardly write the problems fast enough.

"You see, this isn't so bad. Now that you have this down, the next step is —"

Vicaroy's door opened. In marched Nacora, Kuna and Var with Osa in tow.

Vicaroy's gaze instantly fell to the floor and Baya nudged his foot. "Look up." She whispered between her teeth.

Nacora's narrowed eyes were focused on Baya. "Osa has informed me that you are interfering with my son's lessons."

"I'm not interfering. I'm *actually* teaching him." Even Baya had to force herself not to look away from Nacora's intense glower. Instead she straightened her spine.

"Mother, please, look." Vicaroy's voice trembled as he handed her the parchment of problems he had answered.

Nacora snagged the paper from him. Her mouth had been in a severe line but her lips slowly parted as she studied the page. "You did all this … just now."

"Yes. Baya is an excellent teacher. I would ask that you allow her to tutor me."

Nacora sighed and her face softened.

Baya exhaled, realizing that she had been holding her breath.

"Well …" Nacora paused.

Vicaroy gazed up at her with anticipation.

"This is a good technique."

"I was top of my class as well," Baya said.

"As long as you continue to show progress like this then you may study with Baya." She turned to Baya, "Study time is study time. No distractions. No … messing around."

"Of course. I will take his education seriously."

Nacora headed for the exit.

"Madam Unawi, you can't leave the education of your son to a … backward outsider."

"Leave them," was Nacora's reply.

Osa's arms were crossed over her chest. She gave Baya a sharp glare before exchanging a knowing look with her mother.

Baya wondered what that was about.

Kuna was the last to file out of Vicaroy's room. She wore a smirk and gave Baya a wink. Her spear tapped noisily on the stone floor as she walked.

"A small victory," Baya said as soon as they were alone.

But the look on Vicaroy's face caused a tingling sensation to pass through her entire body. She wanted nothing more than to jump on top of him and kiss him all over. She swallowed hard at the look of need in his eyes. "We have to finish your lesson. I promised your mother — no distractions."

"This may be harder than I thought." His voice was rough.

Baya gave him a playful smile. "So, will you escort me to the dance?"

Vicaroy's eyes brightened. "Of course, there's no one else I'd rather go with."

Baya's head fell back in relief as she chuckled. "Anyway." She cleared her throat. "As I was saying before we were interrupted, the next step is to add the numbers this way…"

* * *

Baya spent most of the night staring up at the three bright moons that shone outside her window. First she had been awakened by a nightmare that Tara was being torn away from her in a fierce windstorm. She reached desperately for her but couldn't get ahold of her. When Tara vanished, Baya woke with a start.

Baya took deep breaths to calm herself. Eventually, she dozed off into an uneasy rest. She saw Tara and Mook bounding playfully through a field of flowers, which came in every color. Mook was the same type of animal as Tara and he too had been kept in a cage back in Pathins. But in this dream they ran free through the flower spotted fields that matched their rainbow-colored feathers and scales. Baya chased after them. Her laughter echoed around them.

"Run as much as you like!" Baya threw her arms to the sky. "You're free!"

A faint crackling sound came from behind her. Baya's joy was sucked away as she turned to find a hungry fire consuming the lovely flowers. The fire gained speed and sent everything it touched up into a cloud of black smoke.

"Get out of here!" Baya yelled.

Tara and Mook sped off in the distance, leaving Baya behind. They were soon lost to her. The fire grew closer. Baya needed to find water. She couldn't outrun the flames for much longer. She was forced to come to an abrupt halt as a large drop off appeared in front of her.

"Tara ... Mook," she yelled. But there was no answer and no sign of them. They must have fallen over the cliff. There was nowhere else they could have gone. She looked down. The only thing that could be seen was a swirling grey mist below. The bottom was not visible. Heat engulfed her back, she turned to the fire that was upon her. Her arm came up to cover her face in an attempt to shield it. She took a dangerous step toward the cliff. What if her fate was to fall to her death? Was burning worse than leaping into the unknown abyss?

She decided she had no other choice but to take a chance with the endless darkness. Baya spun around and jumped.

CHAPTER 9

Baya didn't fall far before her feet hit the ground with a painful jolt. The dark fog around her lifted. She had landed on wooden planks. Water lay on either side of her. A pier ... she was on a pier. The island of Pathins rose up in front of her. Low voices drew her attention and caused her to spin around. Standing at the end of the pier was a group of people. A woman held a tiny baby over her head.

"Please, Mighty Ameris, take this baby boy back into the sea where he came from. We are unable to care for him."

The women released the baby and before Baya heard the splash, she was running. "No!"

She pushed her way through the crowd and fell to her hands and knees over the edge of the dock. The baby was slowly sinking. It opened its eyes and Baya gasped. Its large tri-colored eyes stared directly at her. "Bek!" She plunged into the water after him.

Baya's eyes shot open. She was in her room, nothing but quiet and shadows all around. Wiping the sweat from her forehead, she rolled over to gaze at the moons outside her window.

Who knew if Ameris was good or bad? Baya thought. So what if she was a Goddess or just a woman. Something had led her and

Vicaroy to Merth. Through the terror and confusion that raced through her mind, one thing became clear. There was a Goddess, Ameris or not, and that higher-being had guided them.

Was the Goddess now telling Baya that she needed to return home? That she needed to save the boys of Pathins or at the very least Bek? And what of her promise to Mook? She had told the beast that she would set him free. But now Tara was also locked up. Baya sighed. She didn't dare allow herself to fall back asleep for fear of her dreams.

* * *

"YOU DIDN'T GET much sleep last night, did you?" Vicaroy asked.

"Is it that obvious?" Baya said.

Baya had joined Vicaroy in his room for breakfast. They preferred his spacious room and large windows. Not to mention he had his own washroom.

Baya played with her food and opened her mouth to speak, then closed it again.

"What's on your mind?"

"I had these dreams last night. They felt real and they were … terrifying."

"They're only dreams. Try not to let them get to you."

Baya nodded. "What if they weren't. I mean, what if Tara is in danger? I don't know what they do with the animals in captivity but some of them went missing yesterday. Then there is my brother … and Mook back home. What if they need help?"

"I'm sure everything's fine."

"But the dreams were so vivid. What about the fact that Pathins is becoming overpopulated and poor families often kill their baby boys so they have more for their daughters?"

"Surely that doesn't happen very often and besides what are we going to do about it? It's not like we can just go home."

Baya frowned. That was a good point, even if they could survive the journey a second time. There was no way they could find the invisible island. "There has to be a way."

"Are you that unhappy here?"

Baya paused to consider. "I suppose It's ... okay. Well, not really. I hate it."

"It is different." Vicaroy reached across the table and took Baya's hand. "We're stuck here anyway. Unless we think we can survive in the wild. And ..." he paused as if he was considering whether or not he should continue. "It's not your job to save everyone."

Baya nodded solemnly. Maybe he was right.

"Stop worrying. Nothing will come between us and Tara is safe in her cage."

He voiced a concern that she hadn't mentioned but that was very much on Baya's mind — something, or *someone,* pulling them apart. There were too many things to worry about. "Well we might as well get all of our troubles out in the open. What about this business about Ameris and their beliefs about her?"

Vicaroy exhaled sharply. "There's no way of knowing for sure who's right."

"Could everything we were taught be a lie?"

He shrugged.

"We had better get to class."

Vicaroy slumped in his seat and moaned his disapproval.

* * *

THIS TIME VICAROY sat shoulder to shoulder with Baya in class.

"I'm glad to see you decided to join my class again, Baya," Priestess Var issued a wicked smirk.

"Why wouldn't I?"

"During the last class you appeared to be ... rather upset. You remember, when you scurried out in such a hurry."

"She was probably crying," Osa snickered. She sat as close to Vicaroy's right as possible — of course.

He shot her a glare.

Baya tilted her head to one side and gave a slight shrug. "It doesn't matter." Her voice was as cool as a mountain night.

"You mean to tell me," Var said, "that the fact that you believe in the delusional teachings of a madwoman, *does not matter*?" she over-pronounced the last words.

Baya smiled. "Yep."

Var's mouth formed a line and her eyes flashed. She appeared to be incredibly disappointed that she couldn't get a rise out of Baya again. After an awkward silence, Var must have decided that she wouldn't get any more from Baya. "Well. We've wasted enough time on that anyway. Today's lesson is about how the city of Merth rebuilt itself after the devastating effects of Ameris's civil war."

Vicaroy smiled with approval and gave Baya's hand a quick squeeze.

It was a relief when the class turned their attention away from her. Baya took the reprieve as an opportunity to glance around the classroom. Mek was not sitting beside her. She caught a glimpse of red in the back of the class. Baya gave him a quick smile but didn't linger long enough to see if he returned the gesture. The ache of disappointment that crept in was not welcome. There were a handful of towheaded boys sitting too close to her left but they weren't Mek.

* * *

NACORA STOOD in the doorway of Vicaroy's workshop and watched her sons. It wasn't much more than a tiny wooden shed but Vicaroy spent all his free time in "his shop."

"Don't sand in circles. You always go with the grain." Vicaroy ran his hand back and forth over the wood. "Like this."

Rand imitated him. "Is this right?"

"That's it. You got it."

Nacora's sons were so engrossed in their work they were likely to never notice her. She entered the shed. "I'm glad you two are getting along well."

Rand lit up. "Mom, look. Vicaroy's teaching me how to build a boat."

"When it's done, we'll take it out on the river. It's time for dinner, so why don't you run along?"

"Okay, see you tomorrow, Vicaroy." Rand ran out of the shed with all the energy of a child.

"You can join us for dinner, you know?"

"That's okay. I'll eat with Baya."

"Thanks for spending time with Rand."

"He's a neat kid. Maybe Nefer will eventually come around as well."

Nacora chuckled. "He never leaves Wen's side. He won't even do anything with me if Wen's not there."

"He'll grow out of that."

"I hope so." Nacora slowly moved around the shop absentmindedly surveying the tools and piles of wood lying about. "Some of this stuff is old. Let me know if you need me to replace any of it."

"This is more than I could ever have hoped for in Pathins." He chuckled.

"What's so funny?"

"It's ironic. I was banished from my home because I built a boat. Now here I am building one right in front of the Unawi."

"And teaching her son such unfavorable behavior. You are a dreadful influence."

They laughed.

"I hope you will like it here. Merth has much to offer."

Vicaroy kicked at the leg of his workbench, not wanting to tell his mother the reservations he had about being here.

"This place will grow on you, as it did me."

He went back to sanding more vigorously than was needed.

"How are your lessons going?" Nacora quickly changed the subject.

"I actually really like math. Baya says I'm a natural. History, well I can stay awake through class most days and reading ..." Vicaroy rubbed the back of his neck. "It's a pain."

Nacora nodded as she already knew this. She was making small talk in order to get to what was really on her mind. "Has anyone asked you to accompany her to the celebration tomorrow?"

"Oh," Vicaroy appeared taken back by the change in subject. "I'll be going with Baya." Vicaroy's brow furrowed. "Who else would I be going with? You're the one who's always talking about having only one partner."

"But you're not spoken for … yet. Now is your chance to see who else might be out there. Osa, for example, seems interested in you. She's lovely and very skilled with her powers."

"And so is Baya." This came out sharper than Vicaroy intended.

"Very well. I just want you to be absolutely sure. You might find that there's someone who is … even better for you."

"Like Wen is better for you than Azod." He regretted saying it as soon as it came out.

It was Nacora's turn to look away. She pretended to be interested in a lathe that lay conveniently within reach.

"Mom, I'm —"

"It's okay."

"There isn't anyone better for me than Baya."

Nacora pursed her lips. "I suppose I will have to get to know Baya after all. She does seem to treat you well."

"She always has because she truly loves me. She loved me before I was, as you say, 'a prince.' The other girls would not even look at me if I were not your son."

"I'm not so sure about that. When I first came here I was a nobody. Yet, I was a novelty — foreign blood, like you and Baya. Men literally fought over me. I suppose that is how I caught the eye of the prince."

"Actually, that explains a lot."

"You're sure Baya is the one?"

Vicaroy forced himself to hold her stare.

"So be it. This also means that I will have to get her a suitable gown for the celebration tomorrow." She gave Vicaroy a crooked smile.

"Thanks, Mom."

CHAPTER 10

A knock came at Baya's door. She swung it open expecting to see Vicaroy. Instead, she found Kuna, dressed as always in her armor and short tunic. Of course, her spear that doubled as a walking stick dominated her appearance. Baya blinked in surprise. She could have sworn the guard's armor was shinier than usual.

"I'm here to escort you to the women's chambers where you will be prepared for tonight's festivities."

"Hey? You're a woman. Will you be getting *prepared* as well?"

Kuna readjusted her grip on her spear until her knuckles turned white. "All of Merth's most predominant members will be in attendance tonight. Hundreds of people will be allowed into the castle simply so the Unawi can show off her son. I will be on high alert in case anyone tries to harm Nacora." She rapped her knuckles on her metal breastplate. "I'm already *prepared* for the evening."

"Why would someone want to hurt Nacora?"

"The word on the street is that people are happy with the new ruler but you never know, some crazy person could make a move against her. The dance would offer the perfect opportunity. I strongly advised against opening the gates of the palace to the public. But Nacora insisted on letting half the city in."

"With no regard for what a security nightmare this is for you."

Kuna's stern expression softened. "Exactly."

"I'm sure everything will be fine." Baya looked around her room. "Um. I don't have anything special to wear, so I guess I'm ready."

"Nacora has made arrangements for your evening attire."

This was a relief. Baya knew that Osa would be wearing the very best. "Well, no one wants to go to a celebration underdressed." She glanced around. "Wait. Let me grab my bag." Baya stood with her back to Kuna. "Hurry," she whispered.

"Who are you talking to?"

"No one." Baya swung the bag over her shoulder.

"You just told someone to hurry up."

"Oh. Right. I was talking to myself." Baya gave her a mischievous smile. "Let's go."

Kuna narrowed her eyes before spinning on her heel and leading the way.

* * *

THE ROOM KUNA led Baya to was huge, even though it had a low ceiling. Along one wall was a counter. Mounted on the wall above the counter was one long mirror running the entire length. It was well lit with torches and strategically placed candles. The room was full of women, some were seated on stools as they put powder on their faces or sprayed perfumes on their necks. Other women held up different gowns in an attempt to decide which one she liked best.

The room was abuzz with loud excited chatter. Baya couldn't help but smile.

"Baya, darling, over here."

Baya's jaw dropped when she saw who was calling her. It was Nacora.

"I have acquired the perfect gown for you."

"I must get back to the great hall to make sure the perimeter is secured," Kuna said.

"Good luck tonight," Baya told her.

"I may not be the one who needs it," Kuna gave Baya a knowing smile before swiftly exiting.

"She seems happy to be leaving."

"This is not Kuna's style."

"I can't imagine that it's any girl's … *style*. Why would women fuss over their appearance so much?"

"Come. Let me show you. You may decide you like it."

Nacora moved to a metal bar holding up more gowns than Baya had ever seen. Nacora went straight for the one that out-shimmered the others. She held it up and fanned it out with her free arm.

Baya had to deliberately slam her mouth shut after it had fallen open.

The gown was made of a fabric that changed colors. The purples flowed into shades of dark blues and greens. It reminded her of Tara's feathers and scales.

"It has an open back." Nacora flipped the dress around to show her.

And a form-fitted waist, Baya noted.

"Vicaroy will love it," Nacora beamed.

"I'm sure he will."

Nacora tilted her head to examine Baya's face. "Two of my servants will help you with your makeup."

"Makeup?"

Nacora gently placed the gown in Baya's arms as if it were a newborn infant. "Now, go. You don't want to be late."

Baya barely had time to say, "Thank you," before two servants swept her away. They led her to a vacant stool in front of the long mirror.

Osa gave her a wicked smile as she passed by.

By the time the servants were done with her, Baya didn't recognize her own reflection.

Nacora's form appeared in the mirror behind Baya. "You look lovely."

Baya flushed. She felt prettier than … well perhaps, than she ever had. The good food in Merth had restored her body to at least a healthy thin. She tried not to compare herself to Nacora, whose large breasts filled out her gown to the point of bursting. Baya did not have that problem, even though she desperately wished she did.

"It's time to make our entrance." Nacora led Baya out of the women's chamber and down several halls. She stopped at a solid stone wall. With the wave of her hand a door appeared and stone scraped against the floor as it opened.

Nacora smiled warmly. "After you."

Baya narrowed her eyes. "Why are you being so nice to me?"

"I've had a … change of heart. I see it now. My son wants you and no one else. The way he looks at you…" Nacora tucked a strand of Baya's loose hair behind her ear. "Well, it's the same way Wen looks at me. You seem to treat him well, so as long as that is the case then you two have my consent."

Baya searched Nacora's dark almond-shaped eyes for signs that she was lying or, perhaps had been drinking wine all day — something to indicate that this was a joke. All that could be seen was sincerity.

A swelling sensation formed in Baya's chest. Vicaroy wanted her and only her; even with the voluptuous blond, Osa, throwing herself at him. Visions of lovely dark-skinned children running around Vicaroy as they played in the vast palace gardens popped into Baya's head. The future, her future with Vicaroy, had never been so clear. She felt like her chest might burst. They would be together forever, raise a family and … be happy.

"However…" Nacora said.

Baya stopped breathing.

"Must you insist on carrying that bag?"

Baya exhaled. She adjusted the large sack that was slung over her shoulder. "Yes."

"Very well." Nacora gestured for Baya to enter the hidden passageway.

She found herself on a narrow balcony. They were hidden in the shadows high above the Great Hall. The vast room below was full of people. Candle-lit chandeliers and torches filled the room with a gentle yellow glow. It was the largest room she had ever seen.

The narrow balcony led to two wide stairwells that curved elegantly down to the ballroom floor. In between the stairs stood a stage, at the very back of which sat a long table. Behind the table stood two large chairs with plush red cushions. Baya guessed that these were reserved for Nacora and Wen. Many other smaller wooden chairs had been placed on either side of the thrones.

"When you are announced, you will make your entrance via the stairs to the left." Nacora waved to Wen and Vicaroy who waited at the top of the other staircase. "They will enter the Hall from over there."

Wen and Vicaroy returned the gesture.

Vicaroy wore a purple tunic styled in the fashion of Baya's dress. A thick gold belt showed off his lean waist and fabric had been draped over his shoulders, which accented their breadth.

The smile that filled Baya's face was one of the largest she had ever worn.

"You look simply radiant," Nacora said. "I suppose I can see what my son sees in you."

CHAPTER 11

A loud voice boomed through the Great Hall, "The moment you have all been waiting for has arrived. It is with great honor that I give you your merciful ruler, Unawi Nacora."

The crowd came to life. People moved to get a better view of the stairs.

"And your beloved Unatheo, Wen."

Nacora nodded to Wen and they descended the stairs in perfect unison.

The crowd fell silent and like a ripple through water everyone dropped down on one knee.

Nacora and Wen slowly moved to center stage. Nacora took Wen's hand in hers.

"You may rise." Nacora addressed the crowd in a loud voice. Once everyone was standing she continued, "A couple of months ago I was given an opportunity I could never have dreamed of. I have been given the gift of a second chance. You see, I never thought I would see my eldest son again. Yet, despite all odds, he and his companion managed to find their way to this amazing city, just as I once did."

Nacora raised her arms, forming a V shape to draw people's attention to the staircases on either side of her. "I'm proud to introduce you to your new prince, Vicaroy and his lovely companion, Baya of Pathins."

An excited chatter moved through the people and their eyes didn't dare blink as they scanned the stairs for the first sighting of the mysterious foreigners.

Enthusiastic murmurs moved like waves through the crowd as Baya and Vicaroy slowly made their way down the matching stairways.

Baya thought it was odd that they didn't bow to Vicaroy as they had with Nacora. For all their talk about how men were equal, it appeared that they had no real power. It was also strikingly obvious that Vicaroy had the darkest skin out of anyone in the Great Hall. Nacora was in second place and Baya a distant third.

The girls in the front row bounced on their heels. This was accompanied by giggles and squeals.

Baya overheard some of the girls. "He's so handsome!" She worried that they might mob Vicaroy in a frenzy.

Beads of sweat had formed on Vicaroy's brow and his knuckles were pale as they gripped the banister.

Baya was glad he held onto it so tightly. That way he wouldn't fall if he missed a step. She tried to reassure him with a broad smile. She was also trying to remind him to smile as well.

An awkward tight-lipped expression crossed Vicaroy's face.

Baya swallowed a chuckle. With confidence she strode over to him and took his hand. A genuine smile appeared on his lips and spread to his eyes when he gazed at Baya.

The people of Merth broke out in applause. Once Baya was sure they had gotten a good look at their new prince, she led Vicaroy to the long table at the back of the stage. Vicaroy was directed to sit to the left of Nacora, followed by Baya at his left. Wen, Rand, Nefer, Var, and Osa sat on Nacora's right. As she set her bag at her feet, Baya intentionally avoided looking at Osa.

Nacora gave Vicaroy's hand a reassuring squeeze.

He used the elegantly folded cloth napkin to wipe his soaked forehead.

People slowly made their way back to their tables as servants delivered food. Other members of Wen's family flocked to Nacora's table. Mek was quick to take the seat next to Baya. Hopefully this meant that he was not mad at her for refusing him. She greeted him with a nod.

Kuna and a male guard stood like sentinels on either end of the stage. Kuna's eyes were little more than slits as they scanned the room. The notch missing from her ear and its accompanying scar that slashed across the remaining ear made her appear all the more ominous.

As wine was poured, Mek broke the silence. "Did you know that Baya can talk to animals?"

"Oh, it's nothing. All women can do it," Baya said.

"This is true," Nacora said. She was most likely thinking back to her education in Pathins. "But pets are rare, even in Pathins. Most women never learn to use this skill."

"Learning about the different types of animals was my favorite subject in school," Wen said. "It would be wonderful to have a pet that I could talk to."

"It *is* wonderful. I love Doba and Tara very much," Baya said. A tickling sensation moved up Baya's leg. "Doba, no!"

Doba's head appeared over Baya's shoulder. Mek leaned away and a scream came from someone to the right. Baya didn't know if it was Nefer or Var who gave the startled yell.

Kuna was at the table in a matter of seconds, spear at the ready.

"Doba, you promised that as long as I brought you along and gave you fresh table scraps you would stay in the satchel." Baya looked apologetically to those around her. "Sorry. He's getting bored hanging out in my room all day. He begged me to bring him along tonight."

Doba made a series of clicking noises.

"Yes, we were talking about you, Doba, but that wasn't an invitation to come out and scare people."

"Kuna, you can relax. Everything is fine," Nacora said. "I learned to read the mind of a creature like that back when I was in school."

"That may have been one of Doba's parents," Baya said. "Unawi Shema used him to teach us how to communicate with animals."

"We could use an animal like that in our lessons," Var said.

Doba hissed, blinking his four beady black eyes at Var. Mek moved back even farther.

"He says he doesn't want to be used like that anymore. That's why he left Pathins. He was the last of his kind on the island. All he wants is to find others like him."

"The rain forests to the south of Merth are full of septapods," Wen said. "They are different than the desert septapods."

Nacora's expression was full of pride, apparently because of her theo's knowledge of animals.

"As I said, I loved learning about animals in school." Wen winked at Nacora.

Doba jumped on to the table, took a mouth full of food off Baya's plate, and leapt to the floor.

"He said to tell you thanks, Wen," Baya said.

"Thanks for what?"

"I don't know."

Doba jumped off the table and made his way toward the crowd.

"Doba, you promised you would behave." Baya stood. "What do you mean? ... Goodbye? … Doba? …"

His dark segmented body wove through the Great Hall causing a disturbance that rippled through the masses as he went. Men and women jumped to their feet and startled screams followed Doba all the way out the far end of the room.

Baya turned her concerned stare to Vicaroy. "He wouldn't just leave … like that … would he?"

"I don't know." Vicaroy put his arm around Baya. "We didn't have many animals on Pathins. Only fish, birds and insects. I used to see snakes in the garden sometimes. But no predators, which we simply called beasts. So what is the name for Tara's kind?"

Baya knew that Vicaroy was only making conversation in an attempt to get her mind off Doba.

"Tara is the large predator that accompanied you here?" Wen said.

Vicaroy nodded.

"Then Tara is a servine," Wen said.

"A servine." Baya rolled the unfamiliar word around in her mind. "I didn't think any predators existed on the island until they threw me into a pit with one."

"Sounds barbaric," Osa scoffed.

"Yeah. It kind of was," Baya admitted. She spent the rest of the meal poking at the food on her plate, fighting the urge to run after Doba.

"Don't worry," Vicaroy whispered. "I'm sure he went back to your room."

Baya's shoulders relaxed when she looked into Vicaroy's eyes which were full of reassurance.

Var abruptly stood, pulling Baya's attention away from Vicaroy.

"I'm going to retire for the night," Var announced loudly. "It has been simply exhausting planning for this celebration. Not to mention being invaded by a giant insect." A brief shudder passed over Var before she turned to give a slight bow to Nacora.

Nacora nodded. "Get some rest, My Friend."

"Are you feeling well?" Osa said. "Do you want me to go with you, Mother?"

"No, Dear. You stay and enjoy yourself." Var gave Vicaroy a sinister smile before leaving.

An icy sensation ran down Baya's spine. What were they up to? Baya wondered.

Many couples moved to the dance floor after eating their fill. Wen stood and took Nacora's hand. "Would you like to dance, My Love?"

Baya could have sworn that Nacora blushed.

"Why, of course," the Unawi said. "You know how much I love to dance. It feels like it has been ages since we had the opportunity."

As she watched the lovely pair head to the dance floor, Baya was filled with a soft warm feeling. "They love each other so much."

Vicaroy looked at Baya, as if for the first time. "I can't believe I don't know the answer to this but, do you know how to dance?"

Baya chuckled. "No. The dances back in Pathins were only for the daughters and sons of the high priestesses. I was never interested in attending." Baya gave Vicaroy a playful smile.

"Then it's past time that you learned to dance," Osa interrupted. Before anyone could protest she pulled Vicaroy out of his seat by his upper arm and dragged him out to the open floor.

Baya crossed her arms and glared at Osa.

"Would you …" Mek cleared his throat. "I mean, I could teach you to dance … if you like."

"I'm fine right here, thank you."

"You don't look fine. I mean you look beautiful but —"

Baya frowned at Mek, cutting his words short.

Vicaroy barely moved as Osa twisted and twirled around him.

After a long silence Mek leaned in close. "Look." He pointed to a group of young men milling about nearby. "Now that the prince is out of the way, I'm afraid there is a long line of suiters headed your way. They're most likely trying to muster up the courage to ask you to dance."

Baya moaned.

"So wouldn't it be easier if you danced with me, rather than having to turn them all down?"

Baya peeled her eyes away from Vicaroy and Osa to look into Mek's dazzling emerald eyes. His milky skin seemed to glow. The light danced off his hair turning it multiple colors ranging from a fire red, to a deep maroon, to a light brown and finally a golden color. Baya exhaled with exaggeration. "It does seem easier to dance with you."

Mek's eyes sparkled even brighter. He stood and guided Baya to her feet.

As it turned out, Baya wasn't much better at dancing than Vicaroy. She felt silly as they awkwardly moved around the dance floor. Mek's hand on her waist felt … wrong and unfamiliar.

Thankfully after only a couple of songs, Wen and Nacora headed for their seats. Vicaroy took this as an opportunity to get out of further humiliation. Baya quickly followed suit.

"I had better get the boys to bed," Wen announced.

That was when Baya noticed that Nefer sat with his head resting on the table, half asleep.

"Come on, Rand. Let's go," Wen said.

"But why do I have to go? I'm not tired," Rand protested.

"It's getting late. Go with your father, Rand," Nacora said.

"Ahhhh." Rand let his head hang down and followed his father, who carried Nefer, up the stairs leading out the back entrance.

"You were getting so much better at dancing, Vicaroy. Shall we go back out?" Osa beamed.

But before he could answer, a loud horn sounded in the distance. The eerie drone caused the hair on the back of Baya's neck to prickle.

"Close ranks!" Kuna yelled.

CHAPTER 12

Guards seemed to materialize from the shadows. In the blink of an eye they formed two lines in front of Nacora. Kuna and a male guard stood closest to her just in front of the royal table.

The doors at the far end of the Great Hall swung open. The musicians stopped playing and a spine numbing silence befell the previously merry crowd.

Baya gave Vicaroy an uneasy glance and they reached for each other in unison. She strained to see around the guards. People cleared a path in the center of the hall. She instinctively rose to her feet when she saw the mass of people, or creatures, rather, who marched toward them.

Everyone at the table followed Baya's lead and got to their feet.

The creatures made their way toward Nacora's table. They stood taller than regular humans. Some of them had grey skin while others were a sickly green. Their bodies bulged with toned muscles. But what was truly odd about them was that they had four arms and what was even more strange was how they were attached. While they had only two legs, they had double shoulder joints. One set of arms came out in front and the other set faced backwards. Each creature held two spears, one in the front and one in the back.

Baya couldn't imagine why anything would need so many arms. She gasped when she noticed they had wings folded neatly into their sides. The wings consisted of a thin, see-through membrane that was hard to make out from a distance.

"Arges from Aregow," Nacora whispered.

"Who?" Vicaroy asked.

Nacora didn't answer. Her gaze remained focused on the approaching beasts.

Baya searched her face for some clue as to whether or not they were friendly. But Nacora's expression remained sternly impassive. Intense, yes, but no sign of outright fear.

Baya tightened her grip on Vicaroy's hand. She noticed that the women in the audience had moved to stand in front of their theos and children.

To her amazement, the Arges appearance grew even scarier as their faces came into view. All ten creatures were bald. They had four solid black eyes and no other features except small fleshy ears poking up on either side of their head, like tiny horns. No nose, no mouth, only smooth veiny flesh.

Baya shivered and it spread to Vicaroy.

Still another anomaly was that their legs appeared to end in the middle of one large foot as if each leg had a foot facing frontward and another one facing backward.

The Arges stopped in front of Nacora's long table. Many didn't stand front-facing as Baya had expected. They appeared to mill about at random. She swallowed a scream, as the one closest to her turned its back to her, or what should have been its back, instead there was another set of four eyes. The black beady specks blinked at Baya from the back of its head.

"Jetzu." Nacora nodded her head respectfully to the green Arge. "And Hanzu." She repeated the gesture to the slightly taller grey Arge beside Jetzu. "This is a surprise."

"Madam Unawi." Hanzu and Jetzu spoke in unison. Their mouths were nothing more than a thin slit, a slit that all but disappeared when closed.

Baya forced herself not to shudder ... again.

"The reason for your visit must be important if you would travel all this way when it is not time for our annual gathering?"

"It is a matter of utmost importance," Jetzu said. "Since you appear to be in the middle of a celebration we will get right to the point."

"We are looking for the Priestess Var but it appears that she is not here as we had hoped," Hanzu added.

"Var retired early. I'm afraid she is fast asleep. But I'm sure I could help you with whatever it is that is so urgent."

Jetzu and Hanzu gave each other a knowing glance. "It is highly unlikely that Var would share this information with anyone."

Nacora's eyes narrowed. "Var is my most trusted advisor. Are you implying that she would keep secrets from me?"

Jetzu and Hanzu exchanged another glance and Jetzu appeared to roll her eyes.

"Very well," Hanzu said. "It has recently come to our attention that Var has stumbled upon something for which we have searched for centuries. Our mothers passed down legends of this ... missing artifact. We wish to retrieve it."

"And you believe Var possesses this ... artifact?"

"We do. Or at the very least she knows where to find it," Jetzu said.

"I haven't heard her speak of finding anything unusual. Osa do you know anything about this?" Nacora looked to her right but Osa was no longer there. "Osa?"

The entire room seemed to glance around for signs of Osa but she must've vanished in the midst of the chaos.

Odd, Baya thought.

"I'm afraid I can't help you unless you can be more specific," Nacora said.

"The artifact we seek is —"

"Don't tell them," Jetzu interrupted. "Our business is with Var and Var alone."

Nacora's neutral face darkened. "As I've already told you, she is indisposed. If that is all, then please be so kind as to allow us to get back to our celebration. I will confer with Var about this ... object ... whatever it is and send word to you if she knows of anything. Otherwise, we will see you at the usual annual gathering."

Hanzu stamped his spear on the stone floor and a low growl escaped from somewhere deep inside.

Kuna and the other guards grabbed their weapons with both hands and took a step forward.

Baya had the terrible feeling that even though the Arges were far outnumbered, they could make quick work of Nacora's guards.

"Darling," Jetzu placed her five-fingered hand on Hanzu's forearm. They appeared to have no thumb, only long fingers. "Unawi Nacora knows nothing and it is not worth breaking our long-standing peace with Merth." To Nacora she added, "Please let us know if Var will tell you anything about a very old and very powerful artifact. You can send word immediately. We look forward to hearing from you."

"Var won't tell her or anyone else about what she knows," Hanzu barked.

Baya gave a start.

Anger flared to life in Nacora's eyes. "You do not know Var in the least. If you came here to insult me and my court then it is past time you leave." She held Hanzu's four-eyed glare with equal intensity.

"We will find another way, Hanzu," Jetzu said. "We are terribly sorry to have wasted your time Madam Unawi. We look forward to hearing from you and Var regarding this matter." Jetzu lowered her head in respect.

Nacora returned the gesture. "You have my word. I will let you know if I learn of anything out of the ordinary."

Hanzu growled as he walked backward. Two of his arms waved through the air as a signal for the Arges to retreat. It was creepy watching them leave. They didn't turn around but rather used their eyes in the "back" of their heads to see where they were going.

The entire room seemed to exhale once the Arges were out of sight.

CHAPTER 13

"I'm terribly sorry for the interruption," Nacora announced to the masses in the Great Hall. She signaled for the musicians to resume playing. "Everything is fine. Please carry on with the festivities." She sat and raised her glass with a broad smile.

Baya was sure that it was all for show — a strong front.

"Mother, what were those things?" Vicaroy asked.

"And what did they want?" Baya added.

Nacora's smile faded as soon as most of the people had gone back to celebrating. "I have no idea." She mumbled. Her thoughts were clearly not on Vicaroy and Baya.

Kuna moved to stand directly across the table. "Madam, I don't recall Arges flying over our walls uninvited like that before."

"Is that why we heard the sentries alarm only moments before they entered the Great Hall?" Baya asked.

Kuna nodded. "Aye. They simply flew over our walls and right in here."

"Arges are superb warriors." Mek's eyes shone with envy. "They're impossible to sneak up on. You saw the eyes in the back of their heads."

"It's like they were designed to move backward as easily as they move forward," Vicaroy said.

"Technically, they don't have a back, only two fronts," Kuna said.

Mek nodded. "They can survive out in the wild much better than we can. And their women have abilities like ours, so they are basically unstoppable."

"That is why we strive for peace between our two nations," Nacora said. "I hate to think of what would happen if they ever turned hostile toward us."

"I'm afraid it wouldn't be much of a fight." Baya struggled to wrap her thoughts around all this.

Nacora bit her lip. "It would be the end of Merth."

"Ameris's scrolls never mentioned such creatures," Baya said.

"Our history with them dates back about eight-hundred years," Nacora said.

"So Ameris may not have known about them?" Baya asked.

The ruler shook her head indicating that she didn't know the answer.

"Where do they live?" Vicaroy asked.

"Aregow. It's a large territory to the far southeast of Merth," Mek said.

"Mek," Nacora seemed to snap out of her inner thoughts. "Perhaps you should take Vicaroy and Baya with you to combat training."

"What's that?" Baya didn't like the sound of it.

"You didn't learn the art of combat in Pathins?" Mek asked.

"Pathins is peaceful."

"All fighting, violence and weapons of any kind are strictly forbidden," Nacora explained.

"That's too bad. Combat training is super fun. It's my favorite class. Vicaroy you're going to love it." Mek sliced his hand through the air in an attempt to imitate fighting. This resulted in a goblet falling over. Wine spilt across the table.

"Sorry." Mek scrambled to mop up the mess with a napkin.

"I had hoped you two wouldn't need such skills. I see now that it was a naïve hope." Nacora's face grew sorrowful and the color seemed to drain from her.

There was a long silence at the royal table as cheerful chatter and music filled the air.

"Mom, can I talk to you for a minute?"

Nacora rubbed her forehead. She tried to smile but it fell short of convincing. "Sure, Honey."

Once they were off to themselves, Vicaroy asked, "You honestly don't know what that was about?"

Nacora shook her head. "Believe me, I wish I did."

Vicaroy studied her for a moment and decided that she was telling the truth. He also noticed that she looked pale. "Are you okay?"

"I'm fine. A little tired, that's all." She rubbed her head again. "I'm going to retire for the night."

"Mom?"

"I'm fine." She waved Vicaroy off.

Kuna escorted her out of the Great Hall. Nacora appeared to be shooing her away as well.

* * *

Baya left the celebrations shortly after Nacora. She could no longer stand it. She hurried down a long corridor. Her silky gown billowed out behind her. She burst into her room. "Doba! Are you here? You won't believe what we saw tonight."

No rustling came from under her covers or from under her bed. "Doba?" She ripped the blankets back. "You wouldn't dare leave like that … would you?"

"I'm sure he won't go far."

Baya spun around to find Vicaroy — his body relaxed against the door frame. He was his calm and confident self again, his true self. This was in great contrast to how he looked at the celebration. She loved to see him like this and it only happened when they were alone.

Baya sat down hard on the bed. "I'm sure you're right. … Yet, he said, 'goodbye,' at the celebration. It sounded like he meant for good.

You don't think he headed to the south, to the rain forests to find a mate?"

Vicaroy's eyes widened. "I don't know. That is why he came along with us in the first place."

Baya nodded in agreement. "I'm glad you followed me." The last thing she wanted was to be alone in her room without Doba's company.

"It was a relief to get away from all the people." He moved to sit down next to her. "I'm worried about Mother. She looked ill when she left."

"She's probably overwhelmed. I know I am." Baya gazed up at him. His breath seemed to hitch. "I'm proud of your mom, the way she stood up to those creatures."

"She's a very strong woman. Like you." Vicaroy placed his hand over Baya's. "You look wonderful tonight."

"Thank you." Baya flushed. "Although, you were much more of a sight than I was. I thought every girl in the room was going to faint when they saw you."

Vicaroy frowned. "Are you kidding? You didn't see how the guys couldn't take their eyes off you?"

"I didn't notice." Baya chuckled. "I suppose I was too busy glaring at all the girls, Osa in particular."

"I only want you." Vicaroy's golden-brown eyes sparkled in the dim candlelight.

Baya pressed her lips to his.

His hand quivered as he took her waist.

She wrapped her arms around his neck and pulled her lips from his. "You shouldn't be here. What if the guards come by?"

A mischievous smile crossed his lips. "After you left, I excused myself and walked the corridors for a bit. I went by my room and didn't see any guards. They appear to be occupied with all the excitement in the Great Hall. There's a good chance that no one will be by to check on us until morning."

"Let's hope so." A seductive smile crossed her face.

The next thing she knew, Vicaroy was on top of her and she was pinned to the bed. Her legs wrapped around his waist.

He paused to look at her. She pulled him to her by the neck of his tunic. Lips and legs were interlocked in a glorious tangle.

She needed this. He needed this. Baya let her mind go blank except for his caress. Worries about strange creatures and what they wanted, worries about where Doba had disappeared to, worries about other girls chasing after Vicaroy, they all vanished as she lost herself in the desires of her body. The only thing that remained, the only thing that mattered, was their need for each other.

Vicaroy stood and was undressed in a matter of seconds. He pulled on the top of her gown but it didn't budge. "How do I get you out of this thing?"

Baya chuckled. "I have no idea. Servants put me into it." She rose from the bed and turned around. "There must be buttons or a tie or … something."

He tugged at the back for a time. "Can I rip it off?"

"No. Your mother gave it to me. I'm sure it's very expensive."

Vicaroy growled.

"Your mother isn't even here and she's still finding ways to stop us from being together. She most likely gave me this dress because it doesn't come off." Hysterical laughter escaped from Baya.

Vicaroy gave up on the gown and bent over with laughter.

Baya took a couple of deep breaths. "Okay. It has an open back. Surely I can squeeze out." She hunched over and pulled on the sleeves, trying to slide herself out the back of the gown. The waist was stuck at the hips. She pushed until some stitches gave way. Finally the dress slid off and fell to the floor.

Vicaroy's laughter was cut short as his eyes combed over her exposed body.

Suddenly self-conscious, Baya wrapped a blanket around herself.

"What are you doing?" Vicaroy slowly removed the cover.

"I'm too skinny."

"You're perfect," he breathed.

The look of longing in his eyes was reassuring. She let his eyes roam over every inch of her. He brushed his lips over her shoulder and kissed his way to her mouth. He ran his fingertips down her arms. Baya shivered.

"Lay down," he whispered.

He moved with her, crawling on top of her. Starting at her throat he kissed his way down her body. Positioning his head between her legs, he placed his arms around her. The palm of his hand spread against the flat of her stomach as the first gentle brush of his tongue sent a shiver of pleasure through her. Baya cried out when his mouth secured itself to her and sucked. Her chin shot up and her eyes rolled back. It seemed like only a matter of moments before the tingling started in her knees and grew more intense as it spread to her lower abdomen.

When she was sure she couldn't stand anymore, the sensation ebbed to a low purr between her legs. She stilled, utterly unable to move a muscle as her entire body relaxed. It was as if she were sinking into the bed.

When her body started working again, she slowly sat up — breathing hard. "Is that what sex is like?"

"That's just the beginning." Vicaroy guided her back down and positioned himself on top of her.

A mixture of excitement and worry consumed her. She wasn't sure if she could handle much more.

Baya was more than ready, so she only felt a twinge of discomfort as he slid himself inside her.

CHAPTER 14

Vicaroy lay on top of Baya, temporarily unable to move. When his breathing slowed, he whispered, "I've been dreaming of this day for a long time."

"Me too." There were tears in her eyes. The utter joy, the pleasure, the closeness. She could never have imagined that life could be this good. She knew she would never lose Vicaroy. "I feel like we … belong to each other. … I mean, it's like we're now officially together."

"We are," his voice was rough and barely a whisper. "Nothing can come between us." He moved to lay behind her, pulling her up against his body.

She ran her fingers over the scars on his arm from the animal attack on the plains. His arm jerked at the soft touch and his muscles tensed as if the white flesh was sensitive. She was glad they were safe and together. A sudden thought caused Baya to pull away and prop herself up to face him.

Her eyes sparkled like golden orbs in the dim light. "How did you know how to … make me feel so good?"

He cocked his head to the side. "What do you mean?"

"It's like you've done this before … a lot."

He chuckled. "I promise you, Baya, I haven't ever been with a woman before. You know … it's what all boys are taught, well in Pathins anyway. I don't know about here."

Baya's eyes narrowed. "What are you talking about? What are all boys taught?"

"How best to please women, of course. They have little models and everything to show us where all the best spots are." He ran his hand gently between her legs, causing a distracting sensation to run up her spine.

She grabbed his hand to stop him. "Vicaroy, that's … awful."

He looked at her in complete puzzlement. His face darkened. "Why? Did I not please you enough."

"Vicaroy, that was amazing. You were … perfect."

He smiled with relief. "Then what's the problem?"

"The problem. Well … it's terrible. Boys are not allowed to be educated in Pathins except in how to give us the most pleasure. Don't you think that's … wrong?"

"I don't know. I like it that I know how to make you feel good."

"It's not fair. I mean I was never taught how to please you." Baya scrambled to push herself up. "It's like men's only purpose in life is to please women."

"Well that's the way it was back home. But we're in a better place now." Vicaroy sat up beside Baya. "And I can think of a lot worse things than what we just did together."

Baya pursed her lips.

He chuckled.

"What's so funny?"

"Men are not that hard to please. We're quite simple."

"So you enjoyed it?" Baya's eyes were wide with concern.

He ran a finger along her jaw. "You have no idea." He leaned into her, pressing his lips to hers.

They made love two more times before the first sun was on the rise and Vicaroy had to sneak back to his room.

Baya had barely slipped off into a deep sleep when an urgent knock came at the door.

* * *

Baya gave Kuna a sleepy smile but the gesture wasn't returned.

"Unawi Nacora is requesting everyone's presence in the Great Hall," Kuna announced. Her body was even more rigid than usual and her formality was concerning.

Baya forced the tiredness aside. She blinked to help her wake up. "Why?"

"I assure you that I have no idea, other than it appears to be important."

Could Nacora have found out about last night? Were they going to be punished for breaking curfew? What did punishment look like in Merth? "Let me get dressed."

"You have to the count of thirty."

"Fine," Baya snapped as she shut the door. She could hear Kuna knock on the next door. With trembling hands she quickly dressed. The entire time she was hoping that she and Vicaroy were not in trouble for having been together. Surely it was not so bad that everyone needed to be called to a special meeting ... or was it?

By the time the Baya entered the Great Hall, Vicaroy was already at Nacora's side. The room had been transformed. The tables and chairs from last night's feast were gone, including the long table that was in front of the royal thrones. People filed into the large open space of the Hall.

Nacora stood in front of her throne, Vicaroy to her right and ... Osa to her left. Osa was dressed in a lovely green gown. She looked as if she were ready to attend another party.

Baya didn't like the smug look on Osa's face and she wished she had worn a gown instead of breeches and a tunic.

When Baya moved to the stage to take her place by Vicaroy, two male guards moved to stand in her way.

"You are not royalty. You don't belong up here," Nacora said. "Your place is with everyone else — at the bottom of the stairs."

"What?" Baya protested. "What happened to —"

A guard grabbed Baya's arm and guided her down the steps.

"Let go of me." She jerked her arm free. Moving to the front of the crowd, Baya gave Vicaroy a questioning look.

He shrugged, indicating that he had no idea what was going on.

Nacora's icy stare told Baya to keep her mouth shut. Baya suppressed a shiver and held her gaze.

Many more excruciating minutes passed before Nacora stepped forward. The crowd fell silent at once.

"I'm sure you all are wondering why I have called this urgent meeting." She smiled as she slowly glanced at all her subjects — clearly enjoying the attention — the power.

Baya pressed her lips together. Nacora was usually more humble than this, or maybe it was that she hadn't yet seen this side of the Unawi.

"I have some disturbing news." Again she paused for effect. "But never fear, I also have a grand announcement to make." Her warm smile broadened. "First, let's get the bad news out of the way. I'm afraid my very dear companion, Var, has fallen ill. She has left strict instructions that *no one,* except her lovely and intelligent daughter Osa, is to enter her chamber while she recovers. Let us pray for the priestess's health."

Nacora took Vicaroy's and Osa's hands, then lowered her head and led the masses in prayer.

What was with all the boasting — calling Osa 'lovely' and 'intelligent?' Baya wondered. Nacora didn't talk like that, did she?

"Now, on to the good news."

Osa bounced on her heels. She hadn't seemed the least bit upset or worried about her mother.

"It is with great pride that I announce the royal coupling of my son, Vicaroy, to the powerful and benevolent Osa."

CHAPTER 15

Vicaroy shot a wide-eyed glance to his mother, then to Baya, whose mouth had fallen open.

"There is no one more powerful or more suited to become my successor than the gifted and capable Osa," Nacora announced to the room full of onlookers. "Any man would be honored to have such a partner." She glanced briefly at her son. "You are very lucky."

The contents of Baya's stomach threatened to come up. It wasn't just the fact that Vicaroy was being forced to couple with another but the disgusting emphasis on how "perfect" Osa was sent bile into Baya's mouth. It was as if the Unawi was trying to make everyone believe that Osa was the greatest thing in the world.

"This royal coupling will take place as soon as the arrangements can be made." Nacora raised both Vicaroy's hand and Osa's hand, joining them. She stepped back to let the masses celebrate their future Unawi and Unatheo.

Vicaroy stared at his feet. The crowd did not cheer. They remained in silent shock, like Baya. They must not like to see a man forced to couple.

People slowly began to applaud but it was less than enthusiastic.

Nacora coaxed Vicaroy to smile.

Baya was consumed with a cold sensation that collided with an equally fierce heat. The fire won over the fear. The flames rose to Baya's cheeks and caused her ears to ring. "No!" she shouted. "Don't force him to smile! He clearly doesn't want this. Nacora, what happened to last night? You said that men have to agree to the coupling as well. You also said that we could be together —"

"Lock her in her room!"

Numerous gasps and murmurs rippled through the crowd and the two male guards advanced on Baya.

A flash of nervousness gleamed in the Unawi's eyes as she glanced at her shocked followers. She quickly issued the sweetest of smiles. "I regret that such actions are necessary but it is clearly stated in the divine laws of Merth that any amount of insubordination is *not* to be tolerated."

As the guards dragged Baya from the Great hall, she strained to see Vicaroy. "Vicaroy! Don't let her do this to you!"

The guards yanked harder on her arms.

Vicaroy didn't dare to look up. His eyes were unseeing as he continued to stare at the floor.

"No!" Thick smoke billowed from Baya's hands, causing the men to gag and cough. This allowed her to slip out of their hold. She ran for the stage.

Kuna appeared in front of Baya. Her expression was more concerned than stern. "Not here. Not now," she whispered. "Trust me." This wasn't a threat, it was a plea.

Baya searched her face for the truth, for options. Her smoke would not affect Kuna and she doubted she was strong enough to muscle her way past the head of the guard. So, Baya did the only thing she could think to do. She held her head high and swiftly moved to the exit.

One of the guards grabbed for her arm and she jerked away from him. "Don't touch me," she said through gritted teeth.

The guards followed close behind.

Just before Baya reached the main doors, someone in the crowd asked. "What about the Arges?"

Someone else added, "Yes. Why would they bother to travel all this way?"

"I assure you that that was nothing," Nacora's voice rang out.

There was some comfort in knowing that everyone's attention was no longer on Baya *and* it was not on Osa and Vicaroy's coupling. The people of Merth had bigger concerns.

Baya was sealed in her room, with two sentries stationed outside.

She paced. Doba was nowhere to be found and there was no way out of her room. She gazed out the window wishing she could fly. She had to get to Vicaroy.

It wasn't until late afternoon when her door opened. It was Osa, a servant and the two male guards. The servant set a tray of food on the desk and retreated.

Baya wanted to claw at the self-satisfied look on Osa's face.

"I wanted to be the one to personally inform you that this is your last night in the palace. At first light you will be escorted into the city and you are never to set foot in here again. Do you understand?"

"Nacora wouldn't do that. I have no money. Where will I go."

"That is no concern of ours. You're not royalty and you should never have been permitted to stay here in the first place." Osa headed for the door.

Baya ran after her but the sentry took her by the shoulders and threw her to the ground. She slid across the floor into the foot of her bed as the door slammed shut.

Baya jumped to her feet and ran for the exit. She shook the handle and banged her fists on the door. It wouldn't budge even when she tried to use her powers.

"You can't treat a woman like this, you heathens. I demand to speak with Nacora. She …" Baya lowered her voice. "She can't just change her mind like this."

Silence.

"Apparently she can." A voice came from behind Baya.

A hand clasped tight around her mouth before the scream could come out.

"Shhhh," someone whispered in Baya's ear. "It's me, Kuna. I'm here to help so don't get us caught by screaming for the guards."

Kuna slowly loosened her grip over Baya's mouth.

Baya spun around with her arms up for protection. "Where did you come from?"

Kuna put her finger over her lips. "Keep your voice down. I snuck in behind Osa, after they opened the door."

"You made yourself invisible just to get in here?"

"Yes, because something's terribly wrong."

"No kidding!"

"Shhh."

Baya lowered her voice to a whisper. "In Pathins, men would never grab a woman and throw her around like that. Ah! I hate this place. Oh, and Nacora is insane. I thought she was coming around but now she's acting like the wretched woman I met the day I came here."

"Even worse." Kuna sat down hard on Baya's bed.

"None of this makes sense."

"Tell me about it."

That was exactly what Baya wanted to do. "Last night Nacora said that she'd had a 'change of heart' and that she had accepted that her son wanted to be with me." Baya growled in frustration. "I'm such a fool for believing her."

"Shhh."

Baya took a couple of deep breaths. "I wanted to believe her." Tears pooled in her eyes. "It had made me so happy …"

Kuna shook her head. "None of this makes sense. Nacora always talked about having a baby girl so that she could be the heir. To suddenly name Osa as her successor …" Her shoulders were slumped, which was very un-Kuna-like.

"Maybe she's decided that she wants to retire earlier and Vicaroy has given her a chance to do that. I can't take all her mind-changing. What am I going to do?" Baya paced. "I have to get Vicaroy and Tara and get out of here." They could find Doba and … make their way home … somehow.

Baya stopped and looked at Kuna as if for the first time. "What *are* you doing here? I mean, shouldn't you be … guarding something?"

"Nacora …" Kuna choked on her words, "relieved me of my duties in the palace."

Baya's heart sank. "What?" She'd been lost in her own miseries and was completely oblivious to the fact that Kuna was scarcely holding herself together. "I'm sorry. What happened?" Baya gently sat down next to Kuna.

"Nacora reassigned me to wall duty."

"What's that?"

"Guarding the city walls. It's a job for first-year infantry. When I asked why I was being demoted she said that it wasn't a 'demotion' but simply a 'new position.'"

"Which, of course, is a bunch of crap. It's clearly a demotion."

Kuna nodded. "That's why I'm not out there on the wall, as I should be. Something's not right, none of this is like Nacora and I have to figure out what's happened."

"So you're here to recruit an ally?"

"With this … *new* Nacora, no one stands to lose as much as you."

Baya's shoulders dropped. "Great. Thanks." Baya rolled her eyes. "It does sound like we could use each other's help." Baya nudged Kuna's shoulder with her own.

Kuna tried to smile but failed.

There was a long silence.

"What do we do?" Baya ventured. Her mind had stalled – she could see no course of action. The future appeared blank.

"I think this has something to do with the Ominot."

CHAPTER 16

Baya's brow creased. "The ... what?"

"The Ominot," Kuna whispered.

A spark of recognition ignited inside Baya. She'd never heard of an Ominot but the memory of the Arges asking Nacora about a mysterious object the previous night flashed through her mind. "You mean the thing the Arges want?"

Kuna looked at her with wide brown eyes. "How did you know?"

"I guessed, sort of." Baya didn't know how to explain how she was able to put the Ominot together with the interruption of the party — she just knew. "It sounds ... important and whatever the Arges wanted last night must have been important as well."

Kuna's eyes narrowed. "You are a clever one, aren't you? The Arges came looking for Var, who apparently knows something about the Ominot. Then she suddenly falls ill, refusing to see anyone but her daughter. That's rather convenient, don't you think?"

"How do you know that it was the Ominot that the Arges are after?"

"You may be too smart for your own good." Kuna's gaze wandered away from Baya. "I'm the head of the guard. It's my job to know all matters of politics."

Baya crossed her arms. "How do you know about the Ominot when the Unawi herself didn't even know about it."

Kuna stood and looked out the window. Baya got the feeling she was stalling and didn't want to meet her gaze.

"Nacora was lying. After all that's not the first time she's done that lately … gone back on her word. Of course, she knew it was the Ominot that the Arges were after."

"Whatever." Baya had no idea what to believe or who to trust at this point. "What does any of this have to do with Nacora forcing Vicaroy …" Baya swallowed hard. "to couple with Osa?"

Kuna shook her head. "I don't know but we need to find out."

"Do you know why the Arges want this thing, whatever it is?"

There was an uncomfortable silence and Kuna shifted her weight from one foot to the other. "I can only go by what they said last night. They have reason to believe that Var possesses something that they greatly desire. I don't know if it's the Ominot, itself, or if Var knows how to find it."

"So if we can figure out what Var knows, then surely all this will make sense?"

"Maybe. We have to try. I may know where we can get more information. When they escort you out of the palace tomorrow, I will follow you, without anyone knowing, of course. Then we will pay the Bangee a visit."

"What's a … Bangee?" Just the word made Baya shiver.

"No one knows for sure. It's an ancient creature … I don't even know if it is a male or female." Kuna looked up at the ceiling thoughtfully. "Perhaps it's a female, as it possesses powers … of sorts. It has managed to keep itself alive longer than any other living being."

"You said, 'Creature.' So, it's not human?"

"Or even an Arge. One legend states that the Bangee was a half-blood but over the years it has morphed into something else entirely."

"A half-blood?"

"Half Arge, and half human."

Baya shook her head, not understanding.

"You know, it had an Arge for a mother and a human father, or the other way around."

"Oh!" Baya blinked. Images that she didn't want unwittingly popped into her mind. "That's … disgusting. You mean we can … reproduce with those things?"

Kuna glared at Baya. "I don't know. I've never tried."

"Well I wouldn't want to."

"I suppose I wouldn't want to either." Kuna began to pace. "Regardless of how old the Bangee is or where it came from, it's … dangerous and it doesn't like visitors."

"It's the only one of its kind?"

"As far as I know."

Baya didn't like the worried look on Kuna's face. "If we need to find out more about what the Arges want with the Ominot, then why don't we go to them and ask?"

"Their city lies far away. I don't know of any humans who have been there. The long journey through the wild would be just as dangerous as the Bangee and it would take too long. We don't have that kind of time." Kuna looked out the window longingly. "If only we could fly … like the Arges."

"Then wouldn't it be easier to ask Var, sick or not?" Anything had to be better than confronting a half-blood monster.

"I tried to sneak into her room before I came here. It's under a powerful protection spell. I couldn't get in."

Baya had run out of ideas. She put her hands over her face to force herself to think. She felt like she didn't have all the information. How could she possibly know what to do? "Okay, so it'll be easy to get me out of here, since I'm being kicked out tomorrow but how do we get Tara and Vicaroy out?"

"We can't. Vicaroy's been locked in his room as well."

"What?" Baya jumped to her feet. "They can't hold him prisoner for no reason. I thought he was a *prince*."

"Oh, there's a good reason. Osa has claimed him. He belongs to her now and she doesn't trust him, so she can take whatever … precautions she thinks are necessary. After all, she can't have him running around looking for you."

"This is insane. I thought Merth was all about men being equal."

"On the surface but men don't have any real power or control, just the illusion of it. It's a sad joke really."

Burning heat rushed to Baya's face. "Vicaroy is a person. No one can *own* him!"

"Shhh!"

A rustling sound came from the door.

Kuna disappeared.

A guard surveyed the room with narrowed eyes. "Who you talkin' to?"

"I'm venting to myself, you idiot. Get out of here!" Baya threw her shoe at the man's head.

He dodged the shoe on his way out. The door was locked behind him.

Kuna appeared seated on the bed.

"But Vicaroy can't make himself invisible," Baya whispered. "How will we get him out."

"You can't."

"Well you're mistaken if you think, for one second, that I'm leaving without him."

"You don't have a choice."

Baya kicked at the leg of her bed. "There's always a choice." She paced in front of Kuna.

"You're a naïve young woman."

Baya crossed her arms and glared at Kuna.

"And you need to forget about your pet as well."

"What?" Baya demanded.

CHAPTER 17

Baya's world spun out of control. She sat down on the bed next to Kuna to stabilize herself. Doba was gone. Vicaroy had been locked away in his chambers. She would soon be homeless and now Tara was in danger. The only things Baya cared about were being ripped out of her life.

This long list of worries did not include the fact that Baya's brother may be in trouble back in Pathins. How could she help him when she couldn't even take care of herself? Baya placed her hand to her head to try and slow the dizziness. It didn't help.

"What are you saying … about Tara? Why should I forget about her?"

"She's as good as dead." Kuna's voice was too calm for the words she spoke.

Baya nodded. A numbness was enveloping her. She'd had suspicions about the animals that were kept in cages and had wondered why some of them disappeared, never to return. She hadn't had a chance to ask anyone about this, or maybe she hadn't known who to ask, or maybe she hadn't wanted to know the real answer. "They kill them, don't they?"

"Yes, once they are full-grown their coats are worth a fortune."

"Their coats, why? I mean, I haven't seen anyone wearing an animal skin like that."

"No. Men only wear them when they venture outside of Merth, which is a rare occurrence. It's the only way they can disguise themselves in the wild. It's not foolproof but it's better than nothing."

"That figures." Her lips hardly moved as she spoke. "Since men can't make themselves disappear, the skins help to hide them from the deadly beasts out there."

Baya moved to the window. As she looked out over the royal gardens she could barely make out the endless city streets and buildings that lay beyond. She'd only been down one street in Merth and that was a frightening time — all the people staring at her and Vicaroy on the day they'd arrived.

Baya had spent most of her life in palaces and tomorrow would change that — forever. For some reason this didn't bother her as much as it should, even though she didn't know where she would go or what would happen to her out on the streets of this strange city.

Her jaw set and her hands tightened to fists. She couldn't afford self-pity. The ones she cared about most needed her help. "I'm not leaving without Vicaroy and Tara."

"Oh yes you will. They will force you out of the palace tomorrow and you will not be allowed back in."

"I will sneak back in and find a way to get them out."

"That is an unnecessary distraction from our mission. All we need to do is find out what the Bangee will tell us."

"I'm not a member of the palace guard. That may be *your* mission but it's not mine. I don't give a shit about the Ominot, whatever that is, and I don't care about Var and whatever she knows. I only care about Vicaroy and Tara. I will not leave them behind."

"We can make it to the Bangee in three or four days and then come right back. Tara is safe until she's fully grown and Osa's coupling ceremony will not take place for some time."

Baya shook her head. "No. Osa will push for the ceremony to take place soon. She won't risk Nacora changing her mind — as she tends to do, rather frequently."

The two women stared at each other for a long moment.

Finally Kuna blinked. "You won't come with me unless we rescue them, will you?"

"Not a chance in hell."

"I'm stuck in here until they let you out in the morning so we have all night to make a plan."

* * *

KUNA AND BAYA didn't come up with much in the way of a plan. Baya fell asleep early out of sheer exhaustion from a lack of sleep the night before and it was a great way to escape the worst day of her life.

However, her eyes popped open early and in no time she was up and packing the few articles of clothing in her room. She didn't know when they would come for her but she had to be ready.

Kuna had only dozed a bit in the chair and now she stared out the window in silence.

When a rustling noise came from the door Kuna disappeared.

Osa, and a servant carrying food, entered.

"Did you come to rub it in one last time?" Baya asked.

"I only wanted to join you for your last meal in the palace."

"I'm not hungry."

"Are you sure? You won't find food this delicious out there on the streets."

"I'll manage just fine."

"I'm not so sure about that." Osa's smile remained sickeningly sweet.

"I'm tired of your smug face. Just get me out of here."

"As you wish." Osa stepped aside and two female guards moved to stand on either side of Baya. They must have been worried that Baya would again use her powers against male guards.

Baya grabbed her bag of clothes and headed for the door.

On her way by Osa held out a small sack. "Some provisions. Consider it a parting gift from Nacora. She hopes that there will be no hard feelings."

"Go to hell," Baya walked by without taking the sack.

"Take it," Kuna whispered.

Baya cleared her throat in hopes of covering up Kuna's whisper. "On second thought ..." Baya grabbed the bag from Osa. "She owes me."

"Smart choice. I hope you won't take offense if I don't accompany you on your way out. I need to pay a visit to my future theo."

Baya let out a low growl. She wanted to yell, "Don't you dare touch him," but of course Osa had every right to. She could make Vicaroy do whatever she wanted. Baya's fists clenched tight.

"Don't do anything stupid," Kuna whispered in her ear.

Baya took a deep breath and marched forward — not giving Osa the satisfaction of a reply or even a second glance.

Baya thought the guards would escort her into town but they merely opened the large iron gates which separated the commoners from the palace grounds. As soon as she was out of the way of the swinging gates they were closed behind her and the sentries retreated back to the palace without so much as a word.

"Now what?" Baya whispered.

"Head that way."

"I don't know which way you're pointing. I can't see you, remember?" Baya spoke through her teeth, trying not to move her lips. She didn't want people thinking she was crazy — talking to herself.

"Right. Head west."

Baya looked to the sky to get her bearings.

But Kuna lost her patience and took her by the elbow, guiding her down the street to their right.

Once they were deep in the city Kuna grabbed Baya's arm and forced her to make a sudden turn around a building.

"Ouch. What are you doing?" Baya rubbed her arm.

"Someone's following us," Kuna whispered.

CHAPTER 18

"Who's following us?" Baya started to look over her shoulder.

"No. Don't look. Pick up the pace," Kuna ordered quietly.

Baya obeyed.

"I can't see who it is. She's wearing a hood," Kuna's voice rang out nearby.

Baya gave a startled scream when an invisible hand jerked her violently into the narrow opening of an alleyway.

"Shhh," Kuna hissed.

Baya could feel the heat from Kuna's body. She was close, almost pressed up against Baya.

Footsteps could be heard running in their direction.

"She's headed right for us."

"Disappear."

Again Baya obeyed. She resisted the urge to reach out for Kuna. A feeling of overwhelming gratitude made her heart swell — at least she was not alone in this unfamiliar city, where strange, cloaked figures were already following her.

The dark outline of a person appeared in the narrow opening. "Baya!?"

It was a familiar voice but Baya didn't fully recognize who it was until the hood was pulled back to reveal bright red hair.

"Mek." Baya exhaled. She let herself appear. "What are you —"

"I've been waiting outside the gates all morning for you. I didn't want anyone to know that I followed you."

Baya held her hand over her heart as if trying to force it to stay in her chest.

"Sorry to scare you."

"I'm glad it's you. But why —"

"I feel terrible about what happened. You shouldn't be kicked out on the streets. I wanted to make sure you had a place to stay." He held out a sack. "This is for you. It's enough coin to get you a room for at least a month."

Baya put her arms around his neck. "Thank you," she spoke softly. Pulling away she added, "But I already have a place to stay."

"That we do." Kuna materialized and Mek jumped in surprise. "But," she continued, "the money could come in handy."

"Kuna?" Mek said. "Shouldn't you be on the wall?"

She narrowed her eyes. "I have better things to do."

"Like what?"

"That is none of your concern."

"Where will Baya stay?"

The worry in Mek's voice filled Baya with warmth. She was not alone.

"With a friend of mine, for a bit, then we'll be leaving the city," Kuna said.

"Leaving? Where?"

Kuna didn't answer. She disappeared briefly, apparently to check the street to see if anyone else had followed them. "You left the palace alone?"

"Yes. Why?" Mek said.

"It doesn't look like anyone else followed us. Let's go."

"Where are we going?" Mek looked hopeful.

"Not you, Mek, just Baya and me."

"Let me come with you. I can help."

"Go back to the palace. We'll let you know if we need you."

"I want to come with you."

"It'll be dangerous."

"I'm top of my class in combat training. I'm telling you, I can help."

"But you haven't seen any real fighting."

"Wait." Baya looked between them with wide eyes. "Are we going to have to fight?"

"Let us hope not."

"I think we should let him come along. More is better, right?" Baya said.

Kuna eyed Mek for a long moment, as if trying to decide whether or not he would be a nuisance or prove to be of use.

"I have this, remember." Mek held up the sack of coins.

"Fine."

"Yes!" Mek pumped his fist in the air.

"I don't want to risk being seen." Kuna disappeared. "As you pointed out, I'm supposed to be on the wall." She took Baya's elbow and led her out onto the street. "It will be faster to go through the center of town."

"You mean through the market?" Mek said.

"Yes."

Mek's eyebrows rose. "Oh boy."

* * *

MERTH WAS A BUSTLING CITY, its streets full of colorfully dressed people. Men hauled goods in wooden wheelbarrows. People were busy selling, buying and trading wares. Merry chatter filled the air. Baya took it all in with wide eyes. She'd spent most of her life sheltered in a palace or alone with Vicaroy and her animals. This all seemed chaotic and noisy and … smelly.

At times she was enveloped with strange and lovely scents, like the burning of herbs or a brewing pot of stew. Yet, other scents accosted her. Passing by a butcher shop, Baya had to cover her mouth and nose. Thankfully this was followed by the lovely vapers of a perfume shop.

People tried to sell Baya all sorts of goods ranging from jewelry to scarves and from cookware to delicious looking pastries. The latter was the most tempting but Mek gently pushed them aside or politely refused. Baya was grateful for his help maneuvering through the market.

After making it through the crowded market they walked for another thirty minutes. The city seemed enormous, as it still stretched on farther than Baya could see. It had to be many times larger than Una Sitka, the city where she grew up.

Kuna materialized in front of a door up ahead of them. "Here we are." She gave the door a knock.

The door swung open. "Kuna!" A woman placed her arms around Kuna's neck and kissed her cheek. "You didn't tell me you were coming." She gestured for Kuna to enter. "And you brought friends." Her tone indicated that this was a pleasant surprise.

"Sorry, Ena. I didn't have time to send word that we were coming."

Ena's brow creased. "Is everything okay?"

"Yes, of course. We ... well some things have come up and we need a place to stay."

Ena had a kind face and sparkling brown eyes. She appeared to be a middle-aged woman with pale skin and bronze hair. Her face was full of concern. "Of course, my dear friend, anything you need." She gently ushered Baya and Mek inside and quickly shut the door.

Baya exhaled, it was a relief to be off the street and she already liked their hostess.

Kuna introduced everyone.

Ena took Baya's hand in greeting and ran her fingers along Baya's forearm. "Such lovely brown skin. Do you spend a lot of time under the suns?"

"No. ... Well, not recently."

"Lovely," Ena murmured.

"Baya is not from Merth. She was born in Pathins."

Ena's wide eyes took Baya in as if for the first time. "And are you two coupled?" She motioned to Mek.

"No," Baya blurted. It came out more forcefully than she had intended.

Ena frowned. "That's too bad. You'd make a lovely pair." Her face brightened. "Let me get you some refreshments. Please take a seat."

The home was small and stuff was packed into every corner. Colorful fabrics and tapestries covered most of the walls, save one, on which a mural had been painted directly onto the surface. It was quite good. It detailed numerous women and men.

Baya closely examined the artwork.

"Do you like it?" Ena asked.

"Yes. It's beautiful."

Ena pursed her lips and tilted her head to the side. "I've painted all of my lovers on this wall."

CHAPTER 19

"All of your … lovers …?" Baya studied the painting filled with many attractive people — men and women.

"It appears I'm running out of space." Ena shrugged and headed into an adjacent room.

Baya raised an eyebrow at Mek.

He responded with a chuckle.

She wasn't sure why she noticed that Kuna had not been painted on the wall. Perhaps it was the warm embrace and the joy Ena displayed when greeting Kuna. Baya shook her head. Apparently they had not been lovers.

The room was furnished with a large bed and numerous over-stuffed divans. There was one larger table and chairs and small side tables. Everything was piled with parchments and blankets and clothes, all strewn about. She clearly had no theo to help with the housekeeping. The only other room was a kitchen. "Do you live here alone?"

"I sure do … most of the time, anyway."

Baya tried to imagine what it would be like to live alone but she couldn't.

"Kuna, darling, will you clear the table," Ena hollered from the kitchen.

In no time, she laid out a large spread of food.

"And I thought we were just going to have refreshments," Kuna said.

"It smells delicious. How did you manage to make all this?" Baya asked.

"It's easy."

"But, I mean, where did you learn to cook?"

"Well, it took some practice." Ena smiled with pride.

Okay, Baya thought, as she realized how much she didn't know how to do. She couldn't paint like Ena or cook like Ena and she doubted that she could live alone like this.

"Alright, my friend. It's time to tell me what's going on."

Kuna shrugged. "It's nothing."

Ena frowned. "Please. You haven't visited me since you became the head of the guard. Not that I'm mad or anything. I know you were busy."

Kuna pushed her food around. "Well, I'm not the head of the guard anymore."

Ena placed her hand on Kuna's forearm. "I'm so sorry. What happened?"

"I don't know, that's what we have to find out. There have been some ... abrupt and rather dramatic changes in the palace as of late."

"I'll say. Well, the Unawi must be insane to let you go. You're simply the best."

"Thanks, Ena." Kuna still hadn't taken a bite.

"You can stay here as long as you like."

"We won't be staying long. Tomorrow we'll prepare to leave the city and then be off the following day."

"So we'll be going back into the palace soon?" Baya asked. "We'll have to ... sneak back in tonight."

Kuna shot Baya a look that said, 'Shut up.'

Ena looked between Baya and Kuna — a million questions

appeared to roll around in her mind. "Why would you have to *sneak* into the palace and why are you leaving the city?"

Mek leaned forward with anticipation.

"Why, indeed." Kuna scanned her surroundings, as if to make certain they were alone. With a heavy sigh she added, "Do I have everyone's word that you won't tell anyone what we're up to."

"Of course," Mek spoke up quickly.

Kuna hardly acknowledged him but Baya studied him for a moment. Why was he so eager to know what they were planning?

Ena's expression was candid and full of concern. "You know that I would never do anything to cause you harm. Your secrets are safe with me."

Kuna smiled. "I know I can trust you." She swallowed hard. "Baya and I are going to see the Bangee."

Ena's silverware dropped onto her plate with a loud clank and Mek looked like he might fall out of his chair.

"After we rescue Vicaroy and Tara," Baya added.

"We've been over this, Baya. There's no way to get them out of the palace. We spent hours trying to come up with a plan and — nothing."

"And I told you that I'm not leaving without them. Vicaroy won't be held prisoner and he can't be forced to couple with Osa. Not to mention, I won't leave Tara behind to be killed for her skin."

Kuna rubbed her forehead. "We leave for the Bangee the morning after next and that is final."

Baya's chair scraped against the floor as she abruptly got to her feet. "Then I'll get them out of the palace without you." She wanted to storm out of the house but where would she go? She moved to a large chair and pushed a stack of papers out of the way. She plopped down, facing away from the table. It was as far away as she could get in this tiny house.

Ena stood. "Mek, will you help me in the kitchen?"

Mek looked longingly at his plate still full of food. "Of course."

Kuna knelt down beside Baya.

"Don't waste your breath. Just show me how to get back in the palace and I'll get them out."

"How will you get them past the guards?"

"I'll find a way." Baya studied her hand, making it disappear into the background. The invisibility spread along her arm, causing her tunic to disappear as well.

"You are a stubborn one, aren't you?"

"You have no idea."

"Fine. If I show you the secret entrance to the palace, will you promise me that you will not get yourself caught, even if they catch Vicaroy and the animal? I want you to save yourself and get the hell out of there ... no matter what. If you are discovered in the palace after being banished, Nacora will imprison you." Kuna shook her head in despair. "The palace prison is made of a rare pink crystal."

Baya gave her a questioning look.

"That means you can't get out. The crystals take away your abilities. You would be trapped forever — powerless."

Baya swallowed hard. Losing her powers was something that she hadn't known was possible. A fearful shiver passed through her entire body. Without her abilities she couldn't protect the people she cared about. She would be ... useless. Was this how Vicaroy felt, stuck in a prison? "I have to get him out," Baya's voice was low and full of determination.

"Do you promise that you *will* return, with or without them?" Kuna's voice was that of a parent reprimanding a child.

"Yes." Baya turned to meet her gaze.

"Also, I want you to promise that you will accompany me to see the Bangee."

Baya's jaw tightened. Kuna's demands were grating on her. "Why? I mean, can't you go alone or with Mek or Ena or someone else, anyone else."

Kuna shook her head. "It has to be you."

Baya raised her eyebrows. "And why is that?"

"We think that the Bangee will only speak with you."

"Really?" Baya's voice was full of skepticism.

"Rumor has it that she will only see the foreign princess."

Baya narrowed her eyes. "And you think that's me?" Baya shook her head. "I'm not a princess."

"You were royalty, back in Pathins, in line to become Unawi."

"And you think I'm this *foreign princess*?"

"Who else could it be? We don't get many visitors."

Baya chewed on her lower lip. "Why will it only talk to a princess?"

"Who knows. It's an eccentric old creature. There's no telling what its motives are."

"I'm not buying it. Who told you this?"

Kuna's eyes shifted away and she adjusted herself uncomfortably. "It's common knowledge. Most people have heard this old legend."

"Whatever." Baya threw her hands up. "One thing at a time. You show me how to get into the palace and I will not let myself get caught."

"And..."

"I'll go with you to see the Bangee." Baya issued a sharp huff. "I promise."

"It won't be easy to get back into the palace," Kuna said. "The secret entrance is buried on the east side of the palace. It will take us some time to remove the dirt to get in, somehow rescue them and rebury the entrance. So it could take most of the night."

Baya pursed her lips. "We'll have to be invisible while we remove the dirt with our powers."

"And incredibly quiet to avoid the sentries." Kuna handed Baya her plate of food. "You'll need lots of energy, so eat up."

Mek appeared in the doorway. "I ... couldn't help but overhear." He glanced around. "It's a small place. But I can help."

"How?" Kuna all but snapped. Her question was full of doubt.

Baya frowned at Kuna. She was beginning to think that Kuna was always dismissive of Mek because he was a man. She never thought he could be of use.

"Well, unlike the two of you, who need to lay low, I'm free to come and go from the palace as I please."

Baya lit up. "I could simply follow you in through the main entrance."

"Yeah and I could ... I don't know ... cause a distraction or something. ... To help you get them out."

Baya wanted to hug Mek. "That's brilliant! Kuna, it just might work."

Kuna paced in the small space. "There's too much going on in the palace during the day. We need to wait until most people are asleep. There are also fewer guards on duty at night."

"But the palace gates are locked for the night at curfew. No one goes in and out at night. If we go back at curfew, then we couldn't get out until the next morning," Mek said.

Kuna tapped her finger to her lips, in deep thought. "If you follow Mek in tonight just before curfew then I could get the secret entrance free and ready for you to sneak out."

"I will help you," Ena said.

Kuna smiled. "Okay. That's what we'll do. I'll draw you a map that will lead you to the secret exit. You enter, unseen, with Mek at curfew and Ena and I will clear the eastern passage for you."

Baya's shoulders relaxed. This might just work. It had to. She forced herself to ignore the uneasy jitters in her stomach.

CHAPTER 20

When the first sun of the day set, Mek and Baya headed out. The second sun would not set for some time. The summer days were long but the palace would still be closed for the "night." Heavy drapes would be pulled tight over bedroom windows. This way the royalty, tucked safely inside, could get some sleep even though it was still light out.

"What was your business in the city?" A guard at the gate recited his line, as if he'd said those words a hundred times that day.

"My mother asked that I fetch her a bundle of Lav from the market." Mek held up the dried herbs as evidence.

"Why didn't you fetch it from the palace supplies."

"They were out." Mek gave the man an innocent smile.

The guard nodded to his companion, who quickly opened the gate without further questioning. An invisible Baya was right on Mek's heels. In fact, she had to focus on his feet so she wouldn't step on him or run into him if he made a sudden stop. Still, the gate closed right behind her, almost shutting on her. Her heart pounded against her ribs.

They quickly crossed the large courtyard to the main entrance.

The sentries at the palace entrance opened the doors with a slight nod to Mek. Just like that, they were back in the palace.

"That was easy," Baya whispered.

"Yeah but this is where it'll get tricky."

When they were alone in a hallway Baya let herself become visible.

"You should stay hidden."

"It's a lot of work to constantly make yourself blend into your surroundings."

"I can only imagine."

When they approached Vicaroy's door, Baya flattened herself against the wall and made her head invisible so she could survey the situation around the corner. Her head appeared when she looked at Mek.

"That is so weird. I wish I could do that."

"Only two guards," she said. "You ready?"

He nodded. The light of excitement sparkled in his sea-green eyes.

Baya disappeared and rounded the corner. She pressed her body against the palace wall to let Mek pass by without tripping on her unseen form.

"Good evening, gentlemen." Mek smiled with innate confidence, the kind that comes from being born a noble.

The two guards outside Vicaroy's door eyed Mek with leery expressions.

Baya remained as close to Mek as possible.

"I was told to deliver this..." Mek held up his bundle of Lav, "to Prince Vicaroy."

"What does the prince want with that?"

"I don't know, I'm just the delivery boy and since when is it your job to question royalty?"

The guards exchanged a concerned look.

"But Sire, the door is not to be opened until his morning meal."

Mek made a clicking noise with his tongue. "Very well, but you will have to explain why you didn't allow the prince to have his Lav. I can imagine that he's already pretty upset with you."

The guards exchanged another wide-eyed glance.

"It's only a handful of Lav — harmless. Has his mother forbidden him even this little pleasure?"

One guard shrugged to the other, as if to say, "It's your call."

"Fine." The head guard reached for the keys at his belt and unlocked the door.

Mek tried to enter the room but one of the men stepped in front of him. "No visitors, strict orders."

"What? He's not allowed to see his best friend?"

The men exchanged a skeptical look.

"Fine, here." Mek tossed the bundle of herbs into the air, causing the guard to have to scramble for it. "Just be sure he gets his Lav."

Vicaroy's door was ajar but the men were in the way. Baya couldn't get into the room.

Mek turned as if to leave then pretended to trip — falling backwards into one of the guards, who was knocked into the door. This caused the door to fly open as the men stumbled into the room.

Mek straightened his tunic. "Sorry. I can be so clumsy sometimes."

This was Baya's only chance. She wove through the men and pressed herself against Vicaroy's wall, hardly daring to breathe. Thankfully, Mek was a quick thinker and skilled at improvising.

Vicaroy sat by the large windows. He watched the spectacle with little interest. The numb expression on his face made Baya want to scream. What had they done to him?

One guard pulled Mek out of the room.

The other laid the herbs on a table by the door. "Your Lav, Sire."

Vicaroy's brow furrowed at the sight of the bundle of tiny purple flowers. He slowly turned his gaze out the window.

The guard locked the door behind him and they were alone. Baya was relieved that the door was not sealed with special powers. She supposed that a key was all it took to keep men imprisoned.

Baya materialized. "Vic," she breathed.

He slowly turned toward her.

She ran across the room, throwing her arms around his neck.

His arms slowly wrapped themselves around her. "It's you." He inhaled her scent. "How did you …"

She placed her finger to his lips, which was followed by her mouth as she pressed her mouth to his.

Vicaroy pulled away.

"What's wrong?" Baya's heart quickened as she searched his eyes. He would not meet her gaze. "What have they done to you?"

His eyes remained on the window but he didn't let go of her.

"Have they … hurt you?"

He shook his head. "No. But they won't let me out. I'm not even allowed to see my mother."

"Vicaroy, I'm so sorry. I'm here to get you out."

"You can't."

"Why not?"

"I have to stay."

Baya gave him an incredulous look. Then her eyes widened. "You mean you *want* to stay." What if it was Vicaroy's desire to be with Osa? Baya stumbled back a step. This thought had not crossed her mind before. Her heartbeat drummed in her ears.

"Osa says that now that we are to be coupled, I can't be with anyone else or …" Vicaroy shook his head.

"Or what?"

"They'll kill me."

CHAPTER 21

Baya's jaw fell open. "You have got to be joking! They threatened to take your life?"

"You see why I can't leave? I'm stuck here or I'll lose my head."

"What kind of a messed-up place is this?" Baya's cheeks felt like they were on fire. "No." She took his jaw and forced him to look at her. "You'll lose your head if you remain a prisoner in here. You'll go mad. So if you stay and couple with … her then you'll still die. It will take a bit longer is all. I'm getting you out of here."

"Where would I go? If I'm caught, even somewhere in the city, I'll be brought back and forced to couple or … be killed." Vicaroy bit his lower lip. "But you're right. Every second I'm locked in here, I feel like I'm fading away … disappearing. I've been slowly dying ever since I came to Merth. They've held me captive the entire time. But what choice do I have? I have no powers. There's no way out."

He looked longingly at the lush grounds below. "I've even thought about jumping … you know through the window."

Baya looked down at the garden far below and shivered. No one would survive such a fall. Her heart felt like it was being torn in two. "You wouldn't really do that, would you?"

"If they don't let me out of here and if they force me to be with Osa then … yes." He sighed. "If I can't be with you …"

"Did you think that I would leave you — that I would just give up and not come for you?"

The ghost of a smile crossed his lips. "That's the reason I'm still alive. I hoped you'd find a way." He lowered his head. "I can't live without you." The words were barely a wisp in the air.

Baya wrapped her arms around his waist and buried her head in his chest. Tears stung her eyes. "I will always come for you. I need you too, you know. When I thought you were … dead, when you fell into the river, I …" She choked on her words. A tear ran down her face.

"I can't imagine what it would be like to lose you — forever," he whispered.

Baya inhaled his scent, stirring her senses. She took a long moment to enjoy having him in her arms — right where he belonged. "They're so strict about sex. We may be worse off here than in Pathins."

Vicaroy nodded. It was a solemn gesture.

Taking his hands in hers, she looked deep into his eyes. "We're running out of time. We'll have to make our escape within the hour." The slightest twinge of guilt twisted in her stomach. Now that Baya understood the full gravity of the situation there was no way she would leave Vicaroy behind to save herself. They would get out of the palace or die trying. This meant she might have to break her promise to Kuna.

Vicaroy would die if he stayed here. She would gladly break a promise if it meant saving him. Baya shook her head. There was no time to be distracted by thoughts of failure — there was no time for tears either. She had to pull herself together and be strong. Vicaroy and Tara's lives depended on her.

Vicaroy had been lost in thought as well. "What if …" He licked his lips. "I should stay and try to be a good son."

A low growl escaped from deep inside Baya. "I *will* get you out of here. Vicaroy, don't you dare fall back into that … that 'I'm a man, I don't have a choice, I have to do as I'm told,' way of thinking."

Baya welcomed the anger — it forced her to focus. "You belong out there, in the garden, in your shop, building things, sailing on the river …"

"Raising our children," he added.

A radiant smile consumed her face. She ran her fingers down his cheek and cupped it with her hand.

He placed his hand over hers. "I know but I can't help the guilt that I feel for being a bad son. It's the way I was raised. It's… all I know."

Baya nodded.

He gave Baya a weary smile. His hand ran through her hair before pulling her into a tight embrace. "No. You can't possibly understand."

"Of course I understand."

"How could you? You're a woman. You're powerful — you have choices."

"So do you."

He shook his head.

She pushed him away. "We *are* leaving and you're coming with us. We're getting out of this horrible city and if that means we can never come back because Osa will kill you and probably me as well, then so be it."

Vicaroy studied her, hearing every word but still unbelieving.

"We won't be alone this time. Kuna's coming with us."

A spark of light slipped into his eyes. "You think you can honestly get me out of here?"

Baya inhaled sharply through clenched teeth. "I hope so. It's our only hope." This was the part of the plan they hadn't entirely worked out.

She gently interlaced her fingers with his. She turned her hand invisible. "I pray this works." The part of his hand that touched hers also disappeared.

"That's … weird." He pulled his hand away.

She tightened her fingers around his and focused harder.

Nothing.

No more of his hand disappeared. "Damn it."

"What are you doing?"

"I'm trying to turn you invisible. But only the part of you that touches me vanishes, like my clothes."

"So you can't get me out." The light vanished from his golden eyes.

"Don't give up." She looked around the room like a caged animal. "I have to think. I can only make what touches me disappear." She bit her lower lip. "We don't have a lot of time. Mek will be causing a distraction any minute."

"Mek? A distraction?"

"Yes, he's going to divert the guards' attention so we can get out."

"I'm surprised he's helping."

"Why is that?"

"I thought he would be glad to have you all to himself."

"Mek's a nice guy. He's been very helpful and generous."

"I bet."

"We're running out of time. I have to focus on getting you past the guards ... somehow."

Vicaroy's eyes widened. "So you were trying to make me disappear like your clothes?"

"Yes but it didn't work. I can't make all of you vanish."

Vicaroy paced. "Perhaps if you ... wore me. Never mind. That doesn't even make sense."

"Wait a minute." Baya pointed with her index finger. "You may be onto something. I need to *wear* you, like my clothes, to make you invisible. As in carry you on my back ..." Baya frowned. "Or something."

"But you can't carry me."

"No." Baya clapped her hands. "But you can carry me." Her arms wrapped around his neck as she leapt into his arms.

Vicaroy saw nothing when he looked down at her. In fact, he couldn't see his own feet. "Ah!" He almost dropped Baya in shock.

She materialized in his arms. "It worked." Her lips found his.

"I'm going to get out of here."

"You better believe it."

They were lost in another kiss when they heard a commotion coming from the hallway.

CHAPTER 22

Baya pressed her ear against the door of Vicaroy's chambers.

"Run," a man's voice yelled. This was followed by the sound of many faint steps, too many to count.

The distant holler of the guard could be heard as he retreated. "Get out of here! The prince will be safe locked in his room."

The sound of many feet running by died down and Baya placed her hand on the lock. She closed her eyes tight and focused on moving the tumblers until they clicked into place. The door opened easily. Vanishing, she peeked into the hall.

No one in sight.

She reappeared and gestured for Vicaroy to follow. "It sounded like they went that way. So we'll go this way." Baya pointed in the opposite direction.

They took off at a full run.

When Baya rounded a corner she ran right into the chest of a man. He'd apparently been running in their direction.

Baya exhaled with relief when she looked up to find a pair of bright green eyes. "Mek! Thank the Goddess. What happened? I thought you were going to sound emergency trumpets."

"Change of plans. I'll explain later. There are too many people between us and the secret passage, so there's no way out. Vicaroy will be caught."

Baya smiled with triumph. "Watch this." She leapt into Vicaroy's arms and they disappeared.

Mek's mouth fell open. "Brilliant. That will make this a lot easier. This way." He set off at a jog down the hallway in the direction he had come from.

As they quickly made their way through the endless palace halls, Mek spoke quickly and quietly to the invisible pair. "Kuna and Ena already cleared the passage, using their powers, of course. She decided that setting off the trumpets wouldn't work as the guards would take Vicaroy with them when they evacuated, so this new plan … well, it seemed like a pretty good idea."

"What's the new plan?" Baya whispered.

"Let me just say, that woman is crazy. She set all the servines loose and herded, or rather, scared them toward Vicaroy's guards."

"She what?"

They fell silent as some people ran past. Mek nodded politely to them.

Once they were out of sight, Mek said, "It appears to be working well. Everyone's focused on a bunch of deadly animals on the loose. The guards didn't have time to take Vicaroy with them."

"Where's Tara?"

"Don't worry, she's still in her cage. That's where we're to meet Kuna and Ena."

"Perfect. Let's hurry. We don't want to be caught by people or angry animals," Baya said.

In no time they entered the servines' chambers. Every cage was empty except Tara's. She paced and flicked her long razor-sharp tail in warning.

Kuna lit up at the sight of Mek. "Did you find them?"

Vicaroy set Baya down and they materialized.

"Good. However, this beast wants to eat me. I don't think we should let it out."

"Tara." Baya ran to her cage.

Tara appeared to shrink to half her size. The bright feathers around her neck fell against her body and her tail stopped flicking its angry twitch. *Where you been?*

"It's a long story but I'm here to get you out." Baya placed her hand over the lock.

"Whoa. You're not going to let that thing out, are you?" Ena wore a look of sheer terror on her face. "We already have enough of those things running around."

"This one's different. She's my friend." Baya unlocked the cage with her powers.

Tara bounded out, causing everyone to step back. She bared her teeth at Kuna and the feathers on her neck puffed out to twice their normal size.

Kuna raised her spear.

"Tara! Be nice. They're my friends and they're here to help."

But that one has a pointy thing that hurts.

"Kuna is not going to use her spear on you unless you keep acting like this," Baya said.

Again Tara seemed to deflate. *Fine. But tell her to keep that pointy thing away from me.*

"That's my girl." Baya rubbed the scales on her colorful nose.

Tara leaned into her hand and a guttural noise of pleasure escaped from somewhere deep inside.

"I missed you too, baby."

"Now, we have to get out of here without being seen … somehow." Kuna still held her spear at the ready.

Baya smiled. "Tara, do you think you're big enough to carry me?"

Tara huffed. *You're as light as my feathers.* She shook her rainbow mane resulting in a glorious flash of iridescent colors.

Baya chuckled. Tara had grown. She looked big enough to carry a person with ease. She swung herself up onto Tara's back.

Kuna and Ena gasped when they disappeared.

"If the men carry the women, then we can all get out of here without being seen." Baya's voice came out of nowhere.

"But I'm allowed to be in the palace," Mek protested.

"Not if you're caught in here. They'll accuse you of setting the animals loose. And it won't look good if you're caught sneaking out the secret passage."

"Good point." Mek didn't hesitate. He scooped Ena up into his arms. Ena closed her eyes in concentration and they vanished.

"This is incredible! I've always wanted to be invisible," Mek said.

Vicaroy rubbed the back of his neck. "You mean I have to carry Kuna?"

Footsteps could be heard heading their way.

"Hurry, Vic! Take Kuna in your arms," Baya said.

Kuna was made of solid muscle. Even though she wasn't as tall as Baya, she still must've weighed twice what Baya did. Vicaroy strained to pick her up. It was painfully awkward to watch. They both looked incredibly uncomfortable having to engage in such an intimate embrace.

They disappeared from sight as a group of men wrestled with a growling servine in a net. They were stuck in the doorway. The animal pulled away even harder at the sight of the cages. Its massive body thrashed and bucked in resistance.

When they managed to make it into the room, Kuna whispered, "Sneak around them."

Being one invisible entity in a room was much easier than being one of six. Not to mention Tara was huge. They ran into each other and even a couple of moans of pain escaped as they all tried to squeeze past the guards and the wild beast.

Baya was sure Tara had stepped on someone's foot, maybe a couple of times.

The men jabbed at the poor servine with long sticks, trying to force it into one of the cages. Thankfully there was enough commotion that they didn't hear Baya and her companions as they fumbled their way to the door.

Baya and Tara had to pass close by the beast, who stopped struggling as its nose sniffed the air. It suddenly seemed to be staring right at them.

CHAPTER 23

He can smell us. Baya thought to Tara.

We should run. Tara lunged forward.

No! You might run our friends over. Slow and steady. Keep moving. Quietly.

The animal swatted one of the men's sticks away and leapt after Baya and Tara.

"What is it looking at?" One of the guards yelled.

"I don't know. It's acting weird. Just get it in the damn cage."

"It's going to be a long night," the other man complained.

The beast's knife-like tail worked its way through the net and slashed at the men. A bloody line formed across a guard's arm.

"Oh, just wait until I get my hands on whoever let these horrible monsters out."

A low growl came from underneath Baya.

One of the guards scanned the room.

Shhh. Baya spoke to Tara through their mental bond. *Don't pay attention to them. This is my only chance to get you out of here, for good.*

Fortunately, the guards had their hands full and the man who'd heard Tara growl was forced to turn his attention back to the captured servine.

Baya exhaled when they made it out the door.

"This way," Kuna said from somewhere to Baya's right.

Tara followed after the sound of her voice.

"Mek, Ena, are you with us?" Baya whispered.

"Over here." Mek's voice sounded close and just to her left.

"Stay invisible and follow the sound of my voice," Kuna said. "It's not far."

Baya's stomach unclenched. She hadn't realized that it had been in knots until now. They were almost free. Everything had worked out even better than she had thought.

Something brushed against her leg.

"Watch it," someone hissed. It was most likely Ena.

"It's not our fault. We can't see you, remember?" Baya kept her voice low.

"Baya, you stop for a second," Kuna ordered. "Try to spread out so we're not walking on top of each other. The last thing we need is to trip and fall, becoming visible just as someone rounds the corner."

Baya and Tara stilled for a handful of heartbeats, which felt like an eternity but this would give the others some time to get ahead of her.

Even then, she heard a shuffling sound and a "Sorry." Vicaroy and Mek must've bumped into each other. So, the going was tediously slow.

If their lives weren't on the line, this would have been incredibly funny. Baya couldn't help but smile.

They followed Kuna's voice commands down a couple of passages. Only a handful of women and men hurried by, completely unaware. Tara had to press her large mass and Baya's leg against the wall to avoid running into them.

Kuna swung herself out of Vicaroy's arms causing them to materialize in front of a small wooden door.

Vicaroy rubbed his lower back, relieving the pressure from his burden.

"Follow me," Kuna said.

Tara barely fit through the door. Baya had to flatten herself against Tara's feathers so as not to hit her head. When the door was shut Mek set Ena down and Baya slid off of Tara's back. They were in a small room that looked like it was used for storage.

Kuna and Ena busied themselves with moving small wooden crates and chairs out of the way of a wall. Kuna waved her hand over the wall revealing an even smaller door.

"Will Tara fit?" Baya asked.

"It'll be tight."

Tara whimpered.

"It's okay." Baya rubbed behind her ear. "This is our only way to freedom."

Kuna opened the door and gestured for the men to go first, followed by Ena. Baya entered, then Tara squeezed herself through.

They found themselves in a roughly mined passageway. The walls were made of dark jagged stone.

When Kuna shut the door their world went black. The three women immediately lit the way with their powers. The glowing orbs cast a gentle glow around them.

Kuna waved her arm over the door. "There. It's sealed. No one will be able to follow us for some time."

Baya smiled. They'd made it. She had managed to rescue them. Of course she'd had help, for which she was grateful.

Everyone hurried forward with Kuna bringing up the rear.

At times the passage grew even smaller and Tara had to crawl.

Being in such a confined space caused Baya's blood to turn to ice. Thoughts of being trapped in the dark, under water, consumed her. She pressed her hands over her heart to try and slow it — it didn't help.

Why you scared? Tara asked. She sounded like she was on the verge of panic as well.

Baya took a deep breath of stale air. She had to be strong … for Tara. "I'm fine. Everything's fine." Baya gave Tara's head a quick pat.

Thankfully the passage wasn't long. The scent of fresh air caused her to exhale with relief. "You see, we're almost there."

Tara gave Baya's cheek a good lick.

Baya laughed and wiped the saliva off with her sleeve.

Up ahead an opening could be seen. It had grown dark and stars filled the exit.

Baya couldn't remember ever being happier to see the night sky.

They ascended a slight incline toward the opening. The second Vicaroy and Mek stepped out of the passage there were scuffling sounds. Dark figures surrounded them.

Baya ran forward but didn't make it far. Someone grabbed her from behind. A large net was thrown over Tara as a deafening roar escaped along with the flash of her sharp teeth.

"No," Baya cried.

Three men forced Mek to the ground. One held his arms behind his back. One of the men also had a bloody lip. Apparently Mek had gotten a good punch in before they overwhelmed him.

A guard wrapped his arms around Ena, immobilizing her. Baya found herself ensnared by a pair of strong arms as well. They felt like they might crush her chest. She couldn't move her arms.

There was no sign of Kuna.

Vicaroy struggled in the grip of two men but stopped short when Nacora stepped forward.

CHAPTER 24

Vicaroy's chin instantly went to his chest at the sight of his mother.

"That's right, *Son*." Nacora emphasized the last word. "You have disobeyed me." A cold smile crossed her lips. "But thankfully I was able to stop you from throwing your life away with this ..." Nacora gave Baya an icy stare. "This nobody."

A cold tingling sensation ran down Baya's spine.

Osa had been by Nacora's side but now she ran forward throwing her arms around Vicaroy. "Thank the Great Goddess we found you. I was so worried. I thought maybe you'd been eaten by those beasts." Her smile dripped with sweetness. "It's okay, Darling. You're safe now."

"Unless you try something like this again." Nacora's voice was dark and flat. "Then I will not be so forgiving."

Baya narrowed her eyes. Nacora had never talked to Vicaroy like that before. Baya and Nacora had their differences but his mother had always shown him love. Now that was gone.

"As for you." Nacora's piercing stare turned to Baya. "I was merciful once with you and you disrespected me by coming back into my palace. A ruler can only be so lenient." She smiled and there was real pleasure in her expression. "You will never see the light of the suns again." She waved her hand dismissively. "You will be locked-up and your powers will be drained from you ... forever."

Nacora crossed her arms and looked thoughtful as she studied her captives. "You must have had help. There is no way any of you would know about the secret escape route. It was meant to be used for emergencies and kept secret. It is only known to the Unawi, her top advisor and ... the head of the guard." Nacora quickly scanned their faces. "Who is helping you?"

The man who held Baya tightened his grip around her, forcing the air out of her lungs. Baya's mind went blank with fear. Being locked up forever without her powers, without Vicaroy. Tara would become a camouflage coat for a man. She shook her head. "No!" More smoke than she had ever released before rose up from her palms. When the man began to choke, his hold loosened. Baya spun out of his grip and disappeared.

Ena followed her lead.

She ran straight to Tara and yanked at the net that held her. Together they pulled and shook it off. Tara sent her lethal tail flying toward the guards and pounced on the nearest one, knocking him down.

When Baya spun around she found that the men who had been holding Mek lay sprawled on the ground. That must've been Kuna's handy work, she thought.

Mek fought off two more guards and an invisible force hit Osa over the head.

Kuna again, Baya assumed.

Nacora screamed as Osa's body went limp and fell to the ground.

Tara's whip-like tail kept the rest of the guards away.

"Retreat." Kuna's voice rang out through the night. "Mek go unseen with ... my friend. Vicaroy —"

"I got him," Baya called out. She was impressed that Kuna had thought to keep Ena's identity a secret by referring to her only as "my friend."

"Split up! You know where to meet," Kuna said.

Mek disappeared.

Baya swung herself up onto Tara causing Tara to vanish as well. "Vicaroy, hold your arm out." *Tara, run right by him.*

Baya grabbed Vicaroy by the arm as they sped by, using the momentum to swing him up onto Tara's back. The effort almost caused Baya to fall off. But Vicaroy managed to get his legs around Tara and his arms around Baya's waist. This allowed her to get a better grip on Tara with both of her hands.

The guards who had been closing in on Vicaroy looked baffled at his disappearance. "How are the men turning invisible?" A guard asked.

Nacora cradled Osa in her arms. "I swear on my life, you'll pay for this."

"Run as fast as you can, baby." Baya patted Tara's head.

Tara's powerful back leg propelled them forward, almost leaving Baya and Vicaroy behind. She had to squeeze her legs against Tara's sides to keep from falling off as they sped away.

Getting away was her only concern, it didn't matter in which direction they were headed.

Once she was sure they were not being followed and her heart slowed a little, they paused to study the stars

"I think Ena's home is this way." Baya pointed to the south. "Are you okay carrying us, Tara."

Me good.

"I'm glad you're so strong. It'll be safer if we can remain invisible."

They didn't speak as they moved through the streets. Thankfully the city was fast asleep. They took a couple of wrong turns and as the excitement wore off, Baya could feel herself grow weaker with each moment that passed. She slumped against Vicaroy. Her powers had been pushed to their limit.

"I hope we can find Ena's soon." The faint light of the first sun of the day sent rays shooting up into the purple sky.

"The city will be waking soon," Vicaroy said. "How are you holding up?"

"I need food and sleep," Baya murmured.

He tightened his grip around her.

They could hear Tara frantically sniff the air. *Your friends ... I smell them.*

"Good girl. Take us to them."

Tara sped forward and it wasn't long before Baya spotted a familiar little home. "Thank the Goddess."

"What are we going to do with Tara?" Vicaroy asked. "That home doesn't look big enough for all of us."

"We can't risk her being seen. She'll have to hide in the back."

Vicaroy and Baya dismounted as soon as they could. Baya's legs were weak and her back ached from the long ride.

Tara's tongue hung out as she plopped down in Ena's tiny back yard.

"Poor thing. You aren't used to all that exertion. Stay as hidden as you can. We're going to leave the city — soon."

Tara's massive jaws opened in a toothy yawn. *When?*

"We were planning to leave morning after next but after tonight's debacle, we may have to leave sooner."

"You got that right." A voice came from Ena's back door. A shadowy figure appeared and Baya knew it was Kuna by the outline of her notched ear. "Mek, get the animal some water and food."

"Hey, just because I'm a man doesn't mean I'm your servant," Mek said. "I *am* royalty, after all."

Kuna glared at him.

"Fine." He huffed and headed for the kitchen.

Ena gently pushed Kuna aside. "You made it! I was beginning to worry." She threw her arms around Baya.

"Oh, Ena," Baya was surprised at the sudden and intimate contact. She took a step back. "This is Vicaroy, Vicaroy, meet Ena."

She smiled warmly at Vicaroy. "Please, make yourself at home." She gestured to the door. "He's very handsome." She gave Baya a wink and headed inside. "Come. You must eat and rest."

Nothing sounded better than food and sleep — in that order.

"You heard Nacora," Kuna said. "She will be scouring the city for us. We have to leave sooner than expected."

Mek carried a large bowl of water and a chunk of raw meat outside for Tara.

Tara's eyes were already closed. Her nose wiggled as it caught the scent of the meat and her eyes flew open.

"Thanks, Mek," Baya said. She patted Tara on the head as the animal devoured the meat.

A slight murmur of satisfaction came from Tara.

The second Baya stepped inside, Ena placed a large plate of food in front of her. Baya gladly took it and shoveled a bite into her mouth using her fingers.

"And there's more where that came from." Ena handed a slightly less full plate to Vicaroy.

"Thank you," he mumbled.

They joined the others at the table but Vicaroy didn't eat much.

"What's the matter. Don't you like it?"

Vicaroy sat up straighter. "It's delicious. It's just that all there was to do while locked in my room was eat. I guess I'm tired of doing nothing but eating."

Baya rubbed his forearm. "You're free now."

He smiled. "Thanks to you."

Baya took a piece of fruit off his plate. "And I'll eat that if you won't."

He pushed his plate over to her.

"As soon as you can't eat another bite, Baya, you need to rest." Kuna had dark circles under her eyes. "The men will pack anything they think we might need, while the three of us sleep for a couple of hours."

Ena was busy laying out blankets on the floor. "Sorry. I'm afraid I only have one bed. It can hold two but the rest of you will have to sleep on the floor."

"Baya, Ena, sleep if you can." Kuna rose from the table and spread out on one side of Ena's bed. "We leave in three hours. We had to use a lot of our powers tonight. If we don't rest we'll be worthless when we try to escape the city. Mek and Vicaroy pack anything you can find that you think we'll need. After you have five packs ready, then you can rest, if you have time."

Mek opened his mouth, as if to protest but then closed it again. It was difficult to argue with Kuna's rational logic. Instead, he headed for the kitchen.

"You'll find some packs in the chest." Ena gestured to the far corner, as she crawled into bed next to Kuna.

Baya eyed Vicaroy's half-eaten plate of food, wondering if she had room to shove some more in. She was sure that there was no way she could sleep after all that had happened.

Vicaroy took her hand. "Come on. You look tired." He led her to one of the blankets.

Baya laid down and he covered her up. When he moved to leave, she took his hand. "Wait. I'm not that tired. I … need you."

"I should be helping Mek."

"I know but …"

He sat down and lifted her into his lap. Baya's body instantly relaxed. He was with her and they were safe … for now. She lay her head on his shoulder and inhaled his scent and her eyes closed at once. Thank the Goddess he still smelled the same. This was the last thing she remembered before exhaustion consumed her.

CHAPTER 25

Every inch of Baya's body resisted waking. Her mind fought against the voices and the jarring movement.

"Wake up! It's time to leave." Kuna roughly shook Baya's shoulders.

Baya growled and tried to roll over.

"Now! Unless you want to be captured and thrown into the palace prisons — forever."

This forced her brain to start working. She slowly opened her eyes. Everyone was up and about. Sunlight poured into the room. They'd only slept a couple of hours at the most.

She slowly got to her feet. Her body ached from the previous night's adventures and she felt like her muscles weighed twice what they should.

"Here's your pack but eat this first." Ena handed her a thick slice of bread.

Baya narrowed her eyes at the food.

"It's travel cake."

She gave Ena a questioning look.

"It's packed with nuts and dried fruits. It'll give us lots of energy for the road."

Baya's stomach growled. Her body burned up the fuel almost

faster than she could eat. She took a hearty bite. Sweetness exploded in her mouth and soon the cake was gone. To her surprise her hunger faded and she felt like maybe she could somehow face the day. After all, the only thing they had to do was escape the city … unseen … somehow.

Kuna quickly gave instructions and they were out the door in no time. Ena was light and easy enough for Mek to carry. Kuna vanished before leaving Ena's home, followed by Mek and Ena.

Vicaroy and Baya went out the back door and vanished atop Tara.

"Ena, take my hand." Kuna's hand appeared so that she could find it. "I'll hold onto Tara's mane. This way we won't lose one another or trip over ourselves like last night."

"That's a good idea," Baya said.

* * *

THE CITY WAS ALREADY ABUZZ with palace guards scouring the streets. Baya and her companions hurried to the southern gates and were able to fall in behind a group of women trying to leave the city.

"What's your business outside of Merth?" one of the sentries asked.

One of the women handed him a parchment. "We have a permit to collect mushrooms in the Evergreen Forest."

The guard studied each of their faces.

"Is it wise to open the city gates when there are fugitives on the loose?" the younger of the two guards asked.

A couple of the women exchanged a worried look. "Please. The mushroom season is short. We have to get into the forest today to start collecting." The woman's large brown eyes pleaded with the guard.

"These women are not our fugitives," the older guard said. "Open the gates."

"But sir —" the young guard started.

"Their livelihoods depend on getting mushrooms to the market. They have to be able to feed their families."

"Maybe we shouldn't —" the young guard said.

"Please. Show us compassion." The woman held her hands together in an imploring gesture.

"I said, open the gates!"

The younger man lowered his head and began raising the chains, which slowly opened the large wooden gates.

Baya exhaled quietly.

One of the women took the older guard's hand. "Thank you."

The group of mushroom gatherers headed east into the mountains, while Kuna steered them south.

"Stay invisible until the city walls are out of sight," Kuna whispered.

They moved in silence for a time. She could hear the faint footsteps of her companions in the quiet of the wilderness. The only other sound was the merry chirping of birds. The wide, lazy river was on their right. Such a contrast from the noisy bustle of the city.

When they were well out of earshot, Baya ventured. "That was easy."

"Yes," Kuna said. "Too easy. We're lucky it's mushroom season. It's quite common for the gates to remain closed for days on end, otherwise. There is usually little need to leave the safety of the city."

"Thankfully the head guard fell for the woman's begging eyes," Ena added.

"If I were still head of the guard, I would fire that man. The young guard was right to question him. That kid deserves a promotion."

"But the older guard's mistake did allow us to get out of the city," Baya pointed out.

"Exactly. Nacora will be furious if she finds out he opened the gates this morning."

"Do you need to be reminded of whose side you're on?" Baya asked.

"Once head of the guard, always head of the guard." Ena chuckled.

In no time they found themselves on a narrow path surrounded by tall trees. Kuna, followed by Ena gave up her invisible disguise. Baya and Vicaroy slid off Tara's back. Her nose sniffed the air with all the energy of a bee in the spring.

Baya had to tune out Tara's endless chatter as the young animal tried to identify all the wild scents. It amazed Baya how much information Tara could take in from smelling a single spot on the forest floor, especially when she was this excited.

Tara wasn't the only one. Everyone seemed to be able to breathe easier out here.

The events of the previous night played in Baya's mind. "Why did Nacora show more concern for Osa than she did for Vicaroy?" Baya voiced her thoughts.

Kuna shook her head. "It was all very unlike the Unawi. Nacora never wielded her power so fiercely before."

"What has gotten into her?" Baya said.

"She's simply disappointed in me," Vicaroy said. "I'm a terrible son."

"Well, if being a good son means being locked up and forced to couple, then so be it," Baya said.

"I suppose so." But Vicaroy didn't sound fully convinced.

"Nacora can go to hell," Baya spat.

"But now you're all in trouble because of me. None of us will ever be able to enter the city again." Vicaroy walked with his head down.

"I had hoped to bring only Baya on this trip," Kuna said. "I'd planned to leave Mek behind —"

"Hey!" Mek said. "You were going to make me stay in the palace and miss my only chance to see the Bangee?"

"You should be in class and you won't see the Bangee, Mek. Only Baya will. It would have been nice to have eyes inside the palace." Kuna bit her lip. "The best of plans don't always work the way you want. I'm sorry we dragged you into this, Ena. It was never my intention to get you in trouble with the Unawi."

"I knew it was risky when I offered to help." Ena gave Kuna a warm smile.

"Nacora won't stop until she finds out who you are. It may not take her long to figure out who my friends are. When she does, she'll have your home searched."

As the full gravity of the situation sunk in, creases appeared in

Ena's brow and lines formed around her mouth as her smile faded. She seemed to age a couple of years in only seconds.

"You see this is all my fault." Vicaroy's eyes shone with anguish. "Maybe I should go back ... turn myself in. Maybe I could convince Mother to be lenient with you."

Baya's eyes shot to Vicaroy. "Just like you were able to convince her to set you free? Your mother is not listening to anyone right now ... except maybe Osa."

"We are not going back." The authority in Kuna's voice made it final.

To further settle the debate Baya decided that a change of subject was needed. "How did they know where and when to find us?"

Ena and Kuna exchanged a worried look. Ena held her hands out and shrugged, indicating she had no idea.

Mek's eyes shifted between the women. He quickly looked away. "Did you see that bird?"

Baya studied him. He was acting strange.

He caught Baya's scrutinizing stare. "What? It was really pretty." He turned and walked away.

Her eyes narrowed as she watched after him.

Kuna stopped. "Ena, Baya, take my hands. We need to set a protection spell. It's the only way we will make it through the wild ... without being attacked."

The three women stood in a circle, with joined hands. Baya could feel the invisible shield spread from them until it surrounded everyone, including Tara.

"It's more powerful with three of us," Baya said. Baya could feel it. Predators wouldn't be able to find them.

The land was full of lush vegetation. Lots of green trees, yellow grass and too many different colors of flowers to count. They passed through open meadows and dense forest. Tara rolled in the tall grass and blended in perfectly with the flowers. She was right at home.

* * *

"TARA," Baya would call after the animal anytime she was out of sight.

"Stop yelling. I'm sure that creature can handle itself," Kuna said.

"This land is most likely crawling with animals like her or perhaps worse and she keeps wandering beyond our protection."

"Tara's kind are apex predators. There's nothing more deadly out there than her," Mek offered.

"But what if her kind is mean? She's still young and —"

"She'll be fine." Kuna gave Baya a firm slap on the shoulder.

Baya conceded and stopped calling for Tara — at least for now.

They walked until it was almost dark. For the last couple of hours Baya had thought only about crawling up on top of Tara and letting herself be carried, so when Kuna said that it was time to stop Baya didn't protest.

"I'll make us a meal," Vicaroy said.

"He's a really good cook," Baya added.

In no time a fire was lit and Vicaroy went to work cutting vegetables.

Ena rubbed her feet and stared blankly at the fire. "So we have lost our home ... for good?"

Baya moved to sit beside Ena and placed her arm around her. She lay her head on Baya's shoulder as they let the full weight of their situation sink in.

"Vicaroy and I have been in this situation before. We left our home and found a new one. We can do it again."

"Where will we go? It's not like we can live with the Arges," Ena said.

Mek snorted. "Definitely not." He was stretched out on his bedroll and didn't appear to be in the least bit upset about the possibility of never being able to return to Merth.

"But all my friends and family ..." Ena said. "I mean what are we supposed to do, wander around in the forest forever?"

"I'm not giving up on Merth," Kuna said. "We will ..." her voice lowered to a whisper. "I don't know what will happen."

They ate their fill of Vicaroy's delicious stew and everyone indulged in seconds. Kuna put Mek on cleanup duty while Vicaroy laid out his bedroll next to Baya.

"Oh no you don't," Kuna said.

"Don't what?" Baya asked.

"The boys will sleep apart from the women."

"Why?"

"You know it's our custom, people of the opposite gender should not sleep together until they've been properly coupled."

Baya rolled her eyes and gave Vicaroy an irritated scowl.

"That's a bunch of crap," Ena said. "Let them sleep next to each other. I forget how proper you all are in the palace, acting all high and mighty. Well, let me tell you, I live amongst real people and everyone sleeps with each other."

"Don't exaggerate, Ena." Kuna gave her a stern look. "Very few people are as … free-spirited as you."

"You'd be surprised." Ena winked at Kuna.

"I'm the leader here and I say men and women sleep separately."

"I'm with Kuna on this one," Mek said.

"I haven't slept in two days," Vicaroy said as he moved his blankets next to Mek. "At this point I don't care where I sleep as long as I get to."

CHAPTER 26

It was barely five hours later when Kuna relentlessly woke everyone. Baya had to force her body to work. Her feet ached with every step they took. She'd lost her walking legs in the short amount of time they'd spent in Merth, being pampered in the palace. That was over.

"How far to … wherever it is we're going," she asked.

"Not too far." Kuna tossed Baya's pack at her.

"That's vague."

"I don't know exactly. I haven't been there before."

"But you do know how to find this …" Baya swallowed. "creature, right?"

Kuna answered with a glare.

"That's not helpful."

Kuna kicked dirt over the campfire. "Come on. It's getting late. The second sun is already on the rise."

* * *

On the fifth day of travel they found themselves in a downpour. Baya shivered against the wetness that seeped through her light cloak, which was, much to her dismay, only partially waterproof.

"The storm is going to make it difficult to find the entrance," Kuna said. "We should be getting close and I might not be able to see the landmarks."

Baya could only make out the ghostly outline of the nearest trees. It was impossible to see much else.

"Let's find shelter until the rain passes," Kuna said.

This sounded great to Baya but how were they going to find a dry place?

Kuna drifted off the path and was soon out of sight.

A yell came from the direction where Kuna had disappeared, followed by a swooshing sound.

Mek and Ena ran forward. Vicaroy took Baya by the arm to hold her back.

A piercing scream rang out.

"Ena!" Baya yelled.

"Careful." Vicaroy moved forward.

Baya scrambled to get in front of him. She took his hand and slowly moved into the misty forest. "Kuna? Mek?"

Fog swirled around their feet. There was no sign of the others. They cautiously moved forward holding onto one another.

"Where did they disappear tooooo..?" Baya felt the ground give way. She desperately clung to Vicaroy. He tried to pull her up as she slipped. He took a step forward to get better footing but lost purchase on the slick mud and they were both swept away down a muddy embankment.

"Nooooo!" Baya tightened her grip on Vicaroy's hand. His eyes were wide with shock. She clawed at the slick embankment with her free hand. It did nothing to slow their descent. After a couple of seconds, they landed next to each other in a muddy pile.

Kuna pulled them to their feet. "You okay?"

Baya did a quick mental scan of her body. "The landing was rather soft, thanks to all the mud."

"Well now I'm certain of one thing," Kuna said.

"What's that?" Mek tried to brush the mud off his pants, which only resulted in smearing it worse.

"If I were to jump off a cliff, you all would follow," Kuna's eyes sparkled with amusement.

"You're our fearless leader," Ena laughed.

The laugh was contagious, even Kuna had to smile.

Tara bounded toward them. Only her paws were dirty. *Why you slide through mud? The path is just over there.* She pointed with her long nose.

"Next time we'll follow the servine," Baya chuckled.

"This is a fortunate turn of events," Kuna said.

Baya frowned at her mud-covered clothes. "And why is that?"

"Because it led me to the rock face I was looking for." Kuna gestured behind her. "It looks exactly as the legends described."

"It appears we were meant to find the Bangee." Ena gazed upward and her mouth hung open.

Through the grey mist rose an even darker grey stone wall. Baya shivered and it wasn't only from the cold rain and mud that worked their way into her clothes and eventually to her bones. It wasn't clear if the wall had been handmade or not. It was almost too even and too smooth to be natural, yet the occasional blemish looked like it might be something found in the wild.

"The entrance has to be close. Ena, you take the boys and head east. Baya and I will head west. Holler if you find anything."

Tara let out a yip to get everyone's attention. *Over here!*

Baya hurried into the mist after her and stopped short when she saw what Tara had found. Double doors made of obsidian stood four times as tall as Baya. The rounded stone walls surrounding the door appeared to consume it — slowly growing — covering up the door.

Baya blinked and the walls stopped moving. "Did you see …"

What?

She blinked again and shook her head. "Never mind."

At the top of the door were two carved faces surrounded by stone leaves. Their mouths hung open and their faces twisted in agony. It looked as if they were being sucked into a tree. Their fingers wrapped around the top of the door, desperate to hold on.

Baya's blood went cold and her face drained of color. One of the stone heads had four eyes and a slick bald head — an Arge, while the other was a human with wavy hair, two large eyes and full lips. It was impossible to tell the gender of either.

Kuna appeared at her side only to state the obvious, "This is it."

There was a long silence as they surveyed the entry. The only sound was the pouring rain.

It was Vicaroy who broke the icy silence. "Baya can't go in there alone."

She placed her arms around his waist and pulled him close.

"There's nothing to worry about," Kuna said. "This is only the Bangee trying to ward off visitors."

"That's our signal then," Vicaroy said. "We shouldn't be here and Baya shouldn't disturb a creature that clearly wants to be left alone."

Baya cocked her head to the side as she studied the tortured faces over the door. "I don't know if this door is a warning to stay away or … something else."

"What else could it possibly be?" Ena asked.

"I'm not sure but maybe it's a … shrine, meant to honor these two figures."

"Honor them — by capturing their last horrific moments … in stone … forever?" Mek questioned.

"I'm sure it's a shrine, nothing more," replied Kuna, although she didn't sound convinced. She took Baya by the shoulders. "Remember why you're here."

Baya shook her head as if to wake up. Why was she there? Oh, that's right, to ask the Bangee about that object. "The Ominot." Her voice was barely audible.

"Yes. Remember, we need to know what Var knows about it."

"You mean, what the Arges want with it?"

"Right." Kuna shrugged. "Same thing."

Baya narrowed her eyes. "I don't know anything about any of this. Are you sure I'm the only one who the Bangee will talk to?"

Kuna nodded.

"Baya ... don't." Vicaroy reached for her, pushing Kuna out of the way.

Baya pressed herself into Vicaroy. His body was warm so she hugged him tighter.

"This isn't our concern," Vicaroy said. "Who cares about this ... thing? Whatever it is. Let's move on ... start over —"

"This *is* your concern," Kuna snapped. "More so than you know. Look, Baya, you must trust me. Only the Bangee can tell us what we need to know. I'm afraid the fate of Merth is at stake, maybe even more."

"What do you mean? What are you not telling us, Kuna?"

"I'm like you, Baya, left in the dark. We need information. That's why we're here."

Baya studied Kuna's dark eyes. They were sincere and pleading.

"Fine," Baya turned to the door.

Vicaroy took her hand to stop her.

"I'll be okay." She ran her fingers along his five-day old stubble. His eyes begged her as well. "I won't be long."

Kuna tried to force the door open. It didn't budge. Placing her hand over the handles she tried to open it with her powers.

Nothing.

She turned to Baya. "You must be the only one who can open it."

Baya waved her hand over the handles and the sound of stone grinding against stone rang out over the pitter-patter of the rain. The black doors opened wide, revealing more dark forest.

When she stepped over the threshold, it was like walking into a giant bubble — a strong protection spell but it let her in ... only her...

"I'm going with her." Vicaroy's voice sounded muffled. He moved with determination toward the entrance.

"Don't!" Baya held up her hands in warning.

The protective layer threw him back in a flash of blinding green light.

"No!" Baya ran for him but the doors slammed shut many times faster than heavy stone should be able to move.

CHAPTER 27

There had barely been enough time for Baya to get her hand out of the way of the stone doors. She tried to use her powers to force them open.

Nothing.

Baya cursed the massive barrier between her and Vicaroy. She was stuck inside the Bangee's land now.

"Let me out! I have to know that he's okay." She pounded her fists on the doors to no avail.

A rustling sound behind her caused her to spin around. Leaves blew across the path in front of her. If it could be called a path. It looked like no one had used it for many years. It was overgrown and hardly visible, yet it was there.

The grey stone walls extended out on either side of her for as far as she could see — which wasn't far. She turned back to the door. She had to know if Vicaroy was okay.

A whisper breezed by on the wind.

She spun around again. "Who's there?"

Silence, followed only by the slight rustling of leaves in the wind. It sounded like someone was trying to talk to her but she couldn't make out the words.

"Speak up. I can't hear you, … whoever you are." She carefully scanned the forest around her but she saw nothing.

The whisper faded. She moved to follow it as if in a trance. "Wait."

In no time, she was completely surrounded by mist. It was so thick she couldn't see the tops of the trees. Every shadow seemed to be hiding something. Several times she caught movement out of the corner of her eye but upon further examination it would turn out to be nothing — her mind playing tricks on her.

The whispers grew louder but remained unintelligible, until a tiny home came into view. The voice or the wind, or whatever it was, fell silent, even the rain calmed to a faint drizzle. The walls were made of large stones and mortar — no windows. The roof was thatched and covered in a yellow moss. Simple yet functional.

What next? Just walk in or should she knock? Baya took a deep breath to try to quiet the drumming heartbeat in her ears. The handle on the small wooden door turned easily and Baya swung it open. Whoever lived here was waiting for her.

"Hello."

Nothing.

Her eyes strained to make out what was inside the dimly lit home. The table and countertops were littered with shadows of what looked to be cups, parchments, large flasks and pots. Bundles of plants hung from the ceiling.

The warmth that escaped from the open door was welcome. The air smelled stale and … it was like nothing Baya had smelled before. It wasn't entirely unpleasant, simply different. Like someone was boiling lots of strange herbs, not the edible kind that made one's mouth water but more like potent medicines.

"Hello?" Her voice sounded loud as it broke the stillness. "May I come in?"

"Enter," came a raspy voice from the shadows.

Baya squinted but couldn't make out any human shapes or movement. The voice appeared to come from every corner of the house. She cautiously stepped over the threshold. The dim light came from a fireplace at the far end of the room. Baya made her way farther into the home.

"Where are you?"

A dark streak caught her eye as something moved across the floor. She swung her body toward it. A black figure faded in and out of the shadows. A long skinny body slowly came into view as something made its way out of the dark corner. It walked on all fours. Baya could make out the shape of its bones, as if it were a skeleton wearing a black skin suit. It had squatty back legs and ...

Baya's entire body shivered.

It walked on its elbows, leaving its forearms and hands sticking out at odd angles. Its long neck held a large bald head and four milky white eyes eerily glowed in the dim light.

Her skin tingled as if insects crawled over every inch of her. Baya was frozen in place, her mouth gaped open.

"You see, my pet," it rasped. "That's why I don't venture beyond my own lands ... not anymore."

Baya couldn't speak, or move, or even breathe.

"The outside world has never known what to make of me. That's why I'm better off here ... alone."

"You're the ... the ...?" was all Baya could force out.

"Bangee, yes." Its voice was a cross between a purr and a hiss. It crawled out of the shadows, revealing its true length.

Baya's back straightened as her body went rigid. Her brain was yelling, "Run!" But her feet refused to budge.

The Bangee's long fingers brushed her legs and Baya flinched. Its head slowly rose higher and higher as it sat back on its hind legs, like Tara often did. Its head almost touched the ceiling.

After studying Baya for a long moment, it swung its head down until it was only inches from her face. The Bangee inhaled deeply.

"Oh," it purred. "How I miss that smell." The creature's breath was surprisingly pleasant.

"What ... smell?" Baya choked. She hadn't had a proper bath in days but she didn't think that was what the Bangee was referring to.

There was no doubt — she was going to be dinner. After all, the creature looked like it was starving.

"Fear, the smell of fear. It brings me the most pleasure." Its solid cream-filled eyes blinked at different times. "It gives me …" it inhaled deeply. "Strength."

That was it. Baya was as good as dead.

The Bangee moved away, once again raising to its full height, sitting back on its haunches. Its short hind legs closed in on themselves and its arms remained bent in an awkward position with its long fingers flopped downward.

Baya exhaled, relieved to have some space between herself and the creature. She might be able to make it to the door before it could. Of course, she wouldn't be able to get over the walls that surrounded this place, not to mention the powerful protection spell, so there was no point in running — still the instinct was there.

"I know why you came here but the question is … do you?"

Baya's eyes widened. All she could do was shake her head no. She didn't know what the Ominot was, or why it was important.

"That's what I thought." A low hiss came from the thin slit that Baya assumed was its mouth. "Either way, I possess the knowledge you seek."

Its mouth opened, exposing pointy yellow teeth. Baya wanted to yell, "Just kill me and get it over with." Instead she swallowed hard.

"As you might have guessed such knowledge does not come for free."

Baya's breath hitched. "What good would it do to tell me what you know if you're going to kill me?"

CHAPTER 28

A low rasping sound came from deep inside the Bangee. It resembled a laugh — somewhat. But in reality, it was more like a phlegmy cough that caused Baya's skin to prickle.

"I see. You think the price for my knowledge is death." It made the raspy sound again until its chest shook causing its ribs to protrude even more. "You think that I plan to kill you?" The Bangee narrowed its many eyes. "Now why would you think that? Because I don't look like you? Because I'm … terrifying?" It shook its head. "Things haven't changed. You are all still the same — assuming the worst — scared to death of anything that is not like you."

Baya lowered her head. "I'm sorry. I shouldn't have …"

"You, like everyone else, assume that I'm evil? That I'm a killer?" The creature finished her sentence.

Sweat trickled down Baya's brow as she nodded.

The Bangee lowered itself on its elbows and crawled over to the small fire. "No. The price for my knowledge is …"

It snapped its head around to look at Baya with four wide eyes.

Baya forced herself not to shiver.

"You must tell me your worst fear. … That is all. And don't bother lying. I can smell a lie almost as well as I can smell fear."

Baya stared at the floor. An odd mixture of relief and guilt occupied her thoughts. She may make it out alive. Yet, there was also shame because she had assumed that this creature was bad, simply because it looked like nothing she could've imagined in her wildest nightmares.

"Well, my pet. Go on. We don't have all day, now do we?"

"Go … on?"

The creature hissed with exasperation. "Tell me your worst fear."

"Oh," Right. This should be easy. Her first thought was of her sister. She had always feared that Tash was better than her — that she would be more powerful and become Unawi.

Baya shook her head. That couldn't be it. She had left that life behind and no longer feared being second to Tash. "I don't know." Baya's voice was barely a whisper.

"Think, my pet. Think."

Baya couldn't focus. Odd emotions consumed her. She had never felt bad for how she'd treated Tash but now, for the first time, it hit her. "I shouldn't have been so hard on her. I should've been a better … sister."

A clicking sound came from the Bangee. "No, my pet. I'm afraid that is not your worst fear. That maybe what you *regret* most but that does not interest me. You have one more chance. Choose wisely."

Baya shook her head. Where had all that come from about her sister? "Okay, my worst fear …" was being eaten by wild beasts. This had been what plagued her night-terrors as a child. But she hadn't had such dreams since she befriended Mook back in Pathins. "Why is this so hard?"

"If it were easy, then it wouldn't be worth the knowledge I possess."

"If you know my worst fears, then why don't *you* tell me."

"What fun would that be?"

Instantly the Bangee's face was only inches from hers. Its eyes were white orbs that Baya felt she was falling into. There was so much there to see in the milky depths, so much knowledge and history … lifetimes. Baya wanted to ask it how old it was but refrained.

"My pleasure comes from watching *you* discover what you fear most."

Baya instinctively took a step back and blinked to break the trance caused by the white eyes.

"Besides, it is a test," it hissed.

"A test?"

"Yes, to see how insightful you are."

"Insightful? But there are so many things to fear. How do I know which is my worst?"

"Think. And remember, you only have one more chance."

Baya paced in the tiny space in front of her. Think! She feared for her safety, for Vicaroy's, her brother's... The list went on and on. How was she to choose? She feared losing Vicaroy to another woman ... Osa ... maybe.

She stumbled backward. It felt like the answer literally hit her. She was overwhelmed with how it had felt when she thought she lost Vicaroy, when he fell into the raging river. That had to be it. "I never want to feel that again."

"Yes. Yes. Go on. You're getting closer." The creature's fingers twitched with excitement.

Baya swallowed. This was harder than she had thought. It was as if verbalizing her greatest fear might somehow manifest it into reality. Or maybe it was that she worried the information could be used against her, making her vulnerable.

"Go on." The Bangee's eyes shone with a new light.

"That my powers are taken from me and I can no longer protect the men I care about."

"Yesss," the creature hissed. "That's it."

It moved away from Baya and her muscles relaxed.

"But it doesn't have to be that way."

"What?"

"The vulnerable ones — your men, the ones you care about. They don't have to be helpless."

"I'm ... sorry. I ... don't follow?"

"The Ominot. That's why you're here, is it not?"

CHAPTER 29

The Bangee picked at the coals in the fireplace with a small log before tossing it into the fire with an odd flick of its distorted wrist. Its long fingers moved in an exaggerated wave, like a lady's hand fan. "Take your wet cloak off and sit." The Bangee gestured to a wooden chair.

Baya's eyes had adjusted to the dim light, so she could make out most of the objects in the room. Still, she didn't make a move toward the chair.

"I suppose it's my turn to talk," the Bangee said. "I'll make us some tea. You could use something to warm you."

"That's very nice of you but I have to get back to my friends."

"Oh, they'll survive without you. Sit."

Baya felt compelled to do as she was told. Not to mention, the thought of shedding her soaked cloak was a tempting offer. So she did just that.

With the wave of an arm a water pitcher floated over to the Bangee. Its long fingers folded in on themselves as they grasped the handle. It poured the water into a small pot that hung over the fire.

A cup of hot tea did sound wonderful.

"Where to start? Well it's not actually the Ominot that is most important to you at this time. What is plaguing you now is the Ominox."

"The Ominox?"

The Bangee nodded. "The Ominox has been discovered."

Was it speaking in riddles? Was this another test? She had to figure out what it was talking about. Baya shook her head. "Discovered?"

"Yes. The Ominox — let's simply call it the Ox. It gets so confusing with the Ominox, the Ominot..." The Bangee waved its long fingers dismissively. "The Ox has been found — it has been recovered from its ancient hiding place and it's being used against you. And all of Merth, for that matter."

"Merth is in trouble," Baya whispered. "What does this ... Ox do?"

"It was created to harness the power of the Ominot. Sorry, my pet, I'm afraid I've gotten ahead of myself. Let me start at the beginning." The Bangee glanced impatiently into the pot to see if the water was boiling. Of course it wasn't. "It all started with Ameris. I'm sure you've heard of her."

Baya stifled a moan. "Yes." Of course, this *would* have something to do with Ameris.

"She was an ambitious woman."

"But not the supreme Goddess, I know," Baya said.

The Bangee issued its raspy chuckle. "Goddess or no, she was very gifted. In her fight for control she found a way to rip men's powers from them." It shook its head sorrowfully. "That is a lot of power and it's all stored in the Ominot. It is a very dangerous and volatile thing. Ameris spent many years trying to figure out how to control it. She wanted to transfer men's powers to herself, thus becoming unstoppable, a Goddess, if you will."

The room swirled around Baya. She placed her hand over her stomach to try to keep it from turning upside down. It didn't help. Could it be? Had men once had powers? Had Ameris been able to steal their power?

"However, Ameris's attempts to use the Ominot almost killed her. After innumerable tries she discovered a conduit that she called the

Ominox. This "Ox" enabled her to safely use some of men's powers at will."

Baya was unaware that she was sitting on the edge of her seat. "So someone in Merth has found the Ox and is using its power?"

"Impressive, my pet. You are a sharp one, aren't you? That must be why we were meant to meet."

Baya was slowly starting to see a different side to this creature. It was becoming clear that it was an intelligent female — not simply an odd creature.

The Bangee waved her stick-like fingers again causing herbs to float into two small cups sitting on the counter. The cups followed suit, floating gently over to the wooden table next to her. She poured steaming hot water into them and there they sat untouched to steep. Her movements were gentle. Maybe she was not a threat after all?

"What does all this have to do with me?" Baya asked.

"You're the one who must find the Ox and the Ominot and destroy them both."

"Will that give men their power back?"

"Yes and that's when the struggle will begin."

"What do you mean?"

"One thing at a time, my pet."

"Stop calling me that. I'm no one's *pet*." Baya wasn't sure where her strength had come from or when her fear had subsided but she was definitely more concerned with the story than for her own safety. Maybe it was the warm fire and the promise of a hot brew.

The Bangee's thin lips were downturned and her eyes remained on the floor. Baya was sure she looked sad.

"Are you sure about that — being no one's pet?"

Baya narrowed her eyes. What was that supposed to mean?

"We're all someone's pet." The creature seemed to answer Baya's thought.

Baya shook her head to help her focus. "Do you know where to find the Ominot?"

"First find the Ox. Then, with some luck, you may find the Ominot."

"Who has the Ox?"

"I do not know. All I can tell you is what it looks like." The Bangee floated one of the cups over to a small table beside Baya.

Baya picked up the cup and used it to warm her hands. The steaming tea smelled delectable. She could hardly wait to taste it.

The creature crawled on her elbows to a shelf beside the fireplace. She rummaged through stacks of parchments looking for something.

She clearly wasn't the best of housekeepers.

"Ah, here we are." The creature pulled a parchment out from under one of the piles and blew on it. Dust particles danced through thin streams of light.

Baya's shaky hand took the paper from the Bangee. Her lips parted as she studied the drawing. It was a simple flower shape with five petals. The five "petals" were like pink hands with skinny fingers pointing toward its center. Like a starfish had a baby with an ocean anemone. In the center of the "star" was a circle filled with red and orange swirls. Baya had never seen anything like it. "This is the Ox?" she asked.

The creature nodded.

"It's lovely."

"No. It's a terrible thing that must be demolished."

"How big is it?"

"Small enough to fit in the palm of your hand. And ... one more thing ... it cannot be taken by force. If someone tries to tear it from its current owner, the Ox will kill the thief on the spot." The Bangee flicked its long fingers. "Poof. Vaporized into thin air."

"What about stealing it while its owner is asleep or something?"

The Bangee slowly shook its head. "It cannot be taken without the owner knowing. You see, the Ox embeds itself in the palm of its master."

Baya crinkled her nose at the thought and rubbed her palm. "Sounds painful. So how will I get it?"

CHAPTER 30

"I suppose you're going to have to ask for it," the Bangee said.

"I doubt whoever has the Ox will be willing to give up that kind of power," Baya said.

"It won't be easy. Just don't forget, it must be given willingly."

"This is impossible." Baya's shoulders slumped. "Can you at least tell me what the Ominot looks like?"

"There is no way to know."

Baya gave her an incredulous look. "Then how will I find it?"

The Bangee's head swayed from side to side, as if considering. "That *is* the trick."

Baya narrowed her eyes. Why had she stopped being helpful?

"The Ominot can change form and it can appear as different objects depending on who is looking at it. Probably one of the reasons it has remained hidden for all these years."

"Great." Baya rolled her eyes. The sheer absurdity of the tasks at hand made her want to give up before she even started. "So what you're saying is, this will be impossible."

"I pray not. Difficult, yes but hopefully you will find a way."

"So I find this … Ox and somehow convince its owner to hand it over, then it will lead me to the Ominot."

Another nod. "It is easier said than done."

No doubt, Baya thought.

"The legends state that before Ameris left the corporal realm she tried to destroy these two objects but failed. So she hid the Ox where she hoped it would never come to light. In the hands of the wrong person it could be devastating. She must have done a pretty good job if it has only now been found."

A derisive chuckle escaped from Baya. "You're telling me that I have to accomplish something that Ameris herself was unable to do?" She pressed her lips together. The mission laid out before her kept getting more and more ridiculous by the second. "And the Ominot? Do the legends give any clues as to what was done with it?"

"It naturally hides itself as I've already said. It changes forms and its powers can't be used without the Ox. So as you can see, the Ox is the key and should be your only concern … for now. One step at a time, one day at a time."

"So the Ominot could be hidden in plain sight?"

A clicking noise came from the Bangee as she tsked Baya. "Forget about the Ominot for now. First you need a plan and you need to train."

Baya's head jolted back at the sudden change of subject. "Train?"

"You and your male companion need to learn to fight. There are many challenges ahead of you and knowing how to defend yourself could be of great benefit. You have two good trainers with you, the former head of the royal guard and the boy with red hair."

Baya took a sip from the cup. The liquid was a perfect mixture of sweet and nutty. It was an entirely new taste that instantly warmed her insides, much better than the woman's brew she drank every morning. "How do you know all this?"

The Bangee gave her a crooked smile. "I have my ways. I'm very old and I have a lot of time on my hands. It is amazing what one can accomplish with enough time."

"Then why don't *you* find the Ominot and destroy it?"

The coughing laugh came again. "I'm far too old for adventures. Besides only the foreign princess stands any hope of succeeding."

"And you think that's me?"

"Now that I have met you, any doubts I had are gone."

Baya shook her head. "Why?"

There was a long silence. "I can *see* it." She hissed the word see.

"What do you see?"

"There is no way for you to comprehend what I see inside my mind."

"Then you know that I will succeed?"

The Bangee shook her head. "There is no way to know. One thing at a time. Your job is to focus on the now. What will you do next?"

"I have no idea. That's why I came to you, for answers."

"Eventually, you must head back to Merth."

Baya thought of how every palace guard would be on the lookout for them. "That won't be easy."

"No, it won't. There is a cottage not far to the south. It was my home while I built this place. It may still stand. You and your companions can stay there."

"We'll have to come up with a good plan for getting back into Merth."

The creature nodded.

Baya stood as it felt like the conversation was over. She set her mostly empty cup on the table and retrieved her damp cloak. "Thanks for the tea and … for everything."

The Bangee gave a slight nod.

Baya turned back when she got to the door. "Are you lonely?"

The creature gave a heavy sigh that made her ribs look like they were growing. Baya worried that the bone might rip through her brittle skin.

"No."

Baya didn't believe her. "I'm sorry that I … failed you."

"How did you fail me?"

"I was terrified of you, like all the others you'd come in contact with. I shouldn't have been so quick to judge you."

"I expected nothing different." A grey tongue came out of her mouth as she licked her lips. "The only way you could fail me is if you do not destroy the Ominot."

"What happens if I don't."

"Men will continue to suffer under the rule of women. Eventually, Merth will fall along with the rest of the world including Aregow and Pathins."

"Well if that's all ..." Baya murmured. The familiar pressure was back — the tiny stone base that was forced to hold an entire palace. Yet, this burden was many times worse, like supporting the weight of the entire world.

Her thoughts strayed to Bek and she wondered what life was like for him. Was he in trouble? The longer it took to find these objects the worse things would get ... for men. "I guess there's no time to lose." Baya's eyes snapped to the Bangee. She'd been so lost in her own worries that she felt guilty for not thinking of the creature who was right in front of her. "I hope you find someone who can see you for who you truly are."

"This is my lot in life. I fully accept it."

Baya's heart felt like it weighed many times what it should. "Thanks again."

The Bangee merely turned to stoke the fire as Baya put on her cloak and left.

CHAPTER 31

Baya's thoughts were of the poor lonely creature she'd left behind and how foolish she'd been to be so scared of it. Part of Baya wanted to go back ... to what? Keep the creature company? She shook her head. This was much easier to think about than the monumental tasks that had been laid at her feet.

"Find something that's been lost for a thousand years," Baya mumbled to herself. "Oh, by the way, it changes forms or appears as different things to different people — right. That will be easy."

The large stone doors slid open as Baya approached the exit to the Bangee's fortified lands.

"Baya!" Vicaroy's voice roused her from her thoughts.

He was okay!

Vicaroy moved with determination toward the threshold.

"No!" Baya didn't want him to be thrown back again. She took off at a full sprint. As she left the Bangee protective layer, she found herself in his arms.

His hand held the back of her head as he breathed her in. "Are you okay?"

"I ... Well I'm not hurt but ..." raindrops fell on her face in rapid procession. Baya didn't know if it hadn't been raining on the Bangee's land, while it poured on this side of the wall, or if it had just started raining again.

Looking over Vicaroy's shoulder she saw that Kuna and Mek looked relieved. Mek gave her a wink and Ena moved in to give her a hug.

Tara's thick, rough tongue ran up the length of Baya's cheek. "It's good to see you too." She patted the top of Tara's head.

"What did you learn?" Kuna demanded.

Baya shook her head. "Not here. Let's get out of the rain. There should be a cottage not far from here. We can take shelter there." Baya pulled her hood up and headed south.

She wanted them to be sitting down when she told them the Bangee's story and she still needed time to process all the information. It was too much to take in all at once.

Her head began to throb when she thought about where to start. She wasn't even sure how to tell them, let alone what to do next. Yet again, her world had been turned entirely upside down. What she thought was real, all that she'd been taught, was a lie.

* * *

AFTER FIFTEEN MINUTES of walking in the unrelenting rain, Baya and her companions came to a clearing. As promised, in the center of the meadow was a tiny home with walls made of stone. It was a relief to see that its roof appeared to be largely intact. Nothing sounded better than a place to dry off.

What was left of the front door hung uselessly from one hinge. Kuna easily snapped the door loose from the rotten frame and set it aside. It was the most basic of structures, consisting of one room with three windows and one doorway. Any shutters that may have once covered the windows were long gone. This left open holes in the walls. Still, it was dry inside.

Tara was too big to fit through the door. Not to mention, the place wouldn't have been able to hold them all with her inside. Tara curled up in front of the door, under the eaves of the roof so that she was mostly protected from the rain.

Wood remained neatly stacked next to the fireplace and in no time Ena had it blazing. The small space instantly felt warmer. Vicaroy and Mek used branches to sweep the dirt and leaves off the floor, while the three women quickly set a protection spell around the place.

"Alright it's time to tell us what happened." Kuna said as she gnawed on a piece of dried meat.

Baya dried herself by the fire. "You all might want to sit down for this."

* * *

MEK LEAPT TO HIS FEET. "We used to have powers … like women?" His sea-green eyes shone bright in the firelight.

Ena shook her head. "I don't know. It doesn't add up."

"That's what I thought," Baya said. "If men used to have powers, then why are there no records? The island where we came from was founded by Ameris so she was able to write our history however she saw fit. So it's no surprise that we never heard of men having powers. But Merth is older. It existed before Ameris, so how could she have erased all of Merth's history?"

"She did." Kuna's voice was flat. She didn't appear to be overly surprised by all that Baya revealed about her conversation with the Bangee. She had simply remained deep in thought. "In the Great Wars, Ameris burned all of Merth's libraries and schools. Clearly, that was intentional. Any record of men with power or men in power was lost a thousand years ago."

Baya and Vicaroy exchanged a wide-eyed glance. Baya was really starting to hate this new Ameris, the real Ameris.

"Over the generations powerful men have slipped from our minds," Ena's voice was soft, thoughtful. "My father used to say that humans have short memories. Now I think I understand what that meant."

"Do you think it could be true?" Baya asked.

"Could be. There's only one way to find out," Kuna said.

"We have to find the Ox." Mek paced in front of the fire.

"But ... How?" Vicaroy sat on the floor with his elbows on his knees. "Merth is huge. It could be anywhere."

Baya nodded. "It will be difficult enough to get back inside the city walls. Then what? How do we search an entire city for something when every palace guard will be looking for us?"

Kuna stared blankly at the small fire. "We don't have to search." She sounded like she was in a trance. "Var has it."

"Var?" Baya asked. "How do you know?"

"The Ox must be why the Arges wanted to find her so badly the night of Vicaroy's celebration. This information confirms that Var not only knows how to find it but that she already has it in her possession."

"We'd better get to the Ox before the Arges," Baya said.

"There's no telling what they want with it," Vicaroy added.

"Most likely they want to become even more powerful," Ena said.

Kuna's eyes narrowed on Ena. "We don't know what the Arges want with it but they are not our current worry."

Baya studied Kuna. Why was she being so defensive about the Arges? Something told Baya that they *did* need to get the Ox before the Arges.

"Are you saying that we not only have to get back into the city but also back into Mother's palace ... somehow?" Vicaroy said.

Kuna nodded.

"Then why did you all work so hard to break me out of there? I, for one, have no desire to go back to that prison."

"So don't go," Kuna said. "We leave for Merth at daybreak — the ones who wish to return. So get some rest." Kuna stood to lay out her bedroll.

"But the Bangee said we need to train and to ... plan," Baya said.

"Train?"

"Yeah. Vicaroy and I haven't had any formal combat training. She said that you and Mek should teach us to fight. Or at least defend ourselves."

Kuna's jaw tightened. "We can discuss this tomorrow. Women over here." Kuna gestured to one side of the small room. "And boys over there."

"Would you stop calling us boys? We're men," Mek protested.

"That's debatable," Kuna said.

Baya gave Vicaroy her pouty lips and reluctantly let go of his hand. "Good night." She kissed his cheek.

"I'm glad you're safe." He pulled her close and pressed his lips to hers.

"That's enough," Kuna barked.

"Thank you!" Mek agreed.

"I don't know. I thought it was just getting interesting." Ena had stretched out on her bedroll as she watched Baya and Vicaroy.

CHAPTER 32

The hard stone floor under Baya caused her to continually move in an attempt to find enough comfort to sleep. She didn't succeed. Her mind was full of odd forms that walked on their elbows and raspy voices in the shadows. She studied two of the moons out the window above her head, or rather the square hole in the wall. One moon was almost full and the other was a perfect crescent. A rustling sound caught her attention.

Baya stiffened at once — her breathing ceased. She could hear the men's heavy breathing on the other side of the room. Out of the corner of her eye she caught a glimpse of a large figure in the doorway. She couldn't stand it, she sat up and surveyed the room.

The figure was gone and only Ena lay beside her. "Kuna?" she whispered.

Ena moaned and rolled over.

Baya got to her feet and ran to the door. "Kuna?" But there was no sign of her.

Baya sighed. *She's just gone to relieve herself.* She lay back down, this time facing the doorway.

* * *

BAYA'S SHOULDER was asleep but she was not. "Kuna just had to pee," she whispered, "for three hours?" She narrowed her eyes. "I don't think so." Baya rolled onto her back in an attempt to ease her aching shoulder. Through the window, only one moon was partially visible. Maybe she's in trouble, Baya thought. She looked at the others, lost in their dreams and debated about whether or not she should wake them to help her search for Kuna.

Thankfully the dark outline of Kuna's form moved through the door. The figure was easy to recognize; the thick muscled body, the cropped hair and, of course, the outline of the notched ear.

Baya resisted the urge to sit up. Instead she lay motionless as Kuna quietly crawled into the bedroll next to hers.

"Where did you go?" Baya asked.

Kuna leapt to her feet. "Baya! You scared me."

Baya kept her piercing stare on Kuna.

"I ... couldn't sleep. I needed some fresh air."

"Because you don't get enough of that?"

Kuna sat down and punched her pack, which doubled as a pillow. She did this with more vigor than was necessary before plopping down with her back to Baya.

"Kuna, what are you not telling us?"

She swiftly rolled over to face Baya and took her hand. "I would never do anything to hurt any of you."

Baya pulled her hand away.

"I need you to trust me." Kuna's gaze was intense.

Baya searched her dark eyes for any sign of deceit. "We're in this together."

Kuna nodded. "To the end."

A slight smile crossed Baya's lips. "I believe you and I respect your need for privacy."

"Thank you." Kuna exhaled with relief.

* * *

Baya and Kuna slept late. By the time they roused, Vicaroy had already gathered plants and made a fresh stew.

The delectable scent woke Baya.

"So are we going back to Merth?" Baya asked.

"If the Bangee said to train, then that's what we'll do." Kuna didn't appear happy about this.

"Alright!" Mek was full of his usual excitement.

"I'll work with Baya and Mek can train Vicaroy," Kuna said.

Mek stuck his bottom lip out in an exaggerated pout. "I wanted to teach Baya."

Kuna glared at him.

"Fine."

After they ate their fill, Mek gave Vicaroy a playful shove. "Let's get started."

Kuna got to her feet. "Yes. The sooner we can come up with a plan and get back into the city the better."

"Damn straight," Mek said.

"Why are you in such a hurry to get back?" Ena asked.

"I want to get my powers back." He threw his arms out. "I'll be unstoppable." He ended his tirade with a deep belly laugh.

Ena smiled. "Giving boys powers could be dangerous."

Vicaroy studied his hands and tried to imagine what it would be like to have power coming from them — he couldn't. He shook his head and got to his feet.

Once in the meadow outside the small shack Mek held up his hands, his palms facing Vicaroy. "Hit me."

"Hit you?" Vicaroy questioned.

"Yeah, hit my hands."

Vicaroy cocked his head to the side. "I've never hit anyone before."

"It's easy." Mek punched his own palm. "Like that." Then held his hands up again. "Come on. Your fists always need to be up — ready to defend yourself."

Vicaroy had thought learning to fight sounded interesting but now he wasn't sure if he could do this. He didn't want to hit Mek. "Where we come from violence isn't allowed."

"Well, you're not stuck on that sissy island anymore. Give it a try. I bet you'll like it."

Vicaroy slowly raised his fists. The gesture made him feel silly. He jabbed at Mek's hand, barely moving it.

"That was pathetic. This is going to be harder than I thought."

Vicaroy glanced over at the women. Baya swung aggressively at Kuna's hands.

"Good. Harder," Kuna said.

Tara bounded around them, wanting to be a part of the game.

With each swing Baya's speed and force increased. She let out a furious yell with each punch.

"You see, that's how it's done. And never let your fists down."

Vicaroy hadn't even noticed that he'd lowered his hands. "I don't think I'm cut out for this."

Mek pursed his lips. "Hmm. You need motivation." Mek took Vicaroy by the wrist and with one swift twist Mek pinned his arm behind his back. Pain shot up his arm. With a swipe of Mek's leg, Vicaroy found himself face down in the grass. He struggled to turn over but Mek had him trapped. Mek's elbow pressed hard into his back. The feeling of not being able to move and the discomfort in his arm that was bent behind his back caused sweat to form on his forehead.

"You know, the only reason I'm here is to steal your woman," Mek whispered only inches from his ear.

An image of Mek and Baya wrapped in each other's arms caused every muscle in Vicaroy's body to tighten. An angry growl escaped as he struggled.

"That's it," Mek said. "Now get yourself out of my hold."

With his free arm Vicaroy was able to throw his elbow back hitting Mek in the shoulder. This sent Mek off balance just enough for Vicaroy to pull his other arm free. With both arms he shoved himself off the ground. This got Mek off of him entirely.

In the blink of an eye both men were back on their feet.

"Good," Mek smiled.

Something inside Vicaroy had shifted. Mek wasn't a woman. He didn't have to take any crap from him. And the only thing he wanted to do was send his fist into that pretty pale face of his. Charging toward Mek, he sent his fists flying.

Mek easily dodged his wild swings. "Okay. Okay. I was kidding." Mek had to jump back to keep from getting hit. "I'm not after Baya." He ducked. "Calm down, so I can show you how to control your punches."

Vicaroy's chest heaved when he stopped swinging but he didn't take his eyes off Mek. He kept his fists raised and this time he didn't feel silly.

"Good. Now. Widen your stance like this." Mek moved to stand beside Vicaroy. "Your punches need to be quick and short. If you swing from way back or in a wide arc your opponent can see it coming." Mek jabbed at the air in front of him, striking with the speed of a snake.

Vicaroy emulated him. The guy clearly knew what he was doing and Vicaroy was determined not to let any man get the upper hand on him again. It was surprising how good it felt to swing at the air as hard as he could, like a great release that he hadn't even known he needed.

When they stopped for a midday snack, Vicaroy took Baya by the hand. "Let's go for a walk."

Baya gladly followed.

"Where's Tara?" he asked.

"She's hunting."

Perfect. The animal wouldn't be in his way. "It's good that she's big enough to hunt on her own."

"It would be difficult for us to find enough to feed her at this point. She's gotten huge. How are you liking training?"

"It's fine," Vicaroy lied.

"It's fun, isn't it? It's like practicing with our weapons in our secret cove."

"I guess." Vicaroy didn't think that it was anything like being in their cove. That had been relaxing and fun, a game. His jaw clenched. Training with Mek was ... infuriating.

Once they were well away from the others, Vicaroy didn't waste any time. He pressed his lips to hers.

"So that's why you brought me out here?" Baya whispered as she enjoyed the gentle tickle of his kisses against her neck.

"We haven't had any time alone."

Their lips met again. "I know, it's maddening," she breathed between kisses.

"Tell me about it." He ran his hands under her tunic.

His movements were so graceful that she didn't't know exactly how she ended up on the soft yellow grass. All she knew was that in an instant she'd been placed gently on her back and he was on top of her. Every muscle in his bare chest was drawn tight. She ran her hands over his body which felt like chiseled stone. The familiar tingling in her lower abdomen caused her to pull him to her. Their lips met.

Then they were joined together as one. Not just in body but in mind and spirit as well. As if they were now one person — complete. She yielded to his every movement, fully giving him all of her.

It was over quickly. They hadn't even bothered to undress.

"I'm sorry," he whispered through heaving breaths.

Baya's laugh was soft. "For what?"

"I just had to know that you're mine."

She pushed him away to stare up at him with wide eyes. "Should I be offended?"

Vicaroy felt like he could fall into those colorful eyes and never come out. "No. I know you love me … I just … needed you. It's hard with people around all the time. I can't wait until we have our own room and I can properly make love to you."

She ran her hand through his hair and traced her finger over the curved scar — which acted as a constant reminder that she never wanted to lose him … again. "There will be plenty of time for that."

* * *

"I'M glad you two got that out of your systems," Kuna said.

"Got what out?" Baya tried to sound innocent.

"Perhaps, now you can get back to work."

"I'm ready." Vicaroy marched toward Mek.

Mek wore a scowl. "Good. It's your turn to block *my* blows."

Vicaroy was glad to see that his usual smirk was gone.

Mek forced Vicaroy back with each jab. "If you don't have time to dodge the blow then take the brunt of the hit with your forearm. You can knock my fist away with your arm, like this." Mek's hand flew through the air as he demonstrated the defensive move.

By the end of the day Vicaroy had a number of bruises and was beyond tired, yet oddly content as he sat down for a fresh meal that Ena had prepared. He'd learned a lot and fighting was challenging ... and satisfying.

"Thank you for cooking," Vicaroy said.

"You were all so busy and I love to cook. I have absolutely no interest in learning to fight. I'm more of a lover at heart." Ena placed a small piece of flatbread delicately on her tongue and smiled.

"It's delicious," Vicaroy said.

Ena swallowed before speaking. "Why do you sound surprised?"

"I don't know of any women who can cook. Baya can't cook to save her life."

Everyone laughed.

"Hey!" Baya protested.

"Well, it's true," Vicaroy said.

"I don't believe in all that men's work and women's work stuff," Ena said. "I live alone and I have to do it all. Whoever has the time and ability should help out no matter what type of work it is or what gender they are."

Baya nodded. She'd been trying to tell Vicaroy this forever but he always insisted on doing the men's work.

* * *

Every muscle in Baya's body protested when she stretched. The discomfort caused her to wake more fully. With a moan she sat up. Ena and Mek were still fast asleep. So it must have been Vicaroy who had set out fresh bread, fruit and nuts for them. Baya made her way to the door. Vicaroy and Kuna were already training. Baya crawled over Tara's massive form that blocked the doorway.

"Somebody sure is motivated," Baya observed.

Vicaroy's face brightened when he saw her.

They quickly settled into a routine that consisted mostly of training during the day. Vicaroy was relentlessly determined to learn all he could about fighting. Baya and Vicaroy would disappear whenever they could. As far as Baya could tell, Kuna didn't sneak out in the night again.

It was a relatively comfortable life but short lived.

CHAPTER 33

With each day that passed Kuna grew more antsy. They couldn't have been there more than five days when Baya was startled awake by a bad dream. She stared out the window without seeing the soft glow of the moons. Baya fought to brush away the hauntingly hollow feeling the dream had left deep inside her.

"What is it?" Kuna whispered.

Baya hadn't noticed that Kuna was awake let alone staring at her. "It was just a dream."

"What about?"

"It doesn't matter."

"Of course it matters." There was a sharpness to Kuna's voice.

Baya studied her. "I don't know. All that's left of the dream is a feeling. I think someone was in terrible pain and now I just feel … empty."

Kuna sat up and nudged Ena. "Get up." Then more loudly she declared, "Everyone up, now. Pack your things. We leave at once."

"Kuna, it was only a dream."

The guard was already moving about the room, gathering her belongings.

"What about our training? We've barely started —"

"What little you've had will have to do," Kuna said.

Baya crossed her arms. "It's the middle of the night." She didn't get up to collect her things. The thought of returning to Merth made her stomach tighten. It would be dangerous and this place was peaceful.

"What's going on," Ena said through a yawn.

"Kuna's overreacting because I had a nightmare." Baya stubbornly refused to get up.

Ena looked at Kuna with wide eyes. She threw her blanket off and started shoving clothes in her pack.

"Why is this such a big deal?" Baya shifted uncomfortably. "I've always had bad dreams. Why should this one be any different?"

"There is trouble in Merth or there will be soon. I just hope we're not too late," Kuna said.

"And you know this because of some vague dream?"

"Baya, if you are the one who is to find and destroy the Ominot, then your dreams are warnings, of sorts. They reveal things that are actually happening or that are going to happen."

"So someone I don't even know is in pain. There are lots of people who are sick and even dying. What does that have to do with us?"

"The stronger the dream the more relevant."

"But we don't have a plan."

"The plan is to get back into the city and find Var."

"But how?"

"I'm not going to waste time arguing with you. If you don't want to return to the city then ... stay here." Kuna headed for the door.

Baya exchanged a concerned look with Vicaroy. She didn't want to endanger him or let him out of her sight. And she couldn't do both at the same time. Either he would be in danger if he came along or he wouldn't have her protection if he stayed behind. There was no good answer.

"We have to go back," Vicaroy said.

Baya sighed and slowly got to her feet. She crammed her few belongings into her pack.

In no time they were hurrying to catch up with Kuna.

Kuna pushed them hard, forcing them to walk late into the night.

Each morning Baya would wake to the same hollowing dream. This convinced Baya that her dreams must be more than her overactive mind making stuff up. Someone was indeed in serious pain or was about to be. This increased her sense of urgency and her sense of dread. She didn't worry the others with the nightmares but they seemed to understand that something was wrong. They made it back to the gates of Merth by the morning of the fourth day.

* * *

THE SUNS SHONE bright in the purple sky with only wisps of orange clouds in the east. Tired and weary, Baya studied the high city walls.

"Now what?" Baya asked. "As you've told us many times, Kuna, the gates are most likely permanently closed while Nacora searches the city for us. Who knows when they'll open again?"

Kuna didn't acknowledge Baya. She was busy pulling stuff out of her pack, eventually coming up with a rope.

"How is that going to help?"

"I need a rock." Kuna continued to ignore Baya as she scoured the ground, only to pick up a fist-sized stone. Holding the end of the rope and the rock in one hand she closed her eyes. Moving her free hand over the rope and the stone, she sealed the rock to the end of the rope with her powers. A golden metallic substance held them together.

Kuna swung the rope around to test the weighted end. Her sights were set on the top of the wall.

The rope was nowhere close to being long enough to reach the top but Baya figured Kuna would not pay any attention to her if she pointed that out.

"Mek, you throw the rope as high as you can. Ena, when the rope reaches the top, use your powers to tie it to an outcropping on the parapet."

Ena nodded. "That's a long way away to project my powers but I'll try."

Mek swung the heavy end of the rope, gaining momentum. Kuna

readied herself by holding out her arms. Mek released the rope, sending it up the wall.

Kuna sent out more of the sparkling golden substance. It clung to the rope, adding to its length as needed.

The rope started to lose momentum. "Baya! Guide the rock to the top of the wall."

Baya raised her hands and narrowed her eyes on the rock at the end of the rope. It picked up speed making its way to the top of the wall.

Ena took a deep breath and closed her eyes. The rock on the end of the rope wound its way around the stone outcropping, neatly securing itself to a parapet. Now, thanks to Kuna, the rope hung all the way to the ground.

Baya's heart fell. She'd hoped this wouldn't work. This also meant that Tara couldn't come with them. Her heart jumped into rapid motion, restricting her chest. "What about Tara?"

"She's safer outside the city. It's time you let go of your pet." Kuna tugged on the rope, testing its strength.

Unfortunately, it held. Baya couldn't breathe. She'd already lost Doba and now she had to leave Tara behind. She went to her knees. Vicaroy was instantly on her right and Tara nudged her from the left.

"Baya, what's wrong?" Vicaroy asked.

You leave me? Tara's voice echoed inside Baya's head.

"No. I can't. This is crazy. Nothing good awaits us in Merth." Baya's chest was so tight she thought it might cave in on itself, crushing her. They needed a plan to get to Var, and Vicaroy needed to know how to fight better. "This is a big mistake," Baya choked. She could hardly take in enough air to breathe, let alone talk.

Someone was in trouble and she needed to save her or him, Baya believed this much about her nightly dreams. She could hopefully take care of herself but how could she sacrifice Vicaroy? She forced herself to suck in air. She got to her feet and took Vicaroy's hands. "You stay here with Tara. She will keep you safe from predators until we return. You know how to live off the land. You'll be safe if you stay here."

"Actually that's a great idea," Kuna spoke quickly. "We have very little time until a sentry sees us. Both boys stay here with the animal."

Tara growled at Kuna.

"The three of us can climb the wall and stay unseen. You two will slow us down. Ena you first. If you have trouble I will help you climb."

"I'm not staying out here." Mek glared at Kuna. "You needed me to throw your rope, right? Don't treat me like I'm useless."

"We have no time. This is not debatable. We'll come for you as soon as we can." Kuna helped Ena onto the wall, showing her how to wrap the rope around her foot to anchor herself while using her arms to pull herself up.

"There's no way I'm —" Mek said.

"We'll wait for you," Vicaroy interrupted. He gave Mek a stern glare.

"Thank you," Baya breathed. She wrapped her arms around Vicaroy. She could return to Merth now that she knew Vicaroy and Tara would be safe and they would have each other. Baya kissed him hard.

"Hey, this isn't goodbye. I'll see you soon." Vicaroy forced a smile.

The restriction in Baya's chest let up. Thank the Goddess he was being so levelheaded about this. She gave Tara a hug and ruffled her feathers. "I won't be gone long. You take care of the men, okay?"

Tara licked her face.

Baya gave Mek a hug. "Stay safe and take care of each other."

Mek wore a deep scowl. "You're the ones heading into danger."

Ena's arms already shook and she was barely a quarter of the way up the wall.

Baya took hold of the rope.

"Head back into the trees before a guard spots you," Kuna barked.

Mek's curses could be heard as Vicaroy led him into the forest.

Baya's light frame made it easier than she thought to climb the wall — at first. About halfway up Kuna had to start pushing Ena upward. This slowed their ascent as Kuna had to shove on Ena's rear with one hand and still move herself up the rope with the other.

"It's a good thing you're so strong, Kuna." Baya's arms had started to protest and she only had to pull one person up the rope.

"You've really got to work on your upper-body strength, Ena." Kuna gave her rump a hearty shove.

"Sorry," Ena said through gritted teeth. "I'm not a warrior like you. I told you, I'm more of a —" she let out a strained grunt. "Lover." She could hardly get her words out.

The sound of approaching footsteps caused Baya to still and her blood went cold.

"Make yourself invisible," Kuna whispered.

Baya focused on making the rope invisible as well. This only partially worked. But thankfully the guard on the wall was focused on the forest that lay beyond the city. He didn't notice the rope tied around the stone outcropping.

"Hurry," Kuna demanded.

But climbing while invisible took a lot of energy and Baya's arms screamed at her.

When the guard was out of sight, Baya exhaled and allowed herself to be seen.

"Faster." Kuna's footing on the rope slipped. She and Ena slipped.

Baya braced herself and suppressed a scream as they sped toward her, stopping only inches from the top of Baya's head. They hung there for a moment catching their breath.

"If only we could fly," Kuna mumbled.

"Well, we're not Arges, so slow down," Ena said. "It's more important that we make it to the top alive even if it takes us longer."

"Easy for you to say." Kuna gave her friend's butt another shove.

The three women were covered in sweat by the time they reached the top. Kuna untied the rope and let it fall to the ground before the women took off at a full run along the top of the city wall.

* * *

Once under cover of the trees, Mek smacked Vicaroy on the arm. "Why did you give into them so easily? We could have convinced them to let us come."

Vicaroy wanted to rub his arm where Mek hit it but refrained. He didn't want to give Mek the satisfaction of knowing that it hurt. "We would have already been caught … all of us. I don't want the women to be captured." Vicaroy gave him a devious smile. "Besides, I have my own plan."

Mek's eyes widened. "So you're not going to sit here and wait for them?"

"Nope."

CHAPTER 34

"That was your plan all along, wasn't it — to leave the boys behind?" Baya asked, as they ran along the top of the city wall.

"I'd hoped there was a way to not put them in danger," Kuna said. "You made it easier for me when you suggested it."

Baya clenched her jaw. She wanted to like Kuna but she could be so … frustrating. "Do you have any other *plans* that we should know about?"

"Get into the palace, find Var and the Ox."

"That's not a plan. That's wishful thinking."

"Don't forget we have to save that person from your dreams," Ena added.

Baya felt as if they were moving forward like a battering ram. The problem was that certain death awaited them once the battering ram broke through the gates. They needed a real plan. "The last time you tried to find Var in her quarters you failed because it was protected with a strong spell. What makes you think we can get to her this time?"

"Because this time, I have you."

A sentry came into view on the wall in front of the three women and they disappeared.

"This way," Kuna whispered from somewhere to Baya's right. That was when Baya noticed the stairs leading down off the wall. She took them two by two until she tripped over something and ended up in a pile at the bottom of the nearest landing.

Ena stared down at Baya and Kuna. "Are you two alright?"

"Ouch." Baya cupped her elbow. It must have been Kuna she'd tripped over.

"Who's there?" A man's voice came from the top of the stairway.

Kuna jumped to her feet. "Take my hands and don't let go." She grasped her companions by their hands and disappeared. "Run."

Once on the street below the wall, Kuna slowed causing an invisible tug on Baya's arm.

"I don't think I can make it all the way to the palace like this," Ena said. "I'm not used to scaling walls and using my powers this much."

"You're the least sought after out of all of us," Kuna said. "So keep your hood over your head and your eyes on the ground. Baya and I will follow you."

Ena exhaled with relief as she materialized. Her hood cast a shadow over her face — that would have to do. Baya and Kuna continued to hold onto each other, as Ena quickly led them through back streets. The streets were eerily empty.

They knew something was wrong when they came to the market. It too was largely devoid of people. Baya's stomach sank. "Where's everyone?"

No one answered but Ena looked worried.

"We have to hurry." Kuna's voice came out of nowhere.

Baya's question was answered as they came to the square in front of the palace. It was packed with onlookers.

Only slight murmurs rippled through the hushed crowd. Standing on an elevated stage near the main palace gates stood Nacora, Osa and a number of armed guards. Var was not with them. The stage looked as if it had been quickly thrown together for this occasion. Behind it rose the numerous spires of the white castle. Its many windows made it look like it was glowing as it reflected the suns' rays.

"Make your way to the front of the crowd," Kuna whispered.

Baya was forced to let go of Kuna's hand as they carefully maneuvered around people. The people closest to Nacora were tightly packed together. Baya took Ena's waist and stayed as close to her as possible as they slowly made their way through the crowd.

A couple of times people brushed against Baya. Thankfully they didn't seem to take much notice.

"This is your last chance," Nacora's voice boomed over the crowd. "I have been very patient and very merciful. Yet, since you will not hand over my son and the outlaws who have taken him, you leave me no choice." She wore her hair in the familiar tight ringlets that hung down to her shoulders. The blackness of her shiny curls caught the light, making it appear as though she had purple streaks in her hair. Her headpiece was incredibly extravagant and one Baya had never seen before. It sat tall atop her head and precious stones shone like a light above her head. Strands of pearls hung from the crown, adding lovely white accents to her dark hair.

Nacora waved her arm through the air and guards led a string of people onto the elevated platform. There were at least a dozen people with burlap sacks over their heads. Their hands were tied behind their backs. One long rope was secured around each of their necks, leaving the prisoners bound to one another.

"Since merely starving these criminals is not enough to motivate you to help me find my beloved son and the wretched people who took him from me, I'm forced to take extreme measures. Believe me, I wish it had not come to this but starting today each one of these men ..." Nacora waved her gloved hand through the air and her guards ripped the bags off the prisoners' heads.

Ena's face paled and a scream escaped her lips. She fell to her knees. Baya quickly glanced around. The gasps from the masses had been just enough to drown out Ena's outcry. Her body jerked with each sob. Baya put her arms around Ena and leaned over her, causing her to disappear as well. "Shhh. What's wrong?"

"They're my … lovers … or were at one time," Ena choked.

"But how did Nacora find …" The mural of the people painted on Ena's wall popped into Baya's head. Nacora had found out who Ena was and had then been able to discover where she lived. Then she rounded up all the men she could find who were in that painting. She cursed to herself. Unbelievable!

"Well, let us find out if this will be enough motivation for you to return my son to me." Nacora raised both arms. Her hands were clad in silky white gloves. A guard rolled a wooden table onto the platform. "This table is designed to pull a person in two. However, this doesn't happen quickly. Oh no, strong healthy men like these will be able to survive for days as each muscle, each ligament, is slowly torn apart."

Gasps and even some outcries came from the captivated audience. Baya felt like throwing up, and she worried Ena might faint.

A guard untied the unlucky man at the head of the line of prisoners. His eyes were wide with fear as two guards took his arms. They dragged him toward the table. The man dug his heels in and tried to pull himself out of their grip. "No!" he cried.

A third soldier rammed the end of his fighting staff into the prisoner's gut. The man doubled over and the soldiers were more easily able to wrestle him onto the table. His arms were tied above his head at one end of the table and his feet were bound to the other end.

This can't be happening, Baya thought. An icy sensation formed in her chest and slowly spread to other parts of her body. What kind of person could torture an innocent man like that?

"Please, Madam Unawi." A woman close to the stage yelled. "We don't know where your son is. Every inch of this city has been searched."

"He must have left Merth," another woman yelled.

Baya's heart warmed. She felt immense gratitude for these brave women who dared to speak up.

"My son could not get past the city walls. No one can." Nacora covered her heart with her hand. "It pains me to have to do this. But I think of what my poor son must be going through. He must be trapped in one of your cellars, in an attic. Scared, alone. Who knows what tortures have been unleashed upon him?" Nacora wiped her eye as if brushing away a tear. "I ask you, mother to mother, what lengths would you go to in order to save your child?"

But Baya could see that her eyes were dry. She was not a very good actress. Baya exhaled hard through her nose as the anger rose.

"At least one of you knows where he is and all you have to do is step forward … now, before it's too late for this poor man." Nacora scanned the crowd with narrowed eyes.

Baya shivered. Pure determined evil radiated from the Unawi. "Oh my Goddess, she's truly going to hurt that man."

"Baya, do something!" Ena demanded.

Nacora issued another hand gesture and a guard turned a crank at the end of the torture table. At first there was nothing as the ropes slowly tightened, stretching the men's body. He jerked his head back and forth in protest. When the man's first painful cry rang out, Baya materialized.

"Stop!" She didn't know she could yell that loud.

All eyes turned to her, including Nacora's. She held up her fist and the guard stopped turning the crank.

"I know where your son —"

"Here, Mother. I'm here," a familiar voice boomed. "Now you can stop this madness."

Baya's mouth hung open. Vicaroy? How? Why?

CHAPTER 35

"Madam Unawi." Mek bowed deep. "I convinced your son to return to you." He wore a self-satisfied smirk.

The crowd moved aside for them as they made their way to the makeshift stage in front of the royal palace gates.

Baya's hands balled into fists. She had a strong urge to punch Mek. If only she were close enough.

"Baya." An invisible hand tugged on her arm. "Disappear," Ena whispered.

But she wasn't going to leave Vicaroy behind — nope. If he went down, so did she. She marched forward.

Nacora's cold gaze moved from her son to Baya and the Unawi's hand slowly raised.

"Vicaroy. What are you — ?" but Baya's words were cut off by a pink light that shot from Nacora's palm. The light shined through the ruler's glove and instantly had Baya surrounded. The glow made it impossible for her to move and the world around her turned entirely pink. Muffled murmurs of awe came from the onlookers.

Baya's body was no longer under her control. Even though Baya wasn't telling her legs to move, she made her way toward the wooden stand.

"That's right, Baya. Come here," Nacora said.

If Baya had been able to, she would have run to Vicaroy and turned him invisible as they made their escape. But she wasn't going anywhere unless Nacora said so.

Osa wrapped her arms around Vicaroy, who didn't return the gesture. "I was so worried about you, My Love."

Baya's teeth clenched. "All you're going to do is imprison him and force him to —" Her mouth slammed shut and she could no longer open it.

"Tie the criminal up and lock her away."

"No!" Vicaroy yelled.

Nacora had been focused on Baya and turned her attention to her son as if she just remembered he was there. "My Darling Boy." Her smile was unconvincing. "I'm so relieved you are home safe." Under her breath she said. "Guards, escort him to his room."

Osa stood tall and proud. When she reached for Vicaroy's arm he jerked away. It looked like he might protest but two guards moved to stand beside him. One of them leaned in to whisper something in Vicaroy's ear. Baya was sure it was a threat of some sort.

Vicaroy lowered his head as Osa took his arm and steered him toward the palace entrance.

Baya tried to yell for him but her mouth remained sealed. As she neared Nacora, Baya was lifted into the air by the pink light. She would have thrown her arms out to help her balance but she was unable to move. It was like being under water, yet she was as dry as could be. The complete lack of control over her own body caused a cold sweat to run down her spine.

Mutterings from the crowd could be heard as they watched Baya move through the air.

When she landed on the stage, two female guards tied her arms behind her back. Nacora released Baya from the pink light causing her legs to buckle momentarily as they came back under her control.

The guards gruffly led Baya into the Palace. Vicaroy and Osa were already out of sight. Her smoke wouldn't work on the women and disappearing wouldn't help as she doubted they would release their iron grips on her arms, whether they could see her or not. She searched her brain for some way out but no brilliant ideas came.

The guards led Baya into the palace. She found herself being forced to walk through narrow hallways. The dark stone walls that surrounded her resembled Unawi Shema's palace. The drabness didn't cause her to miss her former home. Rather, she longed to be outside in the wide open, in a garden that Vicaroy manicured to perfection.

Instead of focusing on where they were taking her and what they were going to do to her, Baya's thoughts were dominated by the pink light that had radiated from Nacora's hand. She'd been able to fully capture Baya with it. Baya had never heard of such powers. Judging by the gasps from the audience, neither had they. One thing was for sure: Nacora possessed some serious abilities.

After being marched down several sets of stairs it became apparent that they were headed deep under the palace. The air grew thick and closed in on Baya — threatening to crush her lungs. She gasped as the panic consumed her. "What ..." she struggled to suck in enough air to speak. "What are you going to do to me?"

Her escorts answered with silence. They didn't even look at her.

"Are you going to torture me ... like that man on the stretcher?"

An obsidian stone wall abruptly appeared in front of them.

"The palace prison is torture enough." The guard's voice was emotionless.

The other guard pulled out a parchment and hid the contents from Baya. "I can never remember the incantation."

"What incantation?" Baya breathed.

The woman didn't answer. She placed a hand on the stone wall. Her lips moved ever so slightly as she read silently from the parchment. The outline of a doorway appeared in the wall and the stone slid back. When there was just enough space for a person to fit through, the guard tried to force Baya into the gap in the stone.

Baya dug her heels in and struggled against the woman's hold. She would have thrown a punch but her hands were still tied behind her back. The guard who opened the prison door grabbed Baya by the arm and together the two women were able to force her through the door.

This caused Baya to fall to the ground. She managed to turn her body just in time to use her shoulder as padding instead of falling flat on her face. Pain exploded through her jarred shoulder. The door slid shut. She was barely able to jerk her feet out of the way before it slammed closed, almost crushing her legs.

Baya tried to get to her feet but a scream escaped from her as pain tore through her body. She instantly curled into the fetal position. The burning pain started in her stomach and spread quickly outward to her chest, arms and head. It shot down her legs. The internal fire was so intense that she opened her mouth to scream again but no sound was allowed to come out.

Against her will, her body straightened in one quick jolting motion. The contents of her stomach came up. She tried to spit the remaining bile out so she wouldn't choke on it.

She curled in on herself again as an agonizing sound involuntarily came from her mouth, it wasn't exactly a scream. She was in far too much pain to waste energy yelling. It felt like her body was being ripped apart from the inside. She didn't think it could get any worse but it did. Visions of every particle inside her body bursting into flames consumed her thoughts. Every muscle was so tight she thought they might tear away from her bones. When there was no more withstanding the explosion within, mercifully her world went dark.

CHAPTER 36

Baya woke slowly from a nothingness. All that existed was a black void, floating, endlessly. There was no ground, no sky, no world, not even a body, only an abyss. Her eyelashes fluttered. There was also no pain. For a moment she was comforted by this. Baya tried to sit up but dizziness consumed her. She lay back down and tried to survey her surroundings. All she saw was a blur of pink, pink walls, pink ceiling.

Her stomach felt like it was collapsing in on itself. She moaned. It wasn't exactly hunger. The hollow feeling was almost worse than the pain. A part of her was missing or maybe it was all of her that had been violently ripped away. She was too weak to move.

"You get used to it," a soft voice came from beside Baya.

Baya blinked in an attempt to force her eyes to focus. A fuzzy figure slowly came into view — an old woman in grey rags. She sat on the floor with her bony legs crossed.

It vaguely registered with Baya that she was lying on a thin mat directly on the hard, pink floor. She was in a small room with a rough-cut opening for a doorway … no door. Beyond that was just more pink stone.

"Get used to what?" Baya murmured. Her voice was hoarse as if she'd been yelling all night. Maybe she had been.

"The empty feeling. Nothing will fill the void but you do get used to it." The old woman stared into the distance, lost in thought. "This must be how men feel all the time, you know, powerless. But it's normal for them ... I suppose."

Empty. That was exactly how Baya felt. "What happened to me?"

The old woman rapped a knuckle on the pink wall. "You see this? It's a very powerful crystal and we're surrounded by it. This prison has the ability to remove every drop of power out of a woman's body. It does this painfully, one particle at a time until ... there's nothing left."

"My powers ..." Baya choked.

"Gone," the old woman said.

"For how long?"

"Forever."

Baya squeezed her eyelids together and tears ran down her cheeks. Her worst fear had come true. Powerlessness. She was utterly helpless to save the people she cared about. Vicaroy...

"You're the first new prisoner we've had in many years. Tell me, what news do you have of the outside?"

Baya rolled away from the old woman. The last thing she wanted was to recount how the Unawi had turned into an evil bitch who wielded some wicked powers. Baya stared at the pink wall. She slowly reached out to touch it. Perhaps it would steady the spinning motion of the room. It didn't.

The rock was cool and hard. It wasn't a polished wall. It was rough cut as if the prison had been mined into a natural bed of these power-sucking stones. Men would have had to form these walls as women couldn't come near them.

Baya was really starting to hate the color pink. Pink. Powers. She was reminded of the flash of pink light coming from Nacora's palm. The Ox was pink and powerful like these crystals. "That can't be a coincidence," Baya whispered.

"What's not a coincidence, Dearie?" the old woman said.

Baya hadn't meant to say that out loud. She focused on the memory of Nacora capturing her, taking control of her body. The light that had come from her palm spun outward in a circular motion, just like the picture of the pink and orange swirls in the center of the Ox. "Var doesn't have it. Nacora does and she's using its power." Baya sat up and the room circled around her even more wildly. She wavered but managed to brace herself with her arms.

"Easy there. Adjusting to losing our powers takes time."

"I don't want to adjust. I have to get out of here."

The old woman chuckled. "No one's ever walked out of here. We're only carried out …when we die."

Baya took a couple of deep breaths and the spinning room slowed … somewhat. She had to think. "Kuna? Are there any other new prisoners?"

"No, Dearie. Just you."

A spark of hope ignited in Baya's hollow chest. Kuna would find a way to get her out of this place and she would know how to get Baya's powers back. That meant there was nothing to do but wait for Kuna. This thought offered her some relief. She let the dizziness consume her and lowered herself back onto the mat.

* * *

SOMETHING GENTLY SHOOK BAYA AWAKE. "KUNA!" she sat up, certain that Kuna had found a way to save her. But it was only the old prisoner. This time, when she sat up she was less dizzy. The room still swirled around her but she could deal with it. A few deep breaths caused the room to slow almost to a stop.

What remained was … nothing. That dreadful hollow feeling. Many times deeper than the most severe hunger pains — it was the feeling of powerlessness.

"My name is Hatha."

"Baya," she mumbled.

"I propped you up and fed you some broth while you were out … after you first got here but you need to eat."

"I'm not ..." The thought of food made her insides somersault. Yet she couldn't be weak and malnourished when Kuna came for her. There was no telling how long it'd been since she'd eaten. She would need to be able to react quickly when it was time to make her escape. "I'll try."

"That's a good girl."

Hatha helped Baya to her feet and supported her when she swayed, almost falling back down.

"Here." Hatha placed Baya's arm over her shoulder. "Use me as a crutch."

Baya leaned heavily into the old woman who didn't falter under the extra weight. She led Baya out of the small pink chamber.

The hall outside was lined on one side with similar stone archways leading to what Baya assumed were the other prisoners' rooms. There were too many to count and none of them had doors. So there was no real privacy in this place.

Hatha pointed a crooked finger toward the end of the hall. "There is a spring down there where we can drink and wash ourselves. But now we're going to the main room."

Baya followed her gaze to the opposite side of the hall. A shear drop-off was in front of them. Baya warily peered over the edge. The pink stone faded to a dark orange then to a pure black as the ravine was so deep that the torchlight could not reach it. Looking into the depths made Baya's head swirl even more. A rotten musty smell consumed her. Baya placed a hand on her stomach as she dry heaved. She would have doubled over if Hatha hadn't been holding her up. When it passed she managed to ask, "What's down there?"

"Only death, if you were to fall," Hatha said.

Baya took an instinctive step back. "Are all these cells full?"

"No. Most are empty. There are only ten of us, now that you've joined us. We have lost many over the years to the cavern."

"You mean they ..."

"They kill themselves, yes. I suppose not everyone gets used to the emptiness that remains when we lose our powers."

Baya was certain that she would *never* get used to the hollow dread that filled her entire body. Thankfully she had Kuna. She would be out of here in no time. There was that tiny spark of hope again. It would drive her forward.

"Do you think you can stand on your own?"

Baya nodded. She felt much less wobbly.

"Good. Because we have to walk single file across the bridge to get to the main cave where they leave the food. If you can call it food."

Her stomach rumbled at the mention of nourishment. That had to be a good sign. Then her stomach dropped when she saw the skinny piece of stone they had to use to get to the open area on the far side.

Hatha removed Baya's arm from over her shoulders and held onto Baya's waist until she was sure she wouldn't fall.

Baya moved her legs farther apart to brace herself. "We have to cross that?" She pointed to the stone bridge.

"Yes." Hatha started across at once, sure-footed as she'd no doubt crossed the stone passage thousands of times.

Baya progressed with greater care. The smell hit her hard, causing another dizzy spell. She squatted down at once and held onto either side of the bridge. The smell made her dry heave again.

"Use your shirt to cover your mouth."

Baya quickly did this. She took a couple of deep breaths. When her stomach settled and her head cleared — somewhat, she slowly stood and inched along the passageway, which wasn't much wider than her foot. "They really don't care if we live or die, do they?" Her voice was muffled as she spoke through her tunic. She wasn't about to breathe in that putrid scent again.

"No one cares about us, Dearie. In fact, the quicker we die off the less mouths they have to feed."

Once Baya was within a handful of paces to the far side she made a run for it. But she was in no condition to sprint. The room swirled around her and she missed the last step. One foot followed by the other found nothing but air underneath them. She slid down the far wall.

CHAPTER 37

Baya's hands were barely able to grip the top ledge. The putrid air filled her lungs and she gagged. She couldn't help but look down into the bottomless chasm she now dangled over.

Hatha scrambled to her knees. "Take my hands."

Baya was afraid to let go of the ledge. Her hand slid as her fingers gave way.

The old woman grabbed her wrists and tried to pull.

There was no way she would be strong enough, Baya thought.

Hatha grunted as she strained. Surprisingly, Baya slowly began to rise out of the ravine. Her feet were able to scrape the sides, occasionally finding purchase and helping Hatha — somewhat.

When Baya's torso lay on the cave floor Hatha let go. Baya was able to swing her legs up, one at a time, onto solid ground. Baya lay still, panting on the floor. "Thank you," she whispered.

"Next time don't try to run."

Baya chuckled, probably because she was going mad. "Why does it smell so bad?"

"We throw our trash down there and … it's our latrine. Not to mention there are a few rotten corpses down there. Although they are so old there's most likely not much flesh left on the bones."

Baya's entire body shivered. The despair that one must feel in order to throw herself into a latrine — and she'd almost joined them. She shivered again. What little appetite she thought she'd had was gone.

"At least it's well ventilated." Hatha pointed to the ceiling far above the cavern. Many small holes let in thin streams of sunlight, which danced off the stone creating a lovely effect of yellow light and every hue of pink ranging from red to orange. "Otherwise, we'd suffocate from our own stench."

Baya could almost see the putrid air as it rose from the dark depths and was sucked out the tiny holes. Plus she realized for the first time that it was not just torches that lit the cave.

"Those holes also allow us to track the days. Although I don't know why we need to do that."

They walked along the ravine until they rounded a corner that led to a wide-open room Baya vaguely recognized it as the place she'd been thrown into on the day she arrived. A handful of ladies sat on the hard floor. They'd been eating something wrapped in waxed paper.

"Did you save any for us?" Hatha asked.

"Not much but there's some bread and broth left," one of the ladies answered.

All of them had wrinkled skin and grey stringy hair. Their clothes were little more than threadbare rags, like Hatha's. A number of the women had a series of wounds on their forearms. Baya looked closer. They were cuts in varying stages of healing. Some were old white scars, while others were freshly healed pink lines and some were bright blue — new lesions.

"The newcomer's up and about already?" one of them asked.

"That was fast. Most women don't take so well to losin' their powers," another added.

Baya wouldn't say that she was doing well. This was the most terrible thing she'd ever experienced. She couldn't imagine how it could possibly be any worse.

"She's healthy and young," Hatha said.

"Well, she won't be for long — not in this place."

"Did they give us any fruit or veggies?" Hatha asked.

"Of course not," one of the women snapped.

"Anything but bread and broth is rare," Hatha explained to Baya.

"Aye and when they give us fruit or veggies they're mostly spoiled."

One of the ladies tossed Baya some bread wrapped in paper.

"Thank you."

"You need some broth too." Hatha scooped some of the liquid into a bowl and handed it to Baya.

It was a watered-down substance so Baya was surprised when its smell made her mouth water. In no time the bread and soup were gone. She'd hoped food would lessen the emptiness that dominated her senses. It didn't.

"What news do you have from the outside?" one of the prisoners asked.

"Oh yes! Please tell us how you got yourself thrown in here."

The women looked at Baya with wide, expectant eyes.

"I ... don't feel like recounting all that." She hated to disappoint them but the mess she was in and the trouble Merth was in were too raw, too painful.

The women seemed to deflate and the light faded from their eyes. Telling stories was their only entertainment and they were desperate for new ones.

Baya glanced around. What else would she do? Sit in her tiny pink room and stare at the walls while she worried about Tara out in the wild all by herself ...while she focused on her annoyance at Vicaroy for turning himself in and while she tried not to let her anger at Nacora consume her. She was better off talking to the prisoners, amusing them. "Okay. I'll try to ... tell my story."

The women sat up straighter. They literally seemed to light up. Some moved closer to Baya. They sat cross-legged on the floor in front of her, not wanting to miss a word. Baya couldn't help but smile. The prisoners were like young school children, eagerly looking up at their teacher while she read to them.

Baya gazed at the high stone ceiling for a long moment before speaking. "Let me start from the beginning. I'm from Pathins."

This brought about whispers of awe.

She recounted the story of her trials and how they came to leave their home. This seemed so long ago and was therefore less painful to relive. She would have to work her way through the past and eventually discuss the evil Unawi and how she wound up stuck in here. She decided to leave out the part about the Bangee and the Ominot.

Every woman listened intently, hardly taking her eyes off Baya or even blinking as she told story after story. This helped Baya to forget about the bottomless feeling in the pit of her stomach, temporarily anyway.

* * *

DAYS PASSED and Kuna never came. No one came. Only food, which was dropped into the main room from a narrow slot next to the only door into the prison.

Baya didn't lose hope. She knew that Kuna was taking the needed time to devise a careful plan to get her out — any day now. Baya spent the days listening to the ladies' stories. They were more than happy to have fresh ears to talk to. One lady had been a rival lover to the former Unawi, which she claimed was her only "crime." The other women had each murdered someone and Hatha stated that she had been wrongfully accused of the charges against her. She did seem to have the nicest disposition out of the lot so Baya thought that she might be telling the truth.

Thankfully their tales helped the hours to slip by.

"How did this happen?" Baya pointed to the cuts on the arm of one of the prisoners. She had an idea of what the answer was but needed to try and understand why someone would do that to herself.

The woman turned her arm over to hide the wounds. She got to her feet and headed for her room.

"I'm sorry. I just ..."

But the prisoner was gone.

Hatha shook her head. "Some of us need to feel something. Sometimes pain is better than the endless numbness."

Baya lowered her head. Was there no end to the misery in this place?

* * *

BAYA HAD BEEN in prison for four days when she woke to the sound of shrieks piercing the air. These were not just any screams. They were the sounds of someone being ripped apart. The screeching vibrated through Baya, sending pain-filled memories of having her powers stripped from her. Her bones felt like they were on fire. She leapt to her feet and was in the main room in no time.

There on the floor lay Kuna. She wrenched and jerked about awkwardly as shrill screeches came from her mouth. Her back twisted and contorted in unnatural ways. Baya could almost see the power leaving her body in waves and being absorbed into the stone walls.

"No!" Baya's mouth fell open as she watched Kuna's short brown hair disappear. Her body grew in size and her skin turned a ghastly greenish color. More screams came as her bones made terrible popping noises.

"Kuna!" Baya was helpless to do anything but stare in bewilderment. Another set of arms grew from her side and her feet lengthened into an uncanny shape. Finally, a thin membrane formed two wings, attached at the shoulders.

When the screaming stopped Baya knelt beside the heaving mass on the floor. "Kuna?"

Four small black eyes blinked up at her. "Baya." Kuna's voice came from the creature. "I'm sorry." All of her eyes closed and her body went limp.

CHAPTER 38

The prisoners gathered around the strange creature lying on the floor. The large green figure was out cold, its chest barely moved with each breath. The deep sleep was solely to help it escape the pain of having its powers torn out of its body. This was all Baya knew or could understand. Everything else about this creature was a mystery.

"What in the bloody hell?!" one of the prisoners said.

"It's an Arge," Hatha spoke to no one in particular.

"No shit," another prisoner said.

Baya's mouth remained open in disbelief and confusion as she studied the oversized body that lay at her feet. She swore that it once had been Kuna but it no longer resembled her in the least. She decided that she had only imagined seeing Kuna morph into this creature. It couldn't possibly be her. Maybe this place caused hallucinations or she was simply losing her mind. Either scenario was plausible, more so than mutating people.

"How did they manage to capture that thing?" Another prisoner asked.

"I have no bloody idea. Arges are impossible for us to imprison," another woman offered.

"They're many times stronger than us and very powerful," Hatha said.

"Nacora possesses ... something that can easily capture an Arge." Of this much Baya was certain. As long as Nacora had the Ox she was capable of just about anything.

"Well, help me carry her to a room," Hatha said.

"You're actually going to care for that ... thing?" one of the women asked.

"Of course I am. It's a living being." Hatha bent down and took the Arge by its bulky armpits. "Besides it's not as if I have anything else to do." She tried to drag the creature but it didn't move. "I can't do this by myself. Help me," she snapped.

With much straining and cursing they got the large creature to the thin bridge over the cavern before giving up. It was too dangerous to carry, or more accurately drag the Arge over the bridge. At least one, if not all of them would have fallen to their deaths.

Both Baya and Hatha struggled to prop it up. Hatha began to slowly pour broth into its thin slit of a mouth.

"So this is your friend ... the one you've been waiting for?" Hatha asked.

"No," Baya answered quickly — too quickly. "My friend is *not* an Arge. I would know if she were." This came out harsher than she had intended. She forced herself to look away from the notch that was missing from the Arge's pointy ear on top of its head and the subsequent scar that ran diagonally across the ear. Baya never had the chance to ask Kuna how she'd gotten that scar. She inhaled sharply and tried to force this thought out. Thankfully, denial was a very powerful tool — one Baya desperately held onto. "No. Kuna is still out there working up a plan to get me out of here."

Hatha pursed her lips, completely unconvinced. "I'm sure she is, Dearie."

* * *

THE NEW PRISONER recovered from losing its powers even quicker than Baya had. It woke with a moan. Two of its arms wrapped themselves around its stomach. Another agonizing groan came from the creature. It used one of its other arms to lift its torso off the ground. Its fourth arm flew to its head and the creature fell back. Its arms outreached as if to stabilize the spinning room.

Baya remembered the out-of-control feeling all too well.

It hollered in frustration then mumbled something that sounded like, "My powers."

The creature's body twisted in abnormal ways as two of its arms flailed about. Baya shivered.

Hatha's eyes shone with sadness. "It never gets any easier to watch."

Baya frowned. Here she was, repulsed by the thing and Hatha was feeling nothing but sympathy for the suffering creature.

It lay on the ground heaving for a time before its four beady eyes focused on Baya. "I'm sorry." It said as it reached a long arm out to her.

It was undeniably Kuna's voice.

"No." Baya shook her head. "Who in the hell are you?" Baya's heart drummed in her chest.

The creature looked at its green hand as if for the first time. "Oh no," it whispered.

"You are not Kuna, you can't be her!" Baya hurried off over the bridge to her room.

"Baya, wait." It tried to sit up again but wavered. "Let me … explain." It fell back as the dizziness took over.

Baya was already out of sight.

* * *

BAYA LAY on her thin bedroll and stared blankly at the pink stone wall. There was nothing else to do. Kuna, who was apparently an Arge, was the only one who could get her out of here. The guard had gone and gotten herself captured and now … there was no hope.

The small spark of light that Baya had held onto in this Goddess-forsaken prison was extinguished. She was stuck in this place ...

"Forever," she whispered.

There was no way to save Vicaroy from his demented mother and no way to find the Ox and destroy it. Not to mention finding the Ominot. That had always seemed like a far-fetched dream anyway.

Emptiness.

That was all that was left, a void, nothing.

Tears can't even fall in a void.

CHAPTER 39

The following day, or maybe it had been two days, Kuna quietly came into Baya's chamber. She lowered herself to the floor by bending her knees to her chest. She was so big that her oversized feet, which allowed her to walk backward or forward with equal ease, touched Baya. Baya flinched away. She rolled over, turning her back on Kuna.

"Hatha, says you aren't eating."

Baya gave an involuntary shrug. She had no intention of eating, ever again. In fact, she'd considered crawling over to the cavern and letting herself fall in. She decided that starving would be the less painful way to go, even if it were not as quick.

"You have to eat so you can help me figure out how to get out of here."

"You go ahead. Good luck with that. There is no way out and now you're as powerless as I am."

Kuna was silent for a time. "The ... emptiness is hard to take."

Baya slowly rolled over to gaze at Kuna. It was difficult to not be repulsed by the odd creature. She watched as Kuna rubbed her stomach to try and force the emptiness away. Baya knew, from personal experience, that the rubbing didn't work to fill the abyss where their powers had once been.

"We can't just give up. Vicaroy is to be coupled in two days."

"Where is he?"

"He's kept locked away in his guarded chambers."

Baya closed her eyes tight. "That has to be the shortest engagement in all of history."

"Yes. Nacora and Osa are in a big hurry … for some reason. They can't wait to officially bind him to Osa."

"Just stop talking. You're not helping." It was suddenly clear what Baya would do; in two days she would throw herself into the cavern. If Vicaroy were promised to someone else then she would have the courage to kill herself quickly.

"I think they plan to instate Osa as the new Unawi of Merth."

"No shit. When Nacora dies, Osa will become the next Unawi."

"I mean they plan to make her Unawi in three days."

Baya couldn't help herself. She slowly sat up. "What?"

"There is a grand coronation ceremony planned for the day after the royal coupling. It's rumored that twice the amount of money was spent for the coronation than for the coupling. Nacora has announced that she will be stepping down and Osa will take her place."

Baya shook her head. "That doesn't make sense. Nacora said she was hoping for a daughter to take her place … someday."

"A lot of things don't make sense. I was once very close to Nacora. I knew her well … or at least I thought I did but she has … changed."

Baya had a theory that the Ox changed people. That was the only thing that explained Nacora's sudden about-face. Having that kind of power must corrupt a person. Baya narrowed her eyes. But then why was she giving up her place as ruler? Nothing seemed to be adding up, so Baya moved onto something that might. "She's not the only one who's different. In fact, I thought I knew you."

"I'm still me. Baya, you *do* know me."

"Apparently not."

"Please understand, the deception was needed."

Heat filled Baya's cheeks. Her jaw began to ache from being

clenched. The sight of the four black eyes blinking at her made her queasy. She lay back down, turning away from Kuna. "It doesn't matter. Nothing matters anymore."

After a long silence Kuna decided to continue anyway. "I'm an elite soldier in the Argeon army. Many years ago I was given a special mission of the highest honor."

Baya bolted upright. "You're an infiltrator. This entire time you were using me to get the Ox so you could hand it over to your ... kind."

"No. I'm not an infiltrator. Baya, you must believe me. I don't have a *kind*. I've sworn to protect both humans and Arges. I'm called a Peacemaker. My job, my sole purpose in life, is to ensure that harmony remains between humans and Arges. It's an honor and the greatest of callings to be chosen to become a Peacemaker."

"Then why were you so determined to find the Ox?"

"It's true. My leaders, Jetzu and Hanzu are looking for the Ox. They gave me orders to find it and return it to them."

"I knew it. You *are* a traitor. I never should have trusted you!" Baya bit her bottom lip and closed her eyes tight. "Leave me alone."

"Wait, Baya. Jetzu and Hanzu are fair rulers. They want what we want —"

"Get out!" She glanced over her shoulder.

Kuna nodded solemnly. She slowly rose. Her bald head almost touched the ceiling. When she turned to leave her second set of four eyes, where the back of her head should be, blinked at Baya.

Baya trembled. Arges were so creepy. She continued to stare at the walls without seeing. If she'd had a sharp cutting stone nearby she would have considered running it down her forearm until blood spilled out. "So that's why they cut themselves." Baya muttered absent-mindedly. She finally understood.

A scream rang through the caverns. It was a startled noise, not the sound of someone in extreme agony, like a new prisoner but someone who'd been surprised.

Kuna and Baya raced to cross the bridge but Kuna was faster. Baya couldn't keep up with her as they ran for the main room. Kuna's black eyes stared at her as they slowed to make their way over the bridge. This distracted Baya and she almost lost her footing … again. "Could you close your eyes in the back of your head?"

"In actuality, we don't have a back and why would you want me to close my eyes?"

"It's … weird. They're staring at me and … you're moving in the other direction."

The eyes closed which made Kuna's head look more normal, even though it was large and hairless and green.

"Better?"

"I guess."

"It's handy knowing who is behind you at all times. If you were born with eyes that could see all around, you would like it. I always felt half-blind when I was disguised as a human."

They rounded the corner to find that the other prisoners had gathered for the evening meal. What was odd was that they were dancing and hollering about some giant insect that had been thrown in with their food.

Then Baya realized they were not dancing but trying to stomp on something.

"I think it ran up my leg!" One of the women spun around frantically as if trying to get something off her back. "Get it off me!"

That's when Baya noticed the dark segmented insect, the size of her arm, clinging to the woman.

"Doba!" Baya screamed. She ran forward. "It can't be."

A prisoner raised her arm to swat the creature. Baya rushed forward and grabbed her hand, stopping her. "Don't. He's with me." She scooped the insect into her arms and cradled him protectively. "You came back." She whispered.

And you thought I wouldn't? Doba's familiar voice rang in her head.

This caused tears to form in her eyes and a laugh stuck in her throat. "It was looking like you'd left for good."

Doba blinked at her. *You look like hell.*

"Yeah, well, I've been through hell or rather, I'm stuck in hell."

He examined his surroundings. *You've got yourself into real trouble this time.*

"Now they're feeding us insects," one of the prisoners complained as she examined the empty food wrapper that Doba must've been hiding in.

"First Arges and now septapods. What next? The Unawi herself?"

The heavy stone door to the prison slid open. Doba buried himself in Baya's tunic. Baya adjusted her top to make it look less lumpy, like she wasn't hiding a giant insect.

Two theos entered the prison carrying a stretcher between them. A human figure lay on the stretcher, but it was covered completely with a thin white cloth. They gently lay their burden on the stone floor and deftly lifted the body off the stretcher. They retreated just as they had entered but without the body.

Once the men were gone, Baya noticed that Osa stood in the doorway. Baya moved forward but Var swung herself into view. Her blond hair was tastefully piled on top of her head in silky clouds.

"Go ahead," Var said. "The shield covering this door will tear you to pieces."

An orange see-through film could be seen covering the opening, the only exit.

"By all means, Baya," Osa jeered. "Make a run for it."

"I wasn't going to try to escape. I was going to kill you by wrapping my hands around your neck and squeezing —"

"That's quite enough," Var's eyes were alight with anger.

Osa, on the other hand, appeared amused. She was clearly enjoying herself. This Baya regretted. She shouldn't have given Osa the pleasure of knowing how much she got to her.

"For the sake of the Great Goddess, at least try to comb your hair," Osa mocked.

Baya's hand instinctively moved to her hair. It was ratty and matted.

"Do you think Vicaroy would choose the likes of you over this," Osa gestured to her lovely light blue gown. Her wavy golden hair flickered with different hues in the torchlight.

The insult worked. Baya was an absolute wreck. In that moment she felt completely inferior, not only to Osa but to any woman. If Vicaroy were to see her like this… "Who is that?" Baya gestured to the covered figure. She wanted to change the subject and was hoping to get any information she could.

"We've decided that this is the best place for her," Var said.

"We're tired of feeding her and washing her," Osa added. "There's no way she will be able to get out of here to make trouble for us."

"We've already ruined her name with her people. No one will miss her now."

Baya blinked at them. "What are you talking about?"

"That is enough. We will ask the questions," Var said. "Where is Kuna?"

Baya glanced around. Her eyes briefly flickered over the Arge, who hid against a wall out of sight. Baya continued to scan the room as if she hadn't seen anything. "Who knows. She probably already fell to her death in the cavern."

"That is too bad," Var said. "Then it was very generous of us to bring you this new companion."

Var glanced to Osa who nodded. She apparently had gotten her fill of provoking Baya and the door slammed shut in the blink of an eye.

Baya ran forward and slammed her fists into the stone where Osa's face would have been. "Doba," she whispered, "my dear friend, you have to get us out of here."

Why do you think I'm here, just to say, "Hi?"

"That's my Doba," Baya breathed. The bug with the attitude. "I've missed you little buddy."

"Holy shit! It *is* the Unawi."

Baya turned to see who had said that. The prisoners had gathered around the figure on the floor. Kuna had lifted the sheet off its head.

Baya moved to get a better look.

It was Nacora.

CHAPTER 40

The lock to Vicaroy's door turned. In the normal quiet of his solitary chambers it sounded loud and his entire body tensed. His arms shook with the effort it took to hold his body weight. It wasn't time for his morning or afternoon meals so he knew at once that he had a visitor. He wouldn't let whomever it was know how the sound of the door opening affected him … unless, of course, it was Baya. But that was impossible. She would not be coming for him this time. Osa had told him about the horrors of the palace prison where Baya now languished. The thought of her trapped and powerless — just like him — caused a fire to course through his body. He could feel the flames in his bones.

No. He would hide his emotions deep inside and he hoped they would never come out. Thank the Goddess, that he'd found a way to focus his rage, not to mention, pass the endless days. He'd invented a series of contraptions to help him practice fighting and discovered ways to keep his body strong since he was unable to do any real work.

He sewed a sheet into a column and stuffed it with blankets and pillows. He fashioned one end to the ceiling and the other to the floor. He would throw blow after blow until the sheet ripped. His mother must've gotten tired of replacing it every day because she "so graciously" brought him a stout leather sack in the shape of a column about the size of a human.

It was filled with something firm, possibly sand. It made the best punching surface, almost like hitting a real person. Which was perfect. He could pretend that it was Mek or one of his male guards — someone strong — a worthy adversary. Although he would never admit it to anyone, he sometimes envisioned that the sack was his mother. There was a twinge of guilt when he thought about hitting his own mother but at this point he couldn't help himself.

After all, Nacora had threatened Baya's life. The day he turned himself in, she'd said that if he tried to get away, she would have Baya killed at once.

Vicaroy could punch the bag for hours on end. It seemed there was an endless supply of anger to fuel him. He lifted heavy objects, anything he had, nightstands, dressers, until his muscles protested and he could not stand to lift them one more time. Physically exerting himself was the only thing that made him feel good. Well, maybe not good but at least it made him feel alive and ... less powerless.

Pushing his body to its limits was also the only way he could sleep at night. He would all but pass out from exhaustion. Otherwise, he would lay there staring at the ceiling until the morning light, thinking of ways to get out, to help Baya. But that was pointless. If she couldn't save herself then he was lost as well.

Since he'd escaped his lavish prison before, Nacora had apparently decided to seal his chambers with her powers. She even covered his windows with an invisible shield so he couldn't fall to his death. There had been moments when he'd considered jumping through a window but his mother would not even allow him that freedom.

No other ideas for his escape had come to him.

At this particular moment, he'd been standing on his hands. His legs gently rested on the wall behind him, while he lowered his head to the floor and then straighten his arms. Up and down, again and again until his shoulders could take no more and sweat dripped from him.

When the door opened his feet hit the floor and he quickly righted himself. He reached for his tunic.

"Oh, please. Don't get dressed on my account." Osa's voice was full of cheer.

His eyes narrowed. "I'd be more comfortable if I were presentable. Surely you'll allow me that."

Her eyes took in every defined muscle.

Vicaroy's jaw was knotted as he swiftly pulled his tunic over his head.

She waved her hand dismissively as if to say, suit yourself. "I have good news. Your mother says that I can take you for walks in the garden, chaperoned, of course."

Vicaroy studied the lush land outside his window — far below — out of reach. His first thought was that perhaps he could escape on one such walk. He quickly dismissed the idea. He would be heavily guarded, or "chaperoned" as Osa misleadingly called it. Plus, he was no match for her powers.

No. Baya was his garden. He would not walk there with another. "I'll pass, although it's a nice gesture." His distain oozed from every word.

"We need to get to know each other. I mean, I'm trying to understand you."

A derisive chuckle escaped from Vicaroy before he could stop it. She had no idea how to gain someone's trust. He bit down hard to keep his thoughts to himself. He wanted to yell, "You can't get to know someone if you're holding them prisoner."

"Well, I suppose your mother is right. You will learn to love me … even if it is after we are coupled."

Vicaroy had other plans. As soon as they let him out of this room, he'd run and if he couldn't save Baya then he'd die trying. Osa was fooling no one if she claimed to love him. One of the many things Baya had taught him was how to treat someone you care about and imprisoning them was not on the list. In fact, forcing someone to do *anything* could not be called love.

Osa moved to stand by him at the large window. "You know everything will go back to normal after we're coupled."

"Everything, huh?" How stupid did she think he was? "So I'll have Baya back and I'll be in school and allowed to work in my shop and the garden."

At the mention of Baya's name, Osa's open expression darkened. Vicaroy thought it was anger that flashed through her large blue eyes. He smiled to himself. At least he knew how to get to her.

"Your mother also assures me that you will forget about her some —"

"You know, there's something that doesn't make sense. Actually, there are many things that don't add up lately. But why is it that Mother no longer cares about my 'oh-so-important' education? Has she gone mad or —" With each word it was getting harder for him to hold back. Half of his brain was telling him to stop before he said something to push her too far. Yet, the other half no longer gave a shit.

"I'm sure your mother will want you to finish your education after we're promised to each other … forever," Osa interrupted. Her voice was wistful.

"And that's another thing, Mother used to visit me daily but now I haven't seen her since she locked me up … for the second time. I keep asking to see her, yet she never comes. Why is that?"

"She's very busy. There's a lot of planning that must be done on top of her normal duties as ruler. I'm sure she will visit as soon as she has time but until then I'd be glad to deliver a message."

Her overly nice tone made Vicaroy want to hurl something at her head. She seemed to be trying hard to say the right things. It was clearly a pretense — all lies. "So she has time to talk to you but not her own son?" Vicaroy crossed his arms and glared down at her.

She tried to smile but it was unconvincing. "I was hoping you'd be happy about going for walks with me. But I see you need more time." She stepped toward him closing the distance between them and gently placed her hand on his forearm. "How did you get these scars?" She brushed her fingers over the sensitive white skin that stood out from his normal obsidian tone.

He instantly jerked away and stepped back.

When he didn't answer, Osa continued, "I wish your mother would allow you more freedoms. I really do. Please know that I'm doing everything in my power to convince her of this."

More lies, Vicaroy thought. Did she really think he was that dense? "Is that all? Because I'm really busy." He turned his back on her and occupied himself by moving a dresser, just for something to do besides talk to her.

Osa issued a loud sigh before leaving the room. "Someday I will win your heart."

This was almost a whisper and Vicaroy wished he hadn't heard it.

CHAPTER 41

"What the ...? How in the ...?" Nothing but curses consumed Baya's mind.

Kuna's black eyes were wide and round when they met Baya's gaze. Kuna shrugged her massive shoulders. She was at a complete loss as well.

Baya studied Nacora's face. It was relaxed, not a care in the world, as the deep peaceful sleep consumed her. Nothing about her resembled the icy malice that Baya had last seen on that face. All Baya saw now was the likeness to Vicaroy — the lovely dark skin, the almond-shaped eyes. Asleep like this she looked kind and caring.

Baya shook her head.

"Well there hasn't been a dull moment since you came here, Baya," Hatha said. "You've added a lot of excitement to our boring existence. You gonna help me take care of her?"

"Absolutely not! That is the woman who threw me in here. She's the one who's forcing her son, whom I love, to couple with another. She can go to hell."

"She is in hell now and she looks harmless."

"Besides I have to plan our escape and fast. We only have two days." She rubbed her finger under Doba's chin. He had secured himself to her as he always did with his head on her shoulder.

Kuna bent down and moved a strand of curly black hair out of Nacora's face. "I'll help you take care of her, Hatha."

"Kuna! Leave her. She imprisoned us and we need to get out of here … now. We only have two days until the coupling ceremony."

"She didn't imprison me. Var did, when I tried to break into her chambers."

Baya stood up straighter. "Var imprisoned you?" Her stomach knotted in anger. "You tried to get to Var without coming for me first? You should have gotten me out of here then I could have helped you and we would have succeeded and we wouldn't be stuck in here…" She stepped forward and banged her fists on Kuna's chest.

Kuna stood perfectly still taking the blows that didn't seem to hurt in the least.

Baya growled in frustration and took a step away — heaving. A silence fell as she waited for a response … anything.

Kuna scooped Nacora up with ease. "I need to make sure Nacora is fine then I'll help you plan our escape."

"I swear to the Great Goddess I want to strangle you, Kuna." Baya bared her teeth and gave her a vulgar gesture as the Arge walked away cradling Nacora in two of her arms.

"I can see you, you know?"

"That's the point," Baya spat.

The other prisoners had been watching with wide eyes.

"This is better than the theater," Hatha said.

Baya paced in the main room. "Calm down. You won't get anywhere this angry," she thought out loud. She was more furious at Kuna than Osa. Osa had never been a friend, never pretended to care about Baya but Kuna …. A knot formed in Baya's throat. She had trusted Kuna. She even would have called her a friend at one time. Breathe. In and out. In and out.

"Okay. Doba got in here easy enough. We have to get him back out — that shouldn't be too hard. Then he can find the keys and open the door. Hah! Easy. I don't even need Kuna."

"There's just one problem, missy — this place ain't got no keys," one of the prisoners said.

"Two problems. It won't be easy to get that insect out of here." another offered.

Actually three problems. If there were keys I couldn't get the door open by myself anyway. Doba added.

"Shit." Baya hadn't been paying any attention to the other prisoners but, of course, they were all still milling around, watching the "show." Some of them were eating as if nothing had happened. Yet, all eyes were on Baya.

"Okay. Think," Baya demanded. "When they put me in here the guards had to use a secret incantation to open the door." One of the women had it written on a piece of parchment. "That's it, Doba! You just have to find the incantation."

"And how do you think that bug is going to do that? The palace is huge."

"If you're not going to offer solutions then shut up." Baya exhaled hard then she lit up. "I got it. Kuna, the former head of the guard, she will know the incantation." Baya ran for the bridge.

She found Kuna and Hatha in a previously unoccupied room. Kuna held the sleeping Nacora while Hatha spooned broth into her mouth.

"What's the incantation that opens the prison door?"

Kuna's many eyes blinked at her. "If I knew that I would have freed you right away."

Baya bit her lip. She felt the hopelessness knocking at the door, waiting to consume her. "There must be a way. Can you tell Doba how to find it?"

Kuna shook her head. "There is only one guard in charge of the incantation. She has it memorized so getting it from her will be difficult. Again, this is why freeing you wasn't easy."

"That's not true. The guard who threw me in here had the incantation written on a piece of paper. She said something about always forgetting it so she had to write it down."

Kuna looked thoughtful. "I don't recall that but then again I was frantic when they put me in here. That would be grounds for a dishonorable discharge if she were caught with the secret incantation on a piece of paper."

"Will you stop thinking like a guard? And start thinking like a criminal who's trying to break out." Baya took another deep breath. It was the only way to keep the panic away. "We need to get Doba out of here and then he can find the paper and bring it to us."

"It won't do us any good. We don't have powers — remember? — and the door can only be opened from outside."

Baya yelled in frustration. "Is there no end to the obstacles?"

"You see why I couldn't just break you out of here?"

Baya pressed her lips together. Her anger toward Kuna wavered somewhat ... now that she knew how hard it would have been to rescue her. Oddly enough, she didn't want the anger to fade. It sharpened her mind and motivated her to push forward. She needed it to help her remain focused and not fall back into the deadness.

I can get the paper from the guard but then what? Doba said.

"Doba thinks he can get the incantation. So how will he open the door?"

"He can't. Only a female with powers can do that ... from the outside." Kuna and Baya looked at each other with wide eyes.

"Ena," they said at the same time.

Baya frowned. "But Doba doesn't know the guard or Ena. How will he find them?"

I can find them, Doba said.

"How?"

Remember what I told you about how animals can read minds. We don't have words, at first, not many anyway. We see the image of your thoughts in our head then as we learn, we translate them into words. So all you have to do is think of the guard with the paper and this Ena woman and I will know what they look like.

"You brilliant bug!" Baya took Doba from her shoulder and kissed the top of his head.

Hatha flinched.

"Gross. You kiss that thing?" Kuna said.

Baya turned Doba around and held him up to Kuna's face.

Kuna shrank away.

"Look into his eyes. He needs to make a connection with you. Then the two of you can communicate and even better you can show him what the head prison guard and Ena look like."

Kuna's brow furrowed with skepticism yet, she turned her gaze to the insect. After a time she declared. "Incredible. He's quite intelligent. This might actually work. He should be able to find the guard and steal the incantation from her easily enough. She's always stationed near the prison. However, Ena will not be easy to find. She's most likely deep in hiding after all the trouble we caused her."

"Where would she go to avoid palace guards?"

Kuna shook her head in dismay. "I wouldn't even know where to start?"

Baya sighed.

Leave it to me. I'll keep my ears open. After all, that's how I found you. I hunkered down and listened to the palace gossip.

Baya smiled at the insect. "Remember we only have two days."

Doba nodded his tiny head.

"Now there's only one missing piece of the plan, getting Doba out of here," Baya said.

"There aren't many options. It'll have to be when they open the food slot for the morning meal."

Baya tapped her finger on her lips. "He'll have to run out the slot when it opens."

"But the guard will see him and do who knows what to him."

"He got in here wrapped in paper. What if we hide him in the food wrappings again and toss him out the slot?"

Hopefully the guard will think I'm rubbish and throw me away, Doba said.

"Or they will uncover you and stomp on you."

Then I'll have to be fast.

"It's our only hope. We'll have to pray that the guard throws the paper into the rubbish heap with Doba inside it."

Kuna nodded thoughtfully. "It'll have to work."

Baya jumped to her feet. "Paper! We need the food wrappings." She ran out the cave opening. The prisoners would be finishing up the evening meal and tossing the food wrappers into the crevice.

CHAPTER 42

All the prisoners were more than willing to help. It was decided that they would throw as much paper as they had out the food slot when it opened in the morning. Doba would be coiled up in one of the wrappers but they planned to distract the guard with a bunch of trash in the hopes of giving Doba a better chance to get away.

"What if we banged on the slot now. Would a guard open it to see what we needed? That would give Doba more time," Baya asked the prisoners.

"No. We've tried that at different times. The guards are trained to ignore us."

"They don't even care if we're dying."

Baya inwardly cringed at the inhumanity of this place.

There was nothing to do now until morning so Baya paced. She ran her fingers through her hair. Well she tried to. They quickly got stuck in the matted mess. "I need to get cleaned up."

"First you need to eat." One of the old ladies handed her a small loaf of bread. "I saved this back for you."

Baya's stomach growled. "Thank you." It had been at least two days since she'd eaten.

"And yes, please wash yourself." Another prisoner wrinkled her nose in disgust and waved her hand as if warding off a foul scent.

Baya couldn't even remember the last time she'd bathed.

The bread was gone before Baya made it to the spring in the far back of the prison. She threw her tunic and pants into the water to soak. Using her fingers as a comb she started at the ends of her hair and slowly worked out the tangles. Eventually, she was able to run her hands through her hair.

The soap they gave the prisoners was terrible. It hardly produced any lather but she washed herself and her only set of clothes the best she could. All the while, she chastised herself for letting Osa see her this way.

By the time she was done, Baya felt more herself. She was full of questions and, more importantly — hope. It didn't even bother her that all she had to "wear" was a ratty old towel that was barely big enough to cover her.

Baya headed straight to where Kuna and Hatha were tending to Nacora, who was still fast asleep. She reached for Nacora's right hand.

Kuna grabbed her wrist to stop her.

Baya jerked her hand free. "I'm not going to hurt her … yet."

Kuna's four eyes pierced Baya as she examined Nacora's palms. Nothing. No swirling pink light. No Ox. Var and Osa must've taken it from her, Baya thought. She moved to sit as far away from Kuna and Nacora as possible, which wasn't far.

Kuna visibly relaxed now that Baya had backed away.

Doba curled up on Baya's lap and was soon fast asleep. After all, he had a big day tomorrow.

Baya wondered if Kuna's protectiveness for Nacora was simply an old habit.

"You look like an entirely new person," Kuna observed.

"And you *are* an entirely new person … or creature. So that brings me to my first question. How did you do it … appear to be one of us?"

"Female Arges are more powerful than human women. Plus Jetzu and Hanzu issued me a very old and powerful stone, called the Shadow Crystal. This stone allowed me to easily appear human. It was like turning myself invisible but I could make myself look like one of you. The crystal allowed me to do this at all times with relative ease, as long as I had it on me."

Baya nodded. She couldn't help but be impressed. "What happened to the crystal?"

"It was confiscated when they threw me in here."

Baya's interrogation wasn't over. "After we visited the Bangee, did you sneak out that night to report what we'd learned to the Arges?"

"Yes. But it's not a bad thing that Jetzu and Hanzu know what we know."

Baya held up her hand to silence her. She didn't want to hear her excuses and there were more pressing matters to discuss. "We'll be useless without our powers. We won't even make it out of the palace without being recaptured. So the first thing we need to do is figure out how to get our powers back."

"I suppose we'll find out if the legend is true," Kuna said.

Baya gave Hatha a questioning look but it was clear Hatha didn't know what Kuna was talking about. They waited for an explanation and when none came both Hatha and Baya asked, "What legend?"

"It's the pink crystals that drain a woman's powers." Kuna gestured to the walls. "It's rumored that once a woman leaves this prison her powers are restored."

It felt like a heavy weight, one that Baya hadn't even known was there, lifted off her chest. She could suddenly breathe more fully as she imagined what it would be like to get her powers back.

"No one, in my time, has actually determined if this is true."

"It has to be." Baya whispered. She narrowed her eyes. "When we get out of here we should go our separate ways."

Kuna's small dark eyes widened. "Why?"

Baya gave her an incredulous look. "Because I can't trust you."

"Baya, we need each other and we want the same thing."

"Do we? My priority is to get Vicaroy out of here. Then I'll worry about the Ox."

"What's an Ox?" Hatha asked.

Her question went unanswered.

"If we're somehow able to get the Ox," Baya continued, "then you have orders to hand it over to Jetzu. I can't let you do that. It has to stay in my possession. The Bangee thinks that I'm the only one who will be able to use it to destroy the Ominot."

"What in the hell is an Ominot?" Hatha asked.

"Jetzu and Hanzu want the same thing. They only want to get men's powers back. Baya, you have to trust me. We're on the same side. I'll help you destroy the Ominot or I will die trying."

Baya crossed her arms. "I chose to trust you before and you betrayed me." She swallowed hard. "I can't do it again."

Kuna lowered her head and shook it. "I'm sorry I didn't tell you that I'm an Arge but you would never have trusted me if I looked like this. No one in Merth would have."

"For all I know you were going to use me to get the Ox and then steal it or, worse, kill me and take it to your leaders for ... who knows what purpose? How do you know that Jetzu doesn't want its power for herself?"

"Jetzu would never do that! Baya, please know that I would never hurt you."

"Would someone please tell me what you two are talking about?" Hatha looked exasperated as her eyes bounced between Baya and Kuna.

Nacora's long dark lashes fluttered and her eyes gradually opened.

CHAPTER 43

Nacora blinked and tried to sit up. She shook her head before focusing on Kuna's large green face and four black eyes. A faint startled sound came from her as she scooted away. She glanced around wildly until she spotted Baya. It looked like relief that flickered across her face. "Baya!" Her voice was scratchy as if she been screaming for a long time. She crawled over to Baya and threw her arms around her. "What happened? Where are we?"

Baya sat in stunned silence. Kuna looked like she was ready to pull Nacora off of Baya if needed.

"Umm. We were hoping *you* could tell *us* what's going on," Baya finally said. There was no response and she had to push Nacora away.

Nacora stared wide-eyed at the pink wall behind Baya. The color had drained from her face. "We can't be … in here. Baya, why are we in my prison?" Her arms wrapped around her stomach and she curled into the fetal position. "My body … It feels like its caving in on itself."

"That's what it feels like when we lose our powers," Hatha patiently explained.

"No." Nacora clawed at the pink wall. "This can't be. We have to get out of here." She tried to get to her feet but her legs were too shaky.

Kuna caught her and gently sat her back down. Once again, Nacora flinched away from the Arge.

"There's no getting out of here ... yet. So just rest and tell us why Var and Osa brought you here?" Baya asked.

"Var? No she would never…" Nacora placed her head in her hands as if it were spinning and she was trying to make it stop. "The dream … the never-ending dream of Var taking my powers."

Baya looked at Kuna for clarification.

All four of Kuna's arms rose as she shrugged — once again, she was as confused as Baya.

Nacora firmly shook her head. "It was just a dream … not true. It can't be true."

"Well, if her powers had already been taken from her then that would explain why she was the only one to ever skip the painful first moments of being here," Hatha said.

"So she must've already been powerless when she came here. How did Var take your powers?" Baya asked.

"She didn't. She wouldn't …"

"In the dream, how did she do it?" Baya's voice was sharp.

"There was a pink light that swirled around. It came from the palm of her hand. It left nothing but pain … as my powers left me."

Baya gave Kuna a knowing look. "The Ox."

Kuna nodded. "Nacora?"

She started before turning to Kuna. "What's an Arge doing here?" She narrowed her eyes. "That voice … it's familiar."

"That's a long story, for another time," Kuna said. "Tell us the last thing you remember, before you were brought here."

Nacora leaned forward and her eyes narrowed farther. She slowly reached up and touched the Arge's scarred ear. "Kuna?"

Kuna exhaled sharply. One set of hands was folded neatly in her lap and the other set stretched out on either side. "Surprise."

Nacora's shoulders relaxed. "Oh thank the Goddess, you're here." She crawled over and placed her arms around Kuna's neck. All her body weight fell on Kuna.

Kuna had to use her back arms to support them so they didn't fall over. She awkwardly patted Nacora's back with her free hands.

Baya abruptly stood causing Doba to fall to the floor. "That's enough, Nacora. What in the name of the Great Mother is going on! You demoted Kuna and you're forcing your son to couple with Osa and you locked me in here. Now you expect us to be best friends because you went and got yourself locked up too?"

Doba quickly scrambled up Baya's leg to re-secure himself on her shoulder.

Nacora's honey-colored eyes revealed her bafflement. "I ... I wouldn't get rid of Kuna. She's my best warrior and I've told you before, I would never force my son to be with someone he didn't love. And I have *never* sentenced *anyone* to prison." Her voice grew stronger as she spoke. "This place is barbaric."

"We saw you. You say all these *nice* things and then you do the exact opposite. You're insane! You even threatened to torture innocent men in the town square." Baya was yelling by the time her tirade ended.

Nacora's mouth hung open as she stared up at Baya. Her eyes were wide with horror as she shook her head. "No. I wouldn't do any of those things."

"Oh, please," Baya spat.

Kuna put her hand up to silence Baya. "Nacora." She spoke softly. "Tell us how you got here."

"I ... I don't know. The last thing I remember was ... was feeling ill after the celebration last night."

"What celebration?" Kuna asked.

"The one for Vicaroy."

"Was it an engagement celebration?" Kuna asked.

"No. Oh Kuna, don't act like you don't remember. It was the celebration for Vicaroy's arrival in Merth."

Kuna and Baya exchanged a concerned look.

"My stomach began to hurt so I excused myself. I don't think I made it to my chambers. This is where things grow fuzzy. I slid down a wall and ... I must've fallen asleep."

"Then what?"

"Then I woke up here."

"That can't be. Vicaroy's celebration was weeks ago."

"Impossible!" Nacora lost even more color from her already paled face. She was now a ghastly pale green, almost the color of an Arge. "Are you saying that I've been asleep for ... weeks?"

Memories of Nacora sprang into Baya's mind, some she'd all but forgotten or replaced with more recent images of her. The night of the celebration, Nacora had told her that she understood that Baya was who Vicaroy wanted. She had all but given them her blessing. There had been kindness and sincerity in Nacora's eyes that night.

Baya and Vicaroy had made love for the first time. It had been a truly magical night. Then everything went terribly wrong the following morning. This caused a stabbing pain in her chest but she forced herself to think about that terrible time. The morning after the celebration Nacora had changed her mind about everything. Her face had changed as well. The kindness had disappeared. Her expression looked a lot like ... Var's — ruthless and stern.

With wide eyes focused on Kuna, Baya spoke quickly. "After the celebration did you ever see Nacora and Var together?"

Kuna frowned and studied the ceiling in concentration. "No. In fact, I remember thinking that it was odd that Var wasn't there the morning after the celebration for the announcement of her daughter's engagement to Vicaroy."

"Nacora had said something about Var being sick. But what if that wasn't true. If you could use a dark crystal to make yourself appear human, then do you think Var could use the Ox to make herself look like Nacora?"

Kuna's eyes blinked at different times then shot open all at once. Baya watched as Kuna put the pieces together. "That's it! The Ox is very powerful, much more so than my Shadow Crystal. It could easily be used to transform someone, in this case, Var into Nacora. It could also be used to keep Nacora asleep for days on end."

"That would explain why Nacora, or rather Var in disguise, was suddenly so determined to have Osa and Vicaroy together," Baya said.

"They're planning to usurp the throne," Kuna said.

"Right ... except I don't know what that means."

"It means to take control of the government by force and usually illegitimately."

"Oh," Baya looked thoughtful for a moment. "Then that's exactly what they're planning. We don't have usurpers in Pathins, the divine calling and all that. Anyway, when they brought Nacora here they said that they'd ruined her reputation with the people of Merth. This was clearly intentional. She said that the people of Merth are calling for a new leader. In three days Osa will be gladly received by the people as the new Unawi. All she needs to do is couple with a prince first ... to seem more legitimate."

"They're taking full advantage of Vicaroy's arrival as a prince of coupling age," Kuna said.

"Wait. What do you mean, 'ruined my reputation'? How?" Tears had gathered in Nacora's eyes.

"That was the whole torturing-innocent-people thing."

Nacora's hand flew to her heart. "Oh Great Goddess, please help us." She covered her ears and rocked back and forth. "I've lost the support of my people and I've lost my powers. We're stuck in this wretched place ... and my head guard is an Arge." Her voice was hysterical by the time she finished.

Baya lowered her head. She was glad Nacora hadn't turned into a crazy woman. Yet, this was a lot to take in, even for Baya and she'd been awake for it all. "I'm sorry, Nacora."

"Don't forget to add that your oldest son is being forced to couple and there's no telling what Var's done with Wen and your other children." Kuna spoke as if she were discussing the weather.

A loud sob burst from Nacora. She covered her eyes as the tears fell freely. Her body jerked with each ragged breath.

Baya glared at Kuna. "That was helpful."

"What? I just wanted to make sure we covered all of our problems."

Baya resisted the urge to smack Kuna.

"Of which you have a lot," Hatha said. "I swear, I don't envy any of you."

You know you've hit an all-time low when an old prisoner feels sorry for you, Baya thought.

Baya knelt down by Nacora and placed her hand gently on her knee. "Hey, don't worry. We have a plan to get out of here."

Nacora's sobs stopped at once. She looked a Baya with puffy eyes and soaking wet cheeks. "No one has ever escaped from here."

"But we have this little guy." Baya rubbed Doba under his chin. "Tomorrow morning, we're going to toss him out the food slot with a bunch of wrappers. He's going to get the incantation to open the prison door and take it to our friend who will rescue us."

Nacora look thoughtful. She absent-mindedly wiped away the tears as her expression grew determined. "That might work. Except I can save him a step. I know the incantation."

Kuna's eyes narrowed on Nacora. "I thought only the head prison guard knew it."

"And the Unawi. Every Unawi is taught the incantation to the prison. There must always be two and only two in the palace at all times who know it."

"Why wasn't I told this?" Kuna's voice had turned dark.

"You did not need to know."

"Why were we not told that you're an Arge?" Baya shot Kuna a glare that said, 'drop it.' She didn't want to get in a fight over stuff that didn't matter at that exact moment. "This is great. Nacora can write the incantation on a piece of paper. We'll tie it to Doba then all he has to do is find Ena. The real problem is going to be getting the Ox from Var." Baya wanted to change the subject before Kuna grew any more upset over something as silly as not being told the incantation to the prison door. "Does anyone have any ideas?"

Kuna shook her head. "I already tried to get the Ox from her and I ended up in here."

A thought caused Baya to straighten. She glanced to the entry way knowing the other prisoners were sticking close by — listening. "Hey," she hollered out the door. "Do any of you know where to find someone who's hiding from authorities?"

A number of faces appeared in the doorway.

"Any tavern would be a place to start."

"You'd just go askin' around until someone was willing to talk to ya."

"You can't go in lookin' all rich though. No one would say a word to ya then."

This was helpful information. "Thank you," Baya said. "Doba did you get all that?"

Yeah, yeah. He sounded sleepy.

* * *

NO ONE CAME up with any brilliant ideas to take on Var and her newfound powers. Kuna helped Nacora to walk around the room. Her legs were unstable but she was determined to keep trying. Soon she didn't need Kuna's assistance anymore but after only a couple of times around the small area she'd had enough for her first day of being awake in weeks.

Kuna and Baya stayed in Nacora's room that night. None of them seemed to want to be alone.

Baya couldn't sleep. She feared she might not wake in time and miss the delivery of the morning meal. There was no way that could be allowed to happen. They had to get Doba out of here. He only had two days before Vicaroy's coupling to find Ena. So she lay wide eyed, staring at the pink walls — walls she hated more than anything else in the world.

"Can you give me one more chance," Kuna whispered, "to prove that I'm on your side?"

Baya rolled over. She was getting used to her in this form. "I want to believe you, Kuna, I really do..."

"But?"

"I suppose, we need each other if we're going to beat Var."

Kuna's thin lips turned upward. "I won't let you down."

A long silence fell upon them.

"I've been thinking," Baya said. "Do you know what they did with your Shadow Crystal?"

Kuna nodded.

"Do you think we can get it?"

"I have a pretty good idea of where to look. All confiscated items are stored in a closet, not far from the prison entrance. It should be there."

"Good. I think we're going to need it."

"What are you planning?"

Baya gave her a devious smile.

CHAPTER 44

The instant Doba landed on the floor outside the prison he scrambled to get free of the food wrappings that surrounded him. More paper fell on top of him as the prisoners continued to shove their rubbish out the food slot. Doba peeked out of his coverings in an attempt to spot the guard.

"What is the meaning of this?" The guard cursed as she surveyed the piles of trash at her feet. "Stop that this instant." She tried to slam the hatch shut. Papers stuck in the small opening making it difficult for the woman to fully close it.

This was Doba's chance, while the guard was distracted with the latch, so he gauged the distance to the door. *Now.* He moved as fast as his thin little legs would carry him. Thankfully he had a lot of them. He left the guard cursing to herself.

Getting out of the palace took effort and lots of patience as he hid in dark corners or under furniture waiting for someone to happen by and open doors for him. He had to be ready to run like hell to squeeze through in time. One such close call ended up being too close. The door caught the note that had been rolled tightly and tied around his neck. This caused the paper to break loose and skid across the floor.

Not the enchantment to open the prison door. Doba hurried after the note.

A startled scream alerted Doba to the fact that he'd been spotted. Using his head he rolled the paper under a table. His body slid out of sight as a dustpan came down where he had just been. He took the paper in his mouth and continued to run, zigging and zagging, dodging the man with the dustpan, until he was out of the room and safely under a large divan. The servant who was after him wouldn't be able to reach him.

He dropped the note in order to get a better grip on it. *If only I had hands. Now I'm stuck carrying this thing in my mouth.*

When he made it to the gardens outside the palace he paused to celebrate with a good roll in the soft yellow grass. But there was no time to delay any further. It had taken hours to get out of the palace. He still had to find Ena in this massive city with only a day and a half until the celebration. He slipped through a crack in the garden wall and headed into the heart of the city.

Moving through the streets was easier. He had more space to avoid people and more dark places to hide and objects to shield him from sight.

Doba needed to find a local establishment. This would be where he could hopefully get the information he needed, namely where people who are hiding from the Unawi would go.

It took him hours to get to the central market. He wove his way through the streets heading in the same direction as most of the foot traffic. Where the masses went, he followed. Doba shimmied up a leg of a merchant's cart and didn't stop until he reached the canvas that shaded the cart's merchandise. This way he had a good view of the market. He watched people's mouths in an attempt to read them. He also listened intently for any word of a tavern or of where fugitives might hide.

Midday came and went. The suns felt like they were burning holes in Doba. There was less than one day until Vicaroy's coupling and he wasn't having any luck. The people appeared to be concerned only with bartering for goods.

Giving up, he took the note in his mouth and turned to make his way off the canvas over the merchant's cart when he heard a woman say, "Can you point me to the nearest tavern?"

Doba poked his head over the canvas so he could see the two people talking below.

"Two streets down and one to the right." The merchant pointed the way. "You'll find it on your left."

"Thank you," the woman said.

Perfect, Doba thought.

"You from the other side of town?" the merchant asked.

"Yes. I'm here to pick up supplies that are hard to find in my neighborhood."

Doba's heart sank. *What if Ena went to the far side of town? That would be the perfect place to go if someone wanted to avoid the Unawi. If so, I'll never find her in time.*

Doba wiggled his backend as he readied himself to jump onto the woman's large pack. He leapt. His lower half didn't make it. He swayed from side to side as his front legs struggled to pull him up. As quickly as possible, he hid himself in the folds of the sack. With his body curled into a ball, he searched for a place to see out.

In no time, the woman entered a building. She swung her pack off and set it on the floor as she took a seat. Doba carefully uncoiled himself as he slid out.

The tavern was dingy. He was used to clean palace floors, so touching the sticky floor in here made him cringe. The windows were shuttered, casting the place in darkness. This was just the type of place for people who didn't want to be seen. The dimly lit room also made it easy for Doba to sneak around unnoticed until he found the perfect place — an overstuffed chair that was located central to the room. From under it he could listen. A pitcher of water that someone left on a nearby table caught his eye. He glanced about to see if he had time to take a quick drink. His thirst won out. As he moved out from under the divan a person walked by, causing Doba to make a hasty retreat.

Listening to the gibberish of the people around him, he stared intently at the pitcher of water.

Nobody seemed to be talking about anything but the weather or how they'd fared at the market that day.

Soon Doba grew hungry as well.

Much to Doba's disappointment, the man took the water pitcher away.

As the day wore on the inhabitants of the tavern increased as did their noisy chatter. It became increasingly difficult to keep track of it all. Doba found himself jerking awake a time or two.

This is an impossible task. After all, I'm only one little bug. I have needs as well, like food and water. Is that asking too much? he grumbled.

Scooping the note into his mouth, he slowly crept out from his sanctuary and ran for the far corner and its accompanying darkness. He slowly made his way toward the bar, careful to stay out of sight when possible. If there were food and drink that could be scavenged it would be there.

The bartender was busy pouring mugs of wine and ale.

Doba eyed some crumbs that had dropped to the floor near the man's feet. *Am I hungry enough to eat off this dirty floor?... Maybe.*

While he studied his chances of being able to get to scraps without being seen he'd forgotten all about listening to the people around him. That was until a woman who'd been sitting at the bar leaned in to whisper to the bartender. Doba inched closer. He couldn't quite hear what she was saying but he read her lips.

It was something about her friend being accused of shoplifting in the market and guards were looking for them. They needed a place to … avoid being seen for a time.

Doba forgot all about the crumbs. He moved in closer to hear better. The bartender said something to the woman but he'd turned his head away and Doba couldn't make out what he'd said. He ventured even closer to the pair of humans. He was now out in the open. It was a scream that reminded him of this fact.

"Now you're letting giant bugs into your tavern?" a customer complained.

Doba ran for cover.

"No. I'm not." The bartender grabbed a broom.

A disruptive chase ensued as Doba wove his way under tables and chairs in an effort to avoid the angry swipes of the broom.

"He's too fast," the bartender yelled.

People had gotten to their feet knocking over chairs as they scrambled to avoid Doba or the broom swinging through the air.

The noise in the tavern increased tenfold. Whoops and hollers and screams sounded all around. The woman whom the bartender had been whispering with, held open the back door. "Over here. Chase that thing outside."

That sounded like the best option so Doba made a break for the exit. The bartender was out of breath and only able to chase him halfway out. The woman slammed the door shut behind Doba.

"Who let that thing in here?" the man's voice was muffled from behind the door.

"Well if you were a better housekeeper maybe you wouldn't attract such filth."

Filth? Filth! Doba hissed. *I'm cleaner than any of you ghastly humans. Why am I subjecting myself to this? Humans hate me and I hate...* Baya's face came to mind. All the times she'd cared for him, fed him, carried him, kept him safe … freed him. *I have to find out what that bartender said to that woman.* He surveyed his surroundings. To his right was a pile of rubbish. From the top of it he could peer in through a knot that had fallen out of the wooden shutters.

Gross. Now I have to climb a pile of stinky trash. I hope Baya appreciates what I'm going through.

CHAPTER 45

From atop the pile of rubbish, Doba peered into the tavern from which he'd been so rudely chased. The bartender and the woman who was looking for refuge for her thieving friend resumed their conversation after things died down.

The problem was Doba couldn't see the man's face. He had no idea what he was telling the woman. She eventually thanked him and slung her pack over her shoulder. She headed for the back door. Doba couldn't let that woman out of his sight. It was getting late. Vicaroy would be coupled with the wrong woman in less than twelve hours. This was his only hope.

He scurried up the wall and waited over the door for the woman to exit. When the door opened he leapt, aiming the best he could for her pack.

The woman was in a hurry and continued down the street. She didn't notice that Doba hung from her bag, which was rather small. He had a hard time holding on, let alone finding a place to hide. Half his body hung out the top flap. But the good news was there was a plump piece of fruit waiting inside. Something that would cure both his hunger and his thirst. The fruit was gone in no time.

The woman made her way deeper into the city. Doba was sure she was headed to pick up her thief of a friend but after an hour of deliberately taking side streets away from the market area it dawned on Doba. There was no "friend." The woman was the one seen stealing goods from the market. He shook his head. *Humans*. She'd probably stolen the fruit Doba had just enjoyed, for which he was grateful.

Several times when someone could be heard coming toward them the woman disappeared. Once she was able to determine that it was not guards patrolling the streets she would allow herself to be seen again.

At last, the woman stopped to knock on a door. Doba carefully peeked over the woman's shoulder — his dark eyes should go unnoticed at night — or so he hoped.

The door opened abruptly but only a couple of inches. The door had multiple chains securing it which only allowed it to be open a short way.

Odd. Doba thought. *Why would anyone chain a door so that it wouldn't open all the way?*

A woman's piercing stare came from the opening. Well half a stare, only part of her face was visible through the crack. Her eye took in every inch of the newcomer. Doba ducked.

The thief shifted uncomfortably.

"Password?" The woman's voice was old and scratchy.

"Ah ... I was told that it was ... Merth Forever."

The woman on the other side of the door narrowed her eyes or at least the one they could see. "You wanna join the resistance?"

"Um ... the resistance? Oh yeah, the resistance to the Unawi. Yes. Yes I do."

Humans are such terrible liars, Doba thought.

The door slammed shut and the thief cursed under her breath.

The sound of jangling chains was heard before the door swung open. The thief sighed with relief.

"Well come on, we don't got all night."

"Thank you." The thief quickly entered.

Doba did his best to cover up with the top flap of the woman's pack but almost half of him was still exposed.

Thankfully the place was just as dark as the tavern. *Hopefully they won't notice me,* Doba thought. *Ena simply has to be here.* His jaw was tired from holding the note but he had to be ready to bolt at any second if they saw him. All would be lost without the paper.

He appeared to be in a common room. A hand full of women and men sat about a table playing games and drinking. They all stopped to examine the newcomer. Doba did his best to make himself as small as possible as he searched their faces. None fit the image from Kuna's mind about what Ena looked like.

I thought human's slept at night. Clearly I have a lot to learn about common folks.

The old woman who'd let them in led them down a hall. They passed many rooms. Ratty old cloths hung over the doorways. *This place is a dump,* Doba thought.

Eventually they entered one of the rooms. A couple of people were asleep on cots and some slept right on the floor.

"We got a spot for you over there." The old woman pointed. "You have a bed roll?"

"Yeah."

"Good. We ain't got any extra. The resistance is grow'n fast since the Unawi tried to torture those poor men."

"I bet." The thief's undertone made it clear that she didn't care one bit about the resistance or the men the Unawi threatened to harm.

The old woman turned to leave.

"Thanks again."

With a nod the old lady was gone.

The thief swung her pack off and Doba jumped to the floor. He was nothing more than a shadow as he hurried under the cots. *This place is as dirty as the tavern.* Doba lifted a couple of his legs off the sticky floor. *So this is how regular people live?* He shuddered. *Ena has to be here and I have to find her so I can get back in the palace where I belong.*

Doba systematically searched the other rooms. Some had fewer people in them than others and some people had actual beds or at least mattresses on the floor. But no Ena. He was running out of options — down to only a handful of rooms. The first of the suns would soon be rising on Vicaroy's coupling day. *If she wasn't here then where else could she be? No. She has to be here.* Doba stopped short as he saw the woman lying in the bed in front of him. Well, it was a mattress on the floor. Nothing like the fancy beds in the palace.

He inched closer comparing the woman's face to the one in Kuna's head. *It's her!* He spun around in a tight circle — a victory dance, of sorts, before hurrying up the small dresser by the bed. From up there he notice the two people that were sleeping next to Ena — a man and a woman. The woman had her arm around Ena and the man held the woman.

Doba shook his head to help him focus. There was no time to ponder the odd mating habits of humans.

He readied himself and jumped onto Ena's stomach.

CHAPTER 46

That did the trick. Ena sat up in bed with a sharp inhale. She found herself staring into four tiny black eyes and let out a screech.

Doba dropped the note in her lap.

The woman next to Ena rolled away with a sleepy moan.

Ena swatted him off. The insect hit the ground running, quickly exiting the room. She stood to make sure there were no more insects in her bed. The rolled-up piece of parchment fell to the floor. She stared at it with half-asleep bewilderment. Had that bug just dropped it in her lap as if delivering it to her? She rubbed her eyes to clear her thoughts. Surely not.

She left the paper where it fell and crawled back into bed. It must have been a dream. That was it — it had to be. Soon she was fast asleep. The next thing she knew was the sound of something shattering as it hit the floor. She bolted upright. There on her nightstand was that giant bug again. His four beady eyes were intent on her … and it held a piece of paper in its mouth. Apparently the thing had knocked her only mug off the nightstand.

One of her companions rolled over pulling a pillow over his head.

Humans are heavy sleepers, Doba thought. *Or maybe this place is noisy all the time and they're used to it.*

"Shoo. Go away," she whispered.

In a flash Doba jumped onto the bed dropped the note in her lap and was gone.

Ena sat staring at the tight roll of paper. A feeling of dread rose in her stomach. She didn't want to know what it said or who it was from. It was undoubtedly trouble. She took the note and lay back down while she pondered what to do.

A smile crossed her lips as she gazed at her lovers, still fast asleep. Ena didn't want any more adventures. No more trouble with the palace. Then again, she'd joined the resistance. And she was happy … again. But the note seemed to burn in her hand — calling her. She sighed and unrolled the paper.

Our Dearest Ena,

You are the only one who can save us and Merth. We hate to ask this of you but please, we beg you, come for us. It is a matter of life and death. Look into Doba's eyes. He's the insect who brought you the note. He will show you everything. The incantation to open the palace prison is below.

Sincerely,

Baya and Kuna

Ena shrieked and jerked away from the black bug whose penetrating stare was fixated on her again. He clearly wanted her full attention. "Look into the insect's eyes. Why?" Ena whispered, not wanting to wake her companions.

Doba inched nearer, never looking away. He didn't so much as blink. Ena leaned back. "You're so … intense and … unnerving. Kuna and Baya sent you?"

Doba nodded.

"You understand me?"

Doba nodded again and moved even closer

"Okay... But I don't know how looking into your eyes will help." She squared herself to face the bug.

Ena stifled a yelp when a foreign voice sounded in her head. "You ... you can..." she was going to say talk but that wasn't the right word.

Yes. I can communicate with humans. Doba's words poured into her mind quickly. She could hardly keep up. Something about Baya and Kuna locked up without their powers. And Vicaroy being forced to couple with ... someone Ena didn't know. And ... it was up to her to save them.

Ena sat in silence for a time. "I almost lost everything trying to help them," she spoke softly. "I ... I'm not royalty so this can't fall on me. I'm a nobody and I like it that way. My life and my friends ... I just got them back..."

Doba ventured even closer. He was almost on her lap. With all his concentration he focused on Baya's face when he first found her in prison. He'd gotten better at this over the years. Looking into Ena's eyes he projected the image of Baya, sunken cheekbone, tangled and matted hair, the circles under her eyes...

Ena's hand flew to her mouth. "She looks dreadful!"

You have to help them, you're our only hope.

Ena shook her head and lay down staring blankly at the wall.

Doba gave her some time to process everything but it seemed like hours passed and she didn't move or say a word. Her thoughts were mostly of how she dreaded leaving and the guilt that would haunt her if she stayed.

We have to go — now. Time is running out. We still have to sneak into the palace and get them out and stop the coupling.

Ena didn't move but at least she blinked.

Fine, I'm going back to see what I can do — alone, if I have to. Even if I have no idea how to help. I'm making sacrifices too, you know?

Nothing.

Doba jumped off the bed and headed for the door.

"Wait." Ena stood. "I'm going to need my strongest herbs to put the prison guard to sleep."

Doba leapt into the air. *Yes!* He scampered up her leg.

Ena did a little dance and giggled. "That tickles."

She quickly put some provisions in a small bag as she stuffed some shortbread in her mouth. When she got to the door she paused. Her friends were sleeping peacefully. A look of envy and longing crossed her face. She gave them each a kiss on the cheek and only the man slightly stirred but didn't fully wake.

"Goodbye," she whispered.

CHAPTER 47

It was approaching midday and soon Osa would be coupled with the handsome new prince. Var entered Osa's chambers. She never bothered to knock. However, now that her daughter was going to have a theo, she might have to start — knocking, that is.

"Osa, Darling. Let me see my baby girl," Var's voice was nauseatingly sweet.

Osa tried to straighten her gown. It was a golden number made out of the softest fabrics. The skirt billowed out around her legs and there wasn't much to the top. She turned toward her mother as Var rounded the corner into the main room of Osa's chambers.

Var frowned. "Is this the best your servants could do? You're all disheveled." Var sighed. "Come here."

Osa didn't move. Her mother had to come to her. Var went to work straightening the long skirt so the thin red flaps hung down in the center of her hips and down her backside. Var adjusted the straps on the skimpy top. Finally, she tightened the belt around Osa's waist.

Osa exhaled with discomfort.

"It's necessary, my dear, to show off your thin waist."

Osa stood frozen as if afraid to move or even speak.

"Relax, my child. Everything will be fine, once we are in power."

Var took a strand of Osa's hair and began pinning it up. "I swear, why do we even have servants?"

"It's... okay. I want to wear my hair down."

Var's frown deepened. "On your coupling day?" Her voice was incredulous. "Darling, you have better fashion sense than that."

Osa brushed her mother's hand away. "Hey ... um ..."

"What is it?"

"I was hoping that you would let me ... hold it."

Var stepped back with a look of surprise on her face. "Hold it?" She rubbed the palm of her right hand. Through the white glove a faint pink light began to glow — the Ox. "You've never asked me to see it before."

"I know but like you said, it's my coupling day. I just want to know what it feels like, please Mother? Just for a minute."

Var stood even taller and her eyes narrowed.

Osa nervously rubbed at the dark stone hidden in the folds of her silk skirt. Her heart pounded in her chest. "You don't trust me?"

"Don't be ridiculous. Of course I trust you."

Osa held out her hand. "Just for a minute. I want to feel it, that's all."

Var studied her daughter for what seemed like ages.

Sweat threatened to break out on Osa's forehead. Don't let her see how nervous you are, she thought.

Slowly, deliberately Var took off her glove, one finger at a time.

"Thank you, Mother."

"After all, it is your big day." Var moaned as she removed the pink stone from her hand where it had been embedded. It wasn't a painful moan but rather one of pleasure. The center swirled with pink and orange light which was held by the star with rounded edges.

Osa struggled not to appear too anxious to take the stone. She waited, with what she hoped was a calm expression, for Var to place the Ox in her palm. When the stone touched her hand it sent a strong electric shock up her arm. She closed her eyes tight as the power moved through her body and the stone set itself into the palm of her hand. An involuntary moan floated off her lips. She clasped her fingers around the stone.

"It is marvelous isn't it?"

Strips of Osa's hair began to change from a pale yellow to a shimmering brown. Her skin transformed from a milky white to an olive tone.

Var's face fell. "What's happening?"

When the girl in front of Var opened her eyes she gasped. Her daughter's crystal blue eyes were gone. Instead tricolored ones stared back at her. The young woman who stood in front of her now had eyes that were light brown, which faded into green and then to a bright gold sunburst around the pupil. "Baya!"

Baya's smile was full of triumph.

"Where's my daughter?" She stepped forward. "Give it back."

Baya shook her head. "I don't think so, Var. I'll keep it … for now."

Var's face twisted in anger. She lunged for Baya. Baya shot a beam of pink light from her palm but the light flew past Var. It evaporated as it hit the wall, harming nothing.

"You don't know how to use it. You'll kill someone or yourself."

"If that's so, then let's hope it's you I kill." Baya raised her palm again but Var was on top of her. The two women fell to the ground. Var clawed at Baya's hand but the stone was already set.

"If you try to force it out of my hand it will disintegrate you," Baya warned.

Var's hand recoiled.

A large foot kicked Var sending her rolling away from Baya.

Kuna reached down to help Baya up.

"Thanks." She stared at her hand in disbelief and shook it but the stone remained embedded in her palm.

"Does it hurt?" Kuna asked. She appeared to be mesmerized by the swirling light in Baya's palm.

"No. It's…wonderful. Almost like getting our powers back."

"Wow," Kuna breathed.

Baya reached into her dress pocket. "Here's your Shadow Crystal." Baya tossed it.

Kuna deftly caught it. "The celebration will start soon. We'd better go."

They looked to Var who'd fallen into a stunned silence. She wore the look of someone who didn't believe what was happening directly in front of her.

"Make her look like Nacora and bring her with us and don't forget to shut her up," Kuna said.

"Is that all you need me to do? I don't know how this works." Baya shook her hand again this time to see if that might make the Ox jump into action.

"It's incredibly complicated. You'll never figure it out. Just give it back to me," The air of authority was back in Var's voice.

"Not a chance in hell," Kuna said. "If Baya can't shut you up then I will."

"It's too powerful for a young girl, especially a weak and insignificant one like you," Var spat.

Baya closed her eyes and encased the Ox with her fingers. Power moved through her blood, warming it. She could feel things that she'd never felt before, like the slightest air movement. It was a gentle change in pressure against her skin. A new awareness of her body and her surroundings consumed her. Its energy pulsed in beat with her heart, which she could now hear clearly.

When her eyes snapped open they were pinned on her prey. She slowly raised her hand, aiming the Ox at Var.

"No!" Var covered her face with her arms as if that would protect her, as if anything could protect her against something as powerful as the Ox.

A pink light shot from Baya's hand and surrounded Var.

Against her will Var was lifted off the ground. Her arms and legs flailed as she tried to grasp something solid. "No! Please! I'll do anything."

"Yes you will. You'll do exactly what I want you to do and you're going to look exactly how I want you to look." Baya smiled with triumph.

Var's form changed until it was Nacora who looked back at them.

"This is impossible." Var studied her hands, which were now black. "No one can learn to use the Ox in only minutes. It took me months."

"I'm going to need you to be quiet."

Var's mouth snapped shut. She still made muffled sounds as she continued to protest.

"And I need your gloves."

Streaks of a lovely flaxen color ran through Baya's hair until it was entirely a golden blonde. Her skin paled and her eyes shone bright blue. "There." Baya studied herself in the looking glass. "I'm ready for my coupling."

"Perfect. Let's get to the Great Hall. Everyone will be gathered." Kuna vanished.

LET'S BACK UP A BIT, SHALL WE?

Perhaps you'd like to know how Baya did it ...

Kuna's eyes roamed back and forth as she watched Baya pace in the pink prison.

"This is the day of Vicaroy's coupling." Baya had already bitten off her fingernails. She'd moved on to chewing on the soft skin around her nails.

"Perhaps we shouldn't have relied on an insect to get us out of here," Kuna said.

"It's not like we had a choice." Baya looked up at the sunlight that filtered in through the ventilation holes. "Come on Doba," she prayed. Of course it was a long shot. How would Doba find Ena in time and how would he convince her to sneak into the castle and break them out?

The prison door slowly ground open. The prisoners all got to their feet. Baya closed her eyes afraid to see if it was Ena or if it was Osa, coming to rub it in one last time.

"Ena," Kuna breathed.

Baya blinked. There she stood, in the flesh, with Doba on her shoulder. Baya ran to throw her arms around them but the second both feet stepped over the threshold, onto the normal grey stone, it was as if she hit a wall head-on. Her entire body was struck with euphoria. The shock passed through her entire being all at once. Every muscle spasmed. Her legs felt too good to support her weight. She fell to the ground and shook violently. There was only a vague recognition of Ena's scream of terror.

If losing one's powers was the most painful experience possible, then getting them back was the most orgasmic feeling in the world. Baya gasped. Her chest heaved as the sensation slowly left her body. She felt her arms and legs come back under her control. But the best part was that the emptiness was gone. She was whole again — powerful. Her arms, followed by her fingers and then her head gave one last twitch as the pleasure faded.

She blinked at the prison door several times, tempted to return and come back out, in hopes of feeling that again.

"Are you okay," Ena's voice was higher than usual.

"Never better," Baya gasped.

Kuna moaned with pleasure and her legs jerked. She lay in a ball on the floor next to Baya.

Nacora just stood there, wide-eyed. "I still feel … empty."

"This prison didn't take your powers. Var did. Let's go get them back."

Kuna slowly got to her feet but remained bent over heaving.

Baya surveyed her surroundings. The prison guard looked like she was sleeping.

"I gave her a heavy dose of herbs. She'll be out for a while." There was obvious pride in Ena's voice.

"Well done." Baya gave her a hug before looking back at the prisoners. They all looked at the open door with gaping mouths. "You're free … if you so choose."

Hatha gave her a nod of approval and the two women exchanged a warm smile. It could have meant, thank you or goodbye or congratulations or many other things … or all of them.

"Holy shit. That was … phenomenal." Kuna's eyes still looked dazed.

"Better than sex."

"Really?" Ena's face lit up.

"Now I can't wait to get my powers back," Nacora said. "Wait! How do you know what sex is like?" Her face fell. "Have you and my son —"

"Now is not the time to discuss this," Baya said.

"Well, we'll have to make your relationship official now."

"That's assuming he's not already coupled to someone else." Baya shook Kuna to help her snap out of it. "We have to go!"

But Kuna's eyes slowly focused on Ena. "You're not surprised that I'm an Arge?"

"No. Doba told me," Ena said. "Actually, it explains a lot, like how you are so much stronger than us."

"Ena, save yourself and Doba," Baya rubbed under Doba's chin. "You've risked too much for us already. Nacora, you know where to meet us." She nodded at Kuna. "Let's go."

With her power back, Baya was ready to take on the suns and the moons. Yet, she wasn't sure which hand of Kuna's to take. She opted for the one closest to her. This way they wouldn't lose each other or worse, trip over each other. The two women, well a woman and an Arge, disappeared.

KUNA SCAVENGED through the closet where they kept confiscated items. Most of the stuff was covered in dust. Her crystal was in her small leather sack on top of a pile of knives.

"Hurry." Baya bounced on the balls of her feet as she kept watch. "What if the ceremony has started?"

Kuna armed herself by tucking a couple of knives into the top of her pants.

"Come on," Baya waved her on with impatience. "Do you know how to find Osa's chambers?"

Kuna took Baya's hand again and disappeared. "Follow me."

Once outside Osa's chambers, Baya placed her ear to the door. She exhaled with relief. "It sounds like Osa's servants are helping her get ready for the coupling." They weren't too late!

Kuna let herself be seen. She rubbed the Shadow Crystal and transformed herself into a human. Not just any human, she was dressed as a royal guard. And not just any guard. Baya only vaguely recognized the face. "Is she the new head of the army, the one who took your place?"

"I assume so. She used to be second in command, under me."

Kuna knocked on Osa's door.

A woman answered.

"All servants are to report to the kitchen at once."

The servant gave a slight bow. "Of course." She slowly turned to inform the others.

Kuna headed down the hall and Baya followed — still invisible.

Once she rounded the first corner Kuna disappeared.

Baya clumsily groped for Kuna's hand. They pressed themselves against the stone walls as they waited for the servants to leave. The women chattered merrily as they exited Osa's room. When their voices faded in the distance, Kuna and Baya made a run for it. Kuna practically dragged Baya behind her. It was all she could do to keep up with the Arge's long legs. Kuna hardly paused as she entered Osa's chambers, which were huge. It was many times bigger than the room Baya had been given.

A large sitting area with comfortable looking divans and chairs gave way to a bedroom which held one of the largest beds Baya had ever seen. The carved posts around the bed almost touched the high ceiling. Heavy drapes hung around it, turning the bed into a room of its own.

Rounding a corner they saw Osa. She sat in front of a vanity, which was topped with a mirror that took up most of the wall. She fussed with a strand of hair as she studied her reflection.

Baya felt Kuna's hand leave hers. An unseen force shoved Osa forward. She cried out as she was dragged to her feet. Kuna let herself be seen as she spun Osa around. She held Osa's arms behind her back with two of her hands and held a knife to her throat with a third appendage.

It would come in handy to have so many arms, Baya thought. She appeared in front of Osa.

The blonde's bright blue eyes were filled with shock and fear. "How —"

"Quiet," Kuna snapped.

Osa's face contorted in pain as Kuna tightened her grip. The knife blade created an indent in her skin. She bit back another scream.

"Easy," Baya said. "Don't hurt her."

Kuna's four eyes snapped to Baya. There was a piercing fury in them. "After everything she's done? ... She's a traitor to the Unawi." Kuna's voice was so full of disdain that it made it clear that Osa and her type — traitors — were the lowest forms of life.

"Remind me never to make you mad."

"What's the meaning of this?" Osa managed.

"I said, quiet!" Kuna must have done something to her because another painful cry escaped from Osa. With her forth arm she tossed Baya the Shadow Crystal. "Hurry."

Baya wrapped her fingers around the dark stone and closed her eyes. Her hand tingled with the pleasant sensation of its power. The stimulating feeling moved up her arm and into her chest. It exploded as it reached her heart. The power spread more quickly through her body. It was exhilarating, not as orgasmic as getting all her powers back ... but lovely nonetheless.

When Baya's eyes opened they narrowed on Osa. She began to shake with concentration as she took in every detail of Osa's face.

"What are you doing?" Osa demanded. "Wait until my mother gets here. She will make you wish you never laid a hand on me." Osa's mouth fell open as Baya began to change. Her hair streaked with gold and her skin paled, her face transformed. In only a dozen heartbeats Osa was staring at herself. Where Baya once stood was now an exact replica of herself.

"I'm glad your mother is on her way. She's the one we really need to see," Baya said.

"How did you —" But Osa's words were cut short when Kuna twisted her arms.

Baya studied the hand that held the Shadow Crystal — *her* hand which was now an odd pale color. She didn't like being so white. Her skin looked sickly compared to her normal bronze color. "It worked," she whispered. "What do we do with Osa?"

"You're going to need her clothes."

Baya gazed at the crystal and wondered if she could use it to put Osa to sleep. The healer had done something to make Baya fall into a deep sleep when they'd first arrived in Merth. But she didn't know how she'd done it.

When Baya looked up she found Osa slung over Kuna's shoulder. Kuna carried her over to the bed and unceremoniously flopped her down on it. Osa's eyes rolled back in her head and her body was limp.

"Did you kill her?" Baya ran toward them.

"No. But I can if you'd like."

"No! What did you do?"

"Pressure points. She'll wake with a terrible headache." Kuna smiled with satisfaction.

Very awkwardly they took Osa's dress off. Kuna tied her arms behind her back and stuffed her naked body into a wardrobe.

Baya quickly pulled the gown on and stopped short at her unrecognizable reflection in the mirror.

"That was impressive. You must be very powerful," Kuna said.

"It was the Shadow Crystal."

"No. That crystal only helped a little. I doubt any human woman would be powerful enough to make herself look like someone else even with the crystal. Maybe that's why the Bangee chose you."

"Osa, Darling," Var's voice came from the foyer.

Baya jumped and Kuna vanished.

"How do I look?"

"Like Osa only … a mess."

"It'll have to do."

"You can do this," Kuna whispered as Var rounded the corner.

CHAPTER 48

Outside the Great Hall Mek caught up with Baya and Var, who were disguised as Osa and Nacora. Kuna remained invisible, hanging back in the shadows, following at a safe distance.

"Osa, wait! Thank the Goddess. I wanted to catch you before the coupling…" Mek paused at the sight of Nacora surrounded by the pink light, floating in the air. "What's going on?"

Baya knew she had to think fast. "I'm giving Nacora … a ride … to the ceremony. She's rather tired from having to plan a royal coupling on such short notice."

"Come on, you can't fool me," Mek eyed her with suspicion.

Oh no. He wasn't buying her lie. Baya's heart thrummed against her rib cage.

"We both know she's not Nacora."

"She's not?" Baya tried to sound casual but her throat tightened.

"Of course not. She's really …" Mek looked around to make sure no one was near, "your mom."

Baya exhaled. "Right." Then realization dawned; Mek knew that Var had been posing as Nacora this whole time. She narrowed her eyes and stared straight ahead as she made her way toward the Great

Hall. Hopefully, everyone was already there waiting for the royal ceremony.

"Anyway," Mek addressed Var. "I was hoping I could ... you know, get Baya out of prison tomorrow morning."

Baya's eyes widened. Think ... fast! "Oh, Var ... Mother is saving her voice for her ceremonial speech." She was aware of how stupid this sounded but it was the best she could come up with on such short notice.

Var glared at Baya but was unable to speak.

Mek's brow furrowed as he looked between the two women. His expression lightened before he addressed Baya, "Okay ... so can I? You said I could..."

"Could what?"

"Don't pretend like you've forgotten. This was our deal, if I brought you Vicaroy then I could have Baya. Once you and Vicaroy were coupled ... of course. You promised that I could get Baya out of prison. I've got to get her out of that place as soon as possible. Well, as soon as you'll let me. The thought of her trapped and wasting away ..." he shivered.

Baya had to force her mouth to close because at some point it had fallen open. After the shock came a rush of angry blood to her cheeks. He'd betrayed them. How deep did the treachery run in this place?

She was about to find out.

"Come on, Osa. You know I'm on your side." Mek must have misread Baya's shocked reaction for mistrust. "After all, I warned you when they tried to escape. You almost caught them, remember? I've proven myself to you so you've got to hold up your end of the bargain."

Baya's hands clenched. She saw it clearly. After Mek helped her sneak into Vicaroy's room to rescue him, Mek had gone straight to Var and Osa and told them of their plan. That was how Osa and Var had found them that night outside the secret entrance to the palace.

The power of the Ox rushed up her arm. She fought the urge to wrap her fingers around his neck and squeeze. Instead, she managed to force a smile. "Of course, whatever you want. You can have Baya." She waved her gloved hand dismissively.

Mek exhaled as if he'd been holding his breath for a really long time. "Thanks, Cuz. I knew you'd keep your promise."

Baya sensed that was a lie. He had in fact doubted his cousin would honor their deal.

"Just picture it," Mek continued. "It'll work out perfectly. Vicaroy will be joined to you and I will be her hero, saving her from bondage."

He sounded like a child who still believed in fairy tales. How ignorant could he be? In that instant he seemed very young. "Yes, I'm sure she'll forget *all* about Vicaroy and fall madly in love with you."

His sea-green eyes were far away and full of a wistful light.

The sarcasm in Baya's voice had been completely wasted on him. What an idiot, Baya thought. "Mek, you're not entering the Great Hall from the royal balcony."

"Come on. I'm your favorite cousin, aren't I? You get to enter as the highest of royalty and you're not even coupled with the prince yet. Let me come with you. I want to make a grand entrance."

Baya rubbed her fingers over the Ox embedded in her hand. Should she try to put him to sleep with it? Maybe Kuna could do her pressure point trick and knock him out? "Mek, you have to enter the Great Hall like everyone else." She tried to sound authoritative, but one thing for sure was that her annoyance was clear. He couldn't be permitted to see the real Nacora and Var masquerading as Nacora at the same time ... not yet. It would be clear that something was amiss and he might try to stop them or screw things up. "We don't have time for this. Everyone is waiting."

"Please, Cuz?" Mek gave her his best pouty face.

Baya's eyes narrowed. The power of the Ox surged through her. She feared that if she used it while she was this angry she might kill him. "Mek, go." She spoke through gritted teeth.

His shoulders sank. "Fine." He spun on his heel and headed for the main entrance to the Great Hall.

Baya's breath pushed her lips out as she exhaled with relief.

Once he was out of sight, Nacora, the real one, stepped out of the shadows. She'd been waiting around the corner, out of sight. Baya had to admit that being in the presence of two people who looked exactly alike made her skin tingle. It was as if every nerve in her body came alive at once. What kind of a world was this? Was anyone who they appeared to be? How could they know for sure?

"Baya?" Nacora approached her cautiously. "Is that … you?"

Baya revealed her true face. "It's me."

"You did it!" Nacora wrapped her arms around Baya.

Kuna let herself appear. This time she looked like her old self — a human warrior — the former head of the royal guard. Baya had to admit that it was good to see her like this again, a relief actually — familiar and normal — no creepy eyes in the back of her green head.

Nacora gave Kuna a warm smile before turning her gaze to Var, causing her expression to harden. Var remained hovering, surrounded by the pink light. "It's uncanny how much she looks like me." Nacora shook her head. "I never would have believed that you would do this to me."

Var tried to speak but only faint muffled sounds could be heard.

"Everyone's waiting and most likely growing impatient," Kuna said.

"What about my powers?" Nacora asked.

"It'll have to wait. I can't risk losing my control over Var," Baya said. It was hard enough to stay focused on using the power of the Ox to make Var look like Nacora and keep her silent. She didn't want to risk breaking that by trying to give Nacora her powers back now.

Nacora nodded. "Let's do this."

Baya took a deep breath.

"Except you still look like you," Kuna said.

"Right," Baya couldn't see herself so she'd forgotten that she needed to look like Osa. She focused on her memory of Osa's face. "Is that better?"

Nacora's eyes were wide. "You make changing into someone else look easy."

"It kind of is, with this." Baya held her palm out.

Nacora's lips parted as she studied the swirling Ox.

Baya nodded toward the small door that led to the royal entrance to the Great Hall.

Nacora shook her head to clear it. "Here we go."

Var thrashed about in protest so Baya stilled her with the power of the Ox. "In fact, people can't see two Nacora's ... yet." With a wave of her hand, Var turned invisible.

Once on the small dark balcony that led to the wide curving staircase, which ended on the stage below, Nacora nodded to the man who was to announce their entrance.

The masses had gathered and they did indeed look impatient for the ceremony to start. When the royal announcer spoke, the energy in the room came into sharp focus. People snapped to attention as they scanned the stairs for any sign of their leaders.

On the other side of the balcony Vicaroy was escorted out by two male guards. As was customary, he was to enter the Hall from the adjoining staircase. Baya's heart jumped into her throat. She wanted to run to him. He was dressed in an elaborate golden tunic and loose long pants to match Osa's gown. Despite the stern expression he wore he looked handsome. It was a relief to see that he was not hurt — physically anyway.

Longing and love and anger for the situation they were in was almost too much. She wanted to scream his name and blast the two guards on either side of him into a million pieces. No doubt she had the power to do so.

When Vicaroy spotted his mother and "Osa," his expression darkened even farther.

Baya was relieved to see how much he despised Osa.

Nacora placed her hand over her heart and whispered, "He hates me."

Baya rested her hand on Nacora's forearm. "No. He hates Var. He just doesn't know it yet. Let's show him and *all* of them the truth."

Vicaroy was marched down the stairs. He kept his head down in protest refusing to look at the crowd or anything but his feet.

It was Nacora's turn. Baya moved around the balcony to get a better view.

The Unawi's expression was far too serious as she ascended the stairs. The coupling of her son should be a time of great merriment but there was no joy in her face. In fact, there was no joy in the room. The crowd didn't cheer for her as they once did.

Halfway down the stairs Nacora caught a glimpse of Wen and her two youngest boys, Rand and Nefer. They sat obediently at the long table for the nobles. The boys didn't even bother to look at their mother. Their heads remained down as well. Baya didn't know if this was out of defiance or out of fear for their mother. What had Var done to them?

Wen gave Nacora the briefest of disapproving glares but quickly looked away. Baya thought Nacora might trip and fall down the stairs but she managed to steady herself with the handrail. Baya could see the shine of tears pooling in her eyes.

"Come on, keep going," Baya whispered encouragement, even though Nacora couldn't hear her.

Nacora finally took the center stage. Vicaroy and his two guards stood to her right. She raised her arms to silence the buzz of the crowd. "I know that you have gathered for a coupling ceremony but there will be no such thing today."

Vicaroy's head snapped up. The room rippled with whispers.

"I know that I have not been myself of late. But I am back now, the real me, your true and rightful ruler. Allow me to explain and to show you..." Nacora surveyed the room to make sure she had their full attention, which she did.

"There was an imposter under my roof. She posed as me, with the goal of ruining my name and instating her daughter as the next Unawi." Nacora paused to let her words sink in. "The culprit was my number one advisor, Priestess Var. She was able to make herself look like me. I have been betrayed by someone whom I trusted. We've all been deceived. But I'm here before you today, all of you, to set things right."

Many in the audience looked at one another in bewilderment.

"How was Var able to do this?" Nacora continued as if reading her peoples' minds. "She had come to possess a very powerful object which allowed her to do many things. One of which was the ability to make herself look like whomever she chose. In this case … me."

"The Ox," Vicaroy whispered.

Baya could all but see his mind churning as he put the pieces together.

Nacora nodded and smiled at her son. "However, I understand if you don't fully believe me. This is all very confusing and it would be perfectly acceptable if you do not know whom to trust or what to believe. So I'm here to *show* you the truth." Nacora raised an arm toward the staircase — Baya's cue.

It was time for the big reveal. It no longer mattered if a guard, or anyone else for that matter, saw her for who she was so she let her hair turn amber and her skin darken. Var, still disguised as Nacora appeared and Kuna, in human form, moved out of the shadows to stand by Baya's side.

They descended the stairs slowly, with Var floating inches off the ground in the pink light of Baya's new powers. They gave the audience time to take them in. Numerous gasps echoed through the Hall at the sight of the second "Nacora."

"Baya!" Vicaroy moved forward. The two guards on either side of him grabbed him by the upper arms.

"Don't you dare touch my son," Nacora boomed. She was back — the ruler of Merth.

One guard instantly let go of Vicaroy but the other looked between the two Nacora's, unsure of what to do.

Vicaroy jerked away from the guard, forcing him to let go. In the same motion he swung a quick jab. His fist connected with the guard's chin. Mek's fighting lessons paid off. The guard's head flew back. He spun halfway away around before hitting the floor.

"My mother said not to touch me." But the guard couldn't hear Vicaroy as he was out cold. Vicaroy ran to Baya taking her up in his arms.

She wasted no time in pressing her lips to his.

A few brave members of the audience sounded their approval with some whoops and hollers.

Someone from the back yelled, "Let the prince be with whomever he chooses."

Nacora nodded politely to the woman. "That was always my intention."

CHAPTER 49

Nacora's declaration that her son was free to couple with whomever he wished brought about a round of genuine applause from the masses gathered in her Great Hall.

The Unawi turned her attention to Vicaroy's remaining guard. "Your services are no longer needed." She gestured for the man to take his leave.

His eyes darted between Nacora and Kuna as he tried to decide what he should do. The ruler had previously made it *very* clear that he was not to leave Vicaroy's side.

"You heard the Unawi. Get off the stage ... *now*." Kuna's eyes pierced the guard.

That did it. He retreated quickly leaving his fallen comrade sprawled on the floor.

Wen had cautiously made his way to stand beside Nacora. "It's really you."

"Yes, I'm back." She took his hand and gave him a warm smile — a smile that put the light back in Wen's eyes.

"Baya, show them."

Vicaroy had to put Baya down first but as soon as she was standing on her own two feet, Baya let the illusion slowly fade, revealing Var's true form.

Gasps and chatter spread through the crowd.

"Var, do you admit to the people of Merth your acts of treason? Did you pretend to be me, destroying my image with the people in order for you and your daughter to take the throne?"

Baya lifted the powers that kept Var from speaking, yet she was careful to keep her trapped in the pink light.

As if relieved to have her voice again, Var's words came quickly, "No, Madam Unawi. I would never betray you."

Baya caught a glimpse of red hair making its way out the far doors of the Great Hall. You better run, Mek, she thought.

"Then explain yourself to the people of Merth," Nacora demanded.

All in attendance appeared glued to every word. No one so much as blinked. The anticipation in the Hall was palpable.

"I … I…" Var must have decided that the evidence was clear and it was *not* in her favor. "Please don't punish my daughter — this was not her fault. She had nothing to do with this."

Nacora smiled and raised both arms to the audience. "That's enough of a confession for me."

The crowd erupted. Some cried out for Var to be imprisoned. Some even wanted her dead.

"I have never had to send anyone to the crystal prison. But for now, this is where Var will go."

"Please Madam Unawi, what of Osa?" Var's face was twisted with defeat.

"She will be held accountable to the people of Merth, just as you are now. Her fate will be decided then."

"No. Please. Be merciful."

At Nacora's signal two female guards stepped forward to seize Var.

Baya released her from the pink light.

"Take her away." Nacora turned to address the audience. "You gathered here today for a celebration. Granted, this was not what you were expecting. But I don't think things could have worked out more perfectly. I hope you will stay and rejoice at my return. Help me eat and drink this bounty laid out before us."

The audience roared with approval.

Nacora took Wen's hand and Baya and Vicaroy moved to her side. Nacora stood proud before her people until the applause died down. "Now if you will excuse me for a moment, I need to catch up with my family."

"Long live Unawi Nacora," the crowd cheered.

The ruler turned to the royal table. Rand ran to his mother and with a jump, wrapped his arms around her neck. Tears squeezed out of her eyes as she hugged him back. Nefer remained seated. Wen picked him up to carry him out of the Great Hall.

"Vicaroy ... Baya." Nacora waved for them to follow her off the stage. Then to the audience she said. "We will return. Until then, eat, drink and be merry."

This brought about the loudest cheers yet.

Kuna escorted them as they exited to the back of the Great Hall.

Once the masses could no longer see them, Nacora let the tears fall as she kissed and hugged Wen and her youngest boys. Nefer didn't appear to enjoy the affection.

Baya and Vicaroy watched them for a moment, before Vicaroy scooped her up. She wrapped her arms around his neck and wasted no time in pressing her lips to his.

"You're the most amazing woman in the world." Vicaroy kissed her harder.

Baya didn't want to ruin the moment with words that paled in comparison to how it felt being this close to him again. She inhaled his strong earthy scent and allowed herself to fully enjoy his embrace.

It was difficult to tell how much time had passed before Baya reluctantly registered what Nacora was saying.

"Var didn't hurt you did she?" Nacora asked her family.

Wen shook his head. "No. You ... well Var slept in different quarters and mostly ignored us. The few times we were able to approach ... her, she would snap at us to leave her alone."

"We thought you didn't love us anymore," Rand said.

Nefer remained silent and hidden behind Wen.

Nacora knelt down to get closer. "My baby boy, I know this is confusing for you. But I want you to understand that I'm back and that I love you very much."

One blue eye slowly came into view from around Wen's leg. "You were mean to me."

"Baby, that wasn't really me. Look, I'll make it up to you, I promise. Will you give me a chance to show you that your old mother has returned, that this is truly me?"

Nefer's frown remained but he slowly nodded.

"Thank you." Nacora stood and turned to Baya and Vicaroy. Vicaroy carefully set Baya down. Nacora wrapped her arms around them both. "We did it."

"Super easy," Baya said.

Nacora laughed. "I'm not so sure about that." She studied her eldest son. "Are you okay?"

"I'm always fine when I'm with Baya."

"Thank the Great Goddess." Nacora's eyes glistened. She put her hands together and gave Baya a knowing nod.

Baya raised her hand and pointed her palm at Nacora. "You're going to enjoy this … immensely."

"What are you doing?" Wen demanded.

Kuna stepped forward ready to hold Wen back if needed.

Baya closed her eyes and pictured Nacora's powers, her essence. Then she imagined her powers flowing back into her. All of Baya's thoughts and energy focused on giving the Unawi strength. A pulsating electricity moved through Baya's chest and down her arm. She felt the pink light leave her body in a swirling mass.

Nacora's mouth fell open and she collapsed in a shaking heap.

"What are you doing to her!" Wen ran forward in an attempt to stand between Baya and his wife.

Kuna grabbed him by the arms.

"Mom!" Rand yelled.

Vicaroy looked wide-eyed between his love and his mother.

"Everyone calm down. Baya is giving Nacora her powers back," Kuna said.

"She's ... powerless?" Wen's naturally pale face grew even more ashen.

"Not for long," Baya said.

Wen went to his knees. His wife's body shook and a sound of pleasure seemed to come from deep inside her ... her jaw had clenched tight.

"Is she in pain?" Wen asked.

"No, quite the opposite actually," Kuna said.

Nacora curled into a ball. Wen placed his hands on her and tried to steady her. He was desperate to help but her entire body continued to jerk violently.

"Darling!" Wen yelled. His boys watched with pale faces from a safe distance.

One last moan was heard as the tremors stopped. It took some time before she slowly sat up and opened her eyes. "Holy Mother of us all." Her chest heaved as she turned her glassy gaze to Baya. "Can you do that again?"

Baya and Kuna laughed, remembering full well the euphoria.

Nacora lit a ball of light in her hand and stared at it in awe.

Wen helped her to her feet. "Perhaps you should rest."

"I've apparently been asleep for weeks. I'm done resting. I want to celebrate," she squeezed Wen's hands. "Will you dance with me?"

Wen slowly let out a long breath. He might have been holding it throughout the entire ordeal. "I've missed you and I didn't even know it."

Rand and Nefer had backed even farther away.

"Sorry you had to see that, my sons. I'm okay now, back to normal, I promise. We have a lot to be grateful for. Will you join me?"

Rand ran forward and hugged her. Nefer ... well it would take him some time to process all this. Wen scooped him up and led them to the Great Hall.

"I'm famished," Nacora said. "Is anyone else hungry?"

CHAPTER 50

It was back to work for Kuna. Once in the Great Hall she issued commands, as if they were at war. Royal guards were to find Mek and Osa at once. Mek was to be held in the regular cells, the ones reserved for men. And Osa was to join her mother in the dreaded pink jail. They would be questioned and eventually held accountable to the people of Merth.

Baya's insides cringed at the thought of the pain that awaited Osa and Var as their powers were stripped from them.

Ena made her way through the crowd.

"Osa should still be asleep in her wardrobe," Kuna was explaining to one of the guards when Ena's arms flew around her neck. Their bodies collided in an embrace.

"Ena, you were supposed to ..."

"Get myself to safety." Ena finished Kuna's sentence. "I know but I had to make sure you were okay."

"That's a nice gesture, yet you shouldn't have risked it."

Ena gave Baya a fierce hug. "You did it! You caught that terrible woman and restored the people's faith in Nacora. You were spectacular!"

Doba took the opportunity to move from Ena's shoulder to Baya's.

Baya blushed. "Thank you." She rubbed Doba's chin. "We couldn't have done it without the two of you."

"Ena, you must join us at the royal table." Nacora hooked arms with Ena. "Tonight you are our guest of honor."

It was Ena's turn to blush. Her cheeks glowed with a purple tint.

"You came back." Vicaroy rubbed the insect's chin.

Doba crawled from Baya's shoulder to Vicaroy's and rubbed his head against Vicaroy's cheek.

Nefer looked as if he'd eaten something rotten and flinched away. "That thing is creepy."

Rand bounced on his heels. "Can I see him? Pleeeeease."

"I don't think that's a good idea," Wen said.

"He's harmless." Baya gently unwound Doba from Vicaroy's shoulders and held him low for Rand. "You can give him a gentle pat."

Rand's small hand shook as he reached for the long insect.

Nefer watched with wide eyes.

Rand ran his hand down Doba's back.

"Do you want to hold him?"

Rand shook his head to indicate that he'd had enough. His curiosity had been appeased.

"Nefer, do you want to pet him?"

Nefer whimpered and hid behind Wen.

"I think that's a no," Vicaroy said.

Baya and Nacora laughed.

They headed for the long table of food, everyone except Kuna that is. She was busy being the captain of the guard. Baya was sure there was nothing else she would rather be doing.

Doba made his way up Baya's arm, to rest on her shoulder, as usual.

Vicaroy stopped halfway to the food table and looked around at the audience. Some people had already finished eating and had started to dance. He took Baya's hand to stop her. "Do you want to get out of here?"

Baya felt her body relax as she looked into his golden-brown eyes. She gave him a playful smile. "Where would you like to go."

He chuckled. "For a walk or … something. Anywhere but here … with all these people. I haven't seen the outdoors in so long."

"Doba is going on and on about wanting us to meet someone."

Vicaroy's brow creased. "Who?"

"I don't know but he's very excited."

CHAPTER 51

From Baya's shoulder Doba guided them through the palace gardens. The last of the suns had recently disappeared for the day. This set the sky ablaze with hues of purple, blue and red. Baya felt like it had been ages since she'd seen a sunset. Vicaroy couldn't help himself. He had to stop several times to pull weeds. Doba clicked at him with impatience.

"This way," Baya said.

"What's the hurry? We have all night. I'm just happy to be in the garden ..." He gave Baya a warm smile, "with you." Vicaroy stopped to pick a flower for Baya.

Doba bared his pointy teeth and hissed.

"I've missed you too, Doba."

At the sound of more hissing, Vicaroy said, "Alright, I'm coming."

The insect led them deeper into the garden.

"I wish he would tell us what the surprise is. I don't know how much more I can take in one day."

In a dark corner against a far wall stood a large tree with knotted roots protruding from the earth. Doba leapt from Baya's shoulder and disappeared into a hole under one of the thick roots.

"You do know that we can't follow you?" Baya said.

Many eyes reflected the light of the two moons. There were too many to be only Doba's. Baya tried to count them but they kept blinking and moving.

Come meet my human companions. Doba's voice was soft in Baya's head.

"Who are you talking to," Baya asked.

Vicaroy crossed his large arms. "What's going on?"

Baya shrugged.

After a time Doba emerged followed by another long, segmented form. A second septapod was slow to reveal itself. It blinked up at them with four dark eyes.

Baya stared into the insect's eyes, making a connection. "You found a mate. She's making a nest in the base of this tree to lay her eggs ..."

I call her Aba. She's making a home for our children, Doba explained.

Baya picked Doba up and twirled around with him held at arms-length. "I'm so happy for you!" When she finally stopped she pressed Doba to her chest in an embrace.

He clung onto her the best he could with all his tiny legs. *Don't do that again,* he breathed.

Vicaroy rubbed his chin. "Nice work, little buddy. I'm glad you found a companion."

Baya bent down to let Doba crawl off her arm onto the ground. She reached to pet Aba but Aba quickly moved away. Her body formed a U shape as she retreated into her nest.

I told her that she doesn't need to fear you and that you know all the right places to scratch but she's never seen humans before.

"It's okay. We'll give her time to get to know us."

I'd better go. She doesn't like it that I've been away so much lately.

Baya chuckled as she translated what Doba said to Vicaroy. "Go. Enjoy your companion."

You too. I'm glad Vic didn't have to mate with that crazy lady.

Baya shuddered. When it was put like that it sounded doubly terrible. "Thank the Great Goddess."

Doba spun around to head into the burrow.

"Thank you for saving us." Baya gave him a slight wave. She was left with an odd mixture of relief shadowed by a twinge of sadness. She was grateful that Doba's dream of finding a mate had come true. Yet, now she would have to share him.

Vicaroy pulled her to him. His lips on hers made the unhappiness vanish. She wrapped her arms around his neck and kissed him harder. Her eyes shot open and she abruptly pulled away. "Tara? You left her alone in the wild. We have to find her."

"We're not going to find her tonight and I'm sure she's fine. She's old enough to take care of herself."

Baya frowned. "I hope you're right. There's not much I can do for her right now anyway." Her eyes narrowed. "That reminds me, what happened after we parted outside the city walls? You told me you would wait in the forest. The next thing I knew, you were turning yourself in."

Vicaroy opened his mouth to speak but nothing came out.

"Did Mek convince you to return to the palace?" Baya's eyes shone like the flames of a fire. "Did he force you to return?"

Vicaroy literally shrank. His broad shoulders deflated. "No. It was my idea." He put his head down. "I knew that the sentries would let me back into the city. After all, they were searching for me."

"Don't." Baya spoke softly as she lifted his chin.

"I know. You don't like it when I lower my eyes. I can't help it."

"You *can* help it. What I don't like is you lying to me. I thought you were safe outside the city ... then there you were, captured as well."

This time he held her gaze. "At least I was able to keep Mother — well, Var actually, from hurting those poor men."

"There is that. Why did you turn yourself in?"

"I thought Mek and I could help."

Baya's jaw tightened. "Mek planned to hand you over to Var and Osa and you happened to play right into it."

"What?"

She shook her head. "Not now. I'll tell you all about it but tonight I want to be happy. We're together and that's all that matters." Baya leaned into him, pressing her body to his. "This is how it should be. You and I, working things out ... as equals."

"I thought you were going to say, 'You and I, alone in a garden.'"

Baya chuckled. "That too." He somehow managed to pull her even closer. His body was hard against her's. She ran her hands over his wide shoulders and down his defined arms. "You're even bigger and stronger then when I last saw you."

"I found creative ways to pass the time and get all my pent up energy and anger out."

"I'm glad." Baya moaned as she breathed in his lovely earthy scent.

What happened next must have been the longest kiss in the history of the planet.

* * *

LATER THAT NIGHT while the Great Hall was still full of loud merriment, Vicaroy and Baya strolled through the royal gardens under the clear night sky. One moon was on the rise and two were already high above them. They stopped to sit on a bench overlooking a pond.

Vicaroy placed his arm around Baya's shoulders and pulled her to him.

She studied the pink flower shaped stone set deep into her hand. The light was gone as she was not using its powers. Faint metallic swirls moved about lazily in its center.

Vicaroy ran his finger over it. "Does it hurt?"

Baya shook her head no. "It's ... well it feels good ... powerful." She didn't have the words to describe the pure ecstasy of it.

"One down, one to go."

"We have the Ox ... now we have to find the Ominot ... somehow." Taking a deep breath through clenched teeth, she dug her nails in between the embedded Ox and the flesh of her hand. She moaned as the stone came loose. Pink light moved in ribbons around the Ox. She took Vicaroy's hand and spread his fingers apart. "I want you to have it."

"What?"

"That way you'll have powers. No one will be able to force you to do something you don't want."

His eyes were wide as they searched hers. "You would give up all that power … for me?"

Baya's face fell. "Are you questioning my love for you?"

Vicaroy looked between the Ox and Baya several times. "Of course not."

"Good. Then take it." She placed it in his palm.

"Baya, I don't know what to do with it —"

The Ox rose into the air and hovered in place.

Baya's brow furrowed. "That's odd. It should melt into your hand and you should feel this wonderful sense of pleasure course through your body as it takes hold."

Nothing. The stone just floated above his hand.

Baya tried to force it into his hand but when her hand was still inches away it flung itself into her skin, resetting itself to her.

"Ahhh." She bent over as the pleasure electrified her body. Her body jerked a couple of times.

"Are you okay?"

It took a couple of deep breaths before she could speak. "I'm …" Gasp. "Fine."

When she could finally sit up, they looked at each other for a long time.

"It looks like you were meant to have it."

"I don't know. Maybe since you don't have your powers back yet it didn't … take."

"It was a generous offer."

Baya sensed a trace of disappointment in his voice. "I'm sorry. I really wanted you to have it. We have to get your powers back."

"We will."

She laid her head against his chest. They watched the reflection of the stars dance across the dark water.

A flash of light caught Vicaroy's eye. His head snapped up to see where it had come from. "Look." He pointed to the sky in the far north. "It's a shooting star."

Baya's lips parted as she watched the bright white light streak across the entire heavens. Unlike most shooting stars this one remained bright for an unusually long time. "It must be a good sign."

Vicaroy closed his eyes as if making a wish. "Hopefully it means that we'll be able to find the Ominot and destroy it."

EPILOGUE

3031 AD Outer Space

As it turns out, what Baya and Vicaroy saw was not a shooting star but rather a space shuttle from a faraway planet called Earth. Maybe you've heard of it?

The large metal craft moved at many times the speed of sound as it approached its destination — the planet they called Thanadox. This was a strange and new planet. Not only new to the earthlings aboard the San Xavier but intelligent life forms had only lived on this planet for just over three thousand years. And even more recently they'd evolved into what we would call "modern man," or something close to that, in about the past fifteen hundred years.

This was in great contrast to the planet these astronauts came from, where mankind had been walking their planet for tens of thousands of years.

The astronauts aboard the San Xavier had studied Thanadox for many years via satellite. They'd watched its people carefully. They had learned to speak their languages and they knew many of their customs or at least they thought they did.

The planet has been nicknamed *A Woman's World* because as far as the earthlings could tell, the females of the species appeared to be in charge. This was also in great contrast to the planet these astronauts came from.

Soon they would land — finally. It had taken many years to travel this far. However, a number of the passengers aboard the San Xavier had nothing but time. They were very old yet, un-aging, making this a much-needed adventure. After all, living forever could get rather boring.

Vallachia and Elijah couldn't wait to set foot on this virgin ground. There was still so much to learn about this strange place — things that satellite feeds couldn't tell them. Like what the planet smelled like, what it *felt* like. What it was like to have two suns and four moons. The planet they came from was unlucky in this way. It only had one of each — one sun, one moon — as we've established, boring. But then again, you may have already known this.

Elijah sat in the captain's chair — his chair. This was a fancy name for the unextraordinary seat. It was made of black vinyl and wasn't much different from an average office chair. After so many years of endless use the armrests were well-worn and the vinyl was cracked in many places. It was nothing like the lavish thrones he'd ruled from in the past.

"Two minutes until we enter the atmosphere," Elijah announced as he pressed the controls on a clear touch screen in front of him.

Every crew member had been busy preparing for landing but now they ran for their seats.

Vallachia, who was often called Val, was Elijah's co-captain. Not to mention, his wife of one-thousand five-hundred and sixty-two years. Val swiftly secured her buckle. She felt like she might, quite literally burst in two. She couldn't remember in all her years ever feeling this much anticipation. She gently placed her hand on Elijah's forearm. "Buckle up, Darling."

This broke his concentration on the screens. His face softened when he looked at her and his handsome crooked smile crept across his lips. Vallachia had not seen this much light in his crystalline grey eyes in some time. Her stomach already felt like it was full of a million bustling ants. Yet, his smile made a million more flood into her stomach. How could he still excite her like this after all this time?

Elijah snapped his harness into place just as the ship jolted. "This is it." He took her hand and squeezed.

"We're entering the atmosphere," she whispered.

It's not like in the movies, you know, the ones from Earth, when the aliens land smoothly and a door that is also a ramp slowly opens with a slight hiss.

No. It's more like a hard jolt as the ship's reverse thrusters engage. Followed by another blow as the legs touch down. This leaves the ship to bounce several more times as their struts absorb the impact — hence the safety belts.

It took the crew an hour to unlock the doors and prepare to disembark. In reality, it was a very noisy process with lots of clanking metal and grinding cogs.

Finally the metal stairs were lowered to the ground. Vallachia and Elijah had had plenty of time to suit up.

He paused on the bottom step. "Let's do this together. We'll jump at the same time."

"That way, both of us will be the first to set foot on this alien soil."

"On the count of three, ready?"

Vallachia nodded. Her head moved but her large space helmet remained stationary.

"One."

Vallachia jumped.

Her bulky boots hit the dry earth sending up a waft of dust. She could hear Elijah's sigh in her headset. "I simply couldn't resist."

He stepped off the last rung unceremoniously. "Well, you ruined that."

Vallachia chuckled. She could hear the laughter of the crew members in her earpiece.

Elijah bent down and picked up a handful of the dry dirt. It had a lovely reddish tint to it. He let it fall to the ground through his gloved fingers.

"We could set up our encampment over there." Vallachia pointed to a flat open space. "We won't have to cut down any trees or clear much underbrush."

They had chosen a very remote place to land, which was easy as the planet, being so new, was sparsely populated. They wanted to learn more about this place before they met any locals.

Elijah didn't answer.

Val turned to see why. He was in the process of unbuckling his helmet from his suit. He flicked the last brace up.

"What are you doing?" Val gasped.

"Testing a theory." He lifted the helmet as Val moved at the speed of light to try and stop him. He managed to toss the helmet away as Val reached him.

Elijah fell to his knees. In almost the same motion, Val was on hers as well. "Elijah!"

His hands went to his throat. "It burns," he choked.

The wheezing and coughing began. He would have fallen to the ground but Val caught him.

"What were you thinking?" She sat with his head in her lap. "Get a medic suited up now," Val yelled into her earpiece.

Elijah's eyes bulged and his breathing slowed. "No." Not his lovely eyes. Screw pretending to be human. He needed help — now! In a nanosecond Val jumped to her feet and scooped him up in her arms.

The End of Book 2

Help others find this book by leaving a review on Amazon.

Sign up to Lynne's email list at www.lynnehill.com to get a free eBook. Plus, never miss a new release.

A COLLISION OF WORLDS

Book 3 in the Woman's World series

Quick note to readers: If you have not read *The Lords and Commoners* series then now is the time to do so. This is a prequel series to *A Woman's World*. Reading the *Lords and Commoners* series first will enhance your enjoyment of this next book in the *Woman's World* series, where these two worlds come together.

You can find the *Lords and Commoners* series on Amazon.

Then Continue the Adventure with **A Collision of Worlds...**

What happens when two cultures collide?

What happens when two species collide?

How about two galaxies?

Well, largely it's one big freaking mess.

And a whole lot of fun.

Come with Baya on a quest to restore what was stolen.

Along the way, she meets strange people from an advanced planet called Earth.

She also faces fierce new enemies who will do anything to ensure she fails.

Get your next adventure today…

What Critics are saying about book 3...

The crescendo of events and twists of fate and revelations turn this "Collision of Worlds" into a masterpiece of suspense, action and surprise. Baya and Vicaroy now understand that the fate of men and indeed their world lies in their hands and they have to act fast and wisely to avoid this catastrophe, but alas, it isn't that easy! Little could anyone guess that visitors from another planet are both their enemies and their supporters. Readers from the "Of Lords and Commoners" series will be delighted to meet old friends in this third and best book in the trilogy.

— Addicted to Books

AN EXCERPT FROM BOOK 3

Vallachia slowly lowered her head to Baya's neck. Val's expression was full of a deep need. It was like the way Vicaroy looked at Baya when they made love. Baya stilled — she was unable to move. The first sharp pain of Val's fangs sinking into Baya's neck caused her to snap out of her frozen state of fear as the realization hit her: this woman wanted her blood.

ALSO BY LYNNE HILL

& THE BEST READING ORDER

The Lords and Commoners Series

Of Lords and Commoners Book 1

Of Princes and Dragons Book 2

Of Gods and Goddesses Book 3

A Gods and Goddesses Novelette

A Woman's World Series

A Woman's World Book 1

Lost Powers Book 2

A Collision of Worlds Book 3

ACKNOWLEDGMENTS

As always I have so many people to thank. I'm sure I'll leave out some for which I apologize in advance. A special thanks to my marketing team, Ed, Alaina and Alyssa. I couldn't have done this without you. Many thanks to my fans and my Street Team. You made the launch of the *Woman's World* series a success!

Thank you to the authors who provided a blurb for *A Woman's World*. Many thanks to IBPA and all the other organizations that provide resources for authors. I'm very blessed to have my amazing editor, Marcia. And last but FAR from least I am eternally grateful for the unwavering support of my friends and family. I love you all very much!

ABOUT THE AUTHOR

Lynne Hill is the author of the *Lords and Commoners* series and the *Woman's World* series. She made the short list for the Chanticleer Book Awards and was awarded a 5 Star Reader's Favorite award. She was born in Colorado and raised in a small town of eight hundred people. Lynne holds a Doctorate of Psychology in criminology and justice studies. She is an advocate for Restorative Justice, a theme that is incorporated into her novels. Her extensive travels overseas and her work as an American Peace Corps Volunteer in Jordan helped to inspire her writing.

Find out more at www.lynnehill.com where you can sign up to her email list to get a free eBook. Plus, never miss a new release.

www.ingramcontent.com/pod-product-compliance
Lightning Source LLC
Chambersburg PA
CBHW030622310726
48979CB00003B/831
* 9 7 8 1 7 3 6 7 2 4 9 9 6 *